Anonymous

Red patriots; the story of the Seminoles

Anonymous

Red patriots; the story of the Seminoles

ISBN/EAN: 9783337305482

Printed in Europe, USA, Canada, Australia, Japan

Cover: Foto ©Andreas Hilbeck / pixelio.de

More available books at **www.hansebooks.com**

RED PATRIOTS:

THE

STORY OF THE SEMINOLES.

BY

CHARLES H. COE.

———

"Adds to the earnestness of historic justice the charm of dramatic interest."
—Gov't Official.

1898:
THE EDITOR PUBLISHING COMPANY,
CINCINNATI.

DEDICATED

TO

MRS. AMELIA S. QUINTON,

Who, as General Secretary, and longer as President, of the

WOMEN'S NATIONAL INDIAN ASSOCIATION,

has labored twenty years for the elevation and christiani-
zation of our native Indian tribes; and under whose leadership more than forty Missions have been established among
them, including one for the

SEMINOLES OF FLORIDA.

ILLUSTRATIONS.

CONTENTS.

CHAPTER XV.

CHAPTER XVI.

CHAPTER XVII.

CHAPTER XVIII.

———

(PART II.)

CHAPTER I.

CHAPTER II.

CHAPTER III.

CHAPTER IV.

CHAPTER V.

CHAPTER VI.

CHAPTER VII.

APPENDIX.

PREFACE.

During a long residence in Florida I became deeply interested in the Seminole Indians, who inhabited the southern part of the State. I also read everything within my reach relating to their history, including the protracted warfare formerly waged between that invincible people and the National, Territorial and State governments.

Circumstances finally enabled me, within the past few years, to take up my residence in the city of Washington and to continue my study in the great libraries and bureaus of information peculiar to the Nation's capital. And the more widely my researches extended, the more absorbing became my interest in the subject, and the firmer my resolve to place upon enduring record the full story of the rights and wrongs, the true patriotism and the heroic fortitude of the Seminole race.

Love of home and country was uncommonly developed in the Seminole people, due no doubt to the genial climate and great natural resources of their sunny land; to their peculiar isolation by ocean waters; and to the presence of the cherished graves of their fathers. All combined to make the Seminoles' home especially dear—

> "—the spot of earth supremely blest,
> A dearer, sweeter spot than all the rest."

Thus, hemmed in by the sea on all sides but one—unable to retreat or to advance—he was compelled to fight or to submit to banishment. Without the slightest hesitation, the former alternative was chosen, and an unequal and atrocious warfare of seven years' duration

—afterward renewed—took place, at a sacrifice on our part of hundreds of lives, millions of money, and repeated violations of solemn pledges.

The latest history of the Seminole War was published soon after the termination of hostilities, more than a half century ago. The present volume has been written more from the standpoint of the Indian, and includes much new and interesting information, and the correction of many erroneous ideas, in connection with almost every leading feature of Seminole history. New light has been shed, not only upon the earlier movements and struggles of this liberty-loving race, but upon their condition and customs in our present peaceful times. When the interest of the subject seemed to justify it, careful detail has been adopted, and in every part of the work the utmost accuracy has been the great end and aim.

I cannot resist the conclusion that most of my readers will gain a better knowledge of the white man's treatment of the Indian, and a more favorable opinion of the race, than they ever had before, as well as be convinced with me that the wronged and despised Seminole fought in no less sacred a cause than did our forefathers in the days of '76.*

My leading object in thus reviving an interest in this long neglected people, has been to create public sentiment in behalf of the deserving remnant still lingering, by sufferance only, in Southern Florida. It is also the earnest purpose of the author, if the avails of this work shall justify it, to renovate the lone and neglected grave of Osceola,—the brightest example of the Semi-

---

* "The annals of this decaying tribe, if written in strict obedience to the laws of truth, and without prejudice, would place them in a better light than the one in which most people are disposed to regard them."—Life and Adventures in South Florida, by Andrew P. Canova, (1885), a native of the State, who served throughout the last hostilities with the Seminoles.

nole nation—the unforgotten hero of an earlier day,—
and to substitute for his broken and defaced headstone
a suitable shaft worthy of the humble patriot.

I gratefully acknowledge my obligations to the following named persons: First, to my valued friend Prof.
Charles E. Aaron, of Philadelphia, who has rendered me
invaluable assistance in the preparation of this work;
to Maj. Wm. S. Beebe, late of the Ordnance Department,
U. S. Army, who kindly placed at my disposal old
letters, diaries, and other valuable material, left by his
late uncle, Capt. John C. Casey, prominent in the Seminole War and later as agent among the remnant; to Dr.
J. E. Brecht, for years the zealous agent and Christian
worker among the present Seminoles of Florida; to the
late Gen. John Gibbon, U. S. Army, (retired), whose
favorable impressions of the Indian were first received in the Everglades; and to many others who
have encouraged me in my undertaking. Nor must I
fail to thank the officials of the various departments and
libraries of Washington, for free access to priceless
volumes and carefully guarded records, without which
this book would have been impossible.

Considerable matter will be found in the appendix,
which could not be inserted in the body of the work;
also a list of the various sources of information which
have been consuted.

THE AUTHOR.

Washington, D. C., June, 1898.

PART I.
EARLY HISTORY AND CHARACTER.

PART I.

EARLY HISTORY AND CHARACTER—THE STRUGGLE FOR
HOME AND COUNTRY—TRIALS OF THE EMIGRANTS—
SEMINOLES IN MEXICO—PRESENT CONDI-
TION IN THE WEST.

CHAPTER I.

ORIGIN AND EARLY HISTORY OF THE SEMINOLES—TESTIMONY
REGARDING THEIR NUMBERS, CHARACTER AND CONDITION.

A great and powerful confederacy of Indians formerly inhabited the present States of Georgia and Alabama.   They styled themselves Mus-co-gul-gees, or Mus-
ko-gees, but by the English they were called "Creeks,"
from the numerous small streams which flowed through
their country.

Col. Benjamin Hawkins, a commissioner appointed
by the United States in the year 1785 to negotiate with
the Creeks, and later residing among them many years
as their agent, states that there were thirty-seven towns
in the confederacy, composed of seven-eights Muskogees, and the balance Uchees, Natchez, Hitchittees, and
Alibamus.*

About the beginning of the eighteenth century, a
portion of the Creeks withdrew from the rest and settled
on the extreme outskirts of the confederacy, in the
northern part of Florida. The name they bore for many
years thereafter was isti-se-mo-le,† or "wild men."   In

* Sketches of the Creek Country in 1798-99.   (A manuscript work left
by Colonel Hawkins, published in 1848, thirty-two years after his death.)

† Various definitions of the term istisemole have been given, the most
common being "runaway," "wanderer," "separatist," and "emigrant."   That
given by the author is according to Colonel Hawkins, the earliest authority,
and is undoubtedly correct.

5

after years this term was corrupted to Sim-e-lo-le, Sim-e-no-le, and finally to Semi-nole. The new comers were kindly received by the Florida tribes, and as the years went by their numbers and strength greatly increased, enabling them to establish settlements over the country. They finally excited the jealousy of their neighbors, and a fierce war resulted, in which the Seminoles were the victors. Those who escaped death joined the new comers and others who had sided with them,* altogether forming a nation of a heterogeneous nature.

Colonel Hawkins thus refers to the Seminoles, in his manuscript work:

" The towns of the Simenolies deserve a place here, as they are Creeks. They inhabit the country bordering on the Gulf of Mexico, from Apalachecola, including Little St. Johns † and the Florida point.‡ They have seven towns: Sim-e-no-le-tal-lau-haf-see, Mic-co-soo-ce, We-cho-took-me, Au-lot-che-wau, Oc-le-wau-hau-thluc-co, Tal-lau-gue-chalico-pop-cau, Cull-oo-sau-hatche. They are called wild people, because they left their old towns and made irregular settlements in this country to which they were invited by the plenty of game, the mildness of the climate, the richness of the soil, and the abundance of food for cattle and horses."

Most writers in referring to the Creek offshoot, claim that their departure from the others was owing to serious tribal quarrels. This common statement is plainly an error, for Colonel Hawkins does not once mention this as being a cause of removal. The reason assigned by him, as above quoted, seems to be the most rational, and is undoubtedly the true one. From the

---

* Territory of Florida, John Lee Williams, 1837. The author of this work had resided in Florida for many years. See also General Jackson's statement, Am. State Papers, Vol. 2, Indian Affairs.

† Suwanee River.

‡ The peninsula part of the country.

time that the Seminoles first renounced all allegiance to
the Creek nation, however, trouble ensued.　But an
open rupture did not take place for many years, notwithstanding the length of time that the offshoot had
been living by themselves.　As late as 1790 they were
recognized as part of the Creek confederacy in a treaty
between that nation and the United States, signed in
New York City, August 7th, of that year; and, as we
have seen, Colonel Hawkins so regarded them nine years
later.

In September 1821, General Jackson held a talk
with Neamathla, the principal chief of the nation, John
Hicks, and Mulatto King, in which the former chief,
through an interpreter, gave the names and locations of
all the Indian (Seminole) towns in Florida.　The whole
number, including both East and West Florida,* was thirty-seven towns, with a total population of about 5,000.†
A few months later, Capt. John R. Bell, acting-agent
for the Indians, reported the same number of souls in
the nation.‡　In 1823, General James Gadsden wrote
the Secretary of War that "these Indians are now
scattered over the whole face of Florida."　When the
offshoot first withdrew from the Creeks they were under
the leadership of a chief named Sac-a-fa-ca, erroneously
referred to by other writers as "Seacoffee," or "Secoffer."　In 1750, this chief was living in what is now
called Alachua County, where he died at the age of
seventy years.§　The Spanish Governor of St. Augustine alluded to the friendly character of Sacafaca in

---

* Under British rule the territory was divided into two provinces
called East and West Florida, the peninsula portion representing the former.

† Am. State Papers, Vol. II, Indian Affairs, p. 439.

‡ In a letter to Hon. John Floyd, House of Representatives.

§ Reference to "Secoffer," in a private diary of Judge Robert R. Reid
afterward Governor of Florida.　Bench and Bar of Georgia, Miller, 1858.

1737, in a correspondence with the Governor of Cuba, thus proving that the Seminoles were then living in Florida,* and that they were friendly toward the whites.

That the Seminoles were also on good terms with the British, while Florida was in possession of the latter, the earnest words of a writer of that period are worthy of note. In considering "by what means England may render Florida useful to her," he suggests "intermarriage with the Indian families."†

It is probable that peaceful relations had been enjoyed by all the inhabitants for a long period of time, as indicated by a report of Captain Bell to the Secretary of War, in 1822, that "this nation was, before the destruction of their settlements in 1812, numerous, proud and wealthy, possessing great numbers of cattle, horses, and slaves."

Captain Bell had previously reported:

"They are honest, speak the truth, and are attached to the British and Americans. The wars, however, of McIntosh (a Creek chief) and the late desolating war with the United States, and depredations of the frontier white settlers on their settlements, have destroyed their confidence. . . . The pure-blood Seminole Indians are about 1,200 in number. . . . They hunt from November to March. Their hunting grounds are north of twenty-eight degrees north latitude. Their principal game is deer. . . Their cattle, on which they formerly subsisted, have been wantonly destroyed. . . The negroes who dwell among these people as their slaves, are

---

* Corroborated by a statement of General Jackson in 1821, that the Seminoles had been living in Florida for a hundred years. (Am. State Papers Vol. II, Indian Affairs, p. 438.) Bartram, writing in 1773, says they emigrated to Florida in 1710.

† Raynal's History, 1782, Vol. VI.

intelligent and speak the English language, having been purchased from the English.*"

Rev. Jedidiah Morse, a United States' Commissioner appointed in 1820 to investigate the condition of various Indian tribes, thus corroborates the above:

"Before the wars of 1812 and since, these Indians with their negro slaves, lived in comfort, and many of them were wealthy in cattle and horses. But these wars have broken them up, destroyed great numbers of their bravest warriors and chiefs; also their villages and cattle, and thrown them into a state most distressing and pitiable." †

* Am. State Papers, Vol. II, Indian Affairs.

† Report to the Secretary of War, Morse, 1822.

CHAPTER II.

Compared with the long, desperate and decisive struggle generally known as the Seminole or Florida War, the first hostilities with the Seminoles were only a series of assaults, in which our race was, with few exceptions, the aggressor. The trouble occurred while Florida was still a province of Spain, at intervals during the years 1812, 1816, 1817 and 1818. It is not the author's intention to dwell on the details of the first hostilities; but the several causes which led up to them, also a few of the more important incidents connected therewith, will receive due notice in this chapter.

In the year 1812, the Seminoles were charged with committing depredations along the southern frontier of Georgia. The white settlers, as usual, disregarded the fact that these forays were almost invariably in retaliation for similar acts against the red men.* In

*.The famous Kit Carson, scout and Indian agent, who knew the Indian and his ways thoroughly, truly said that "all our Indian troubles were caused originally by bad white men, if the truth were known;" also that "Indians rarely commit outrages unless they are first provoked to them by the border whites."—Life of Kit Carson, Ellis.

September of the above year, a party of Georgia volunteers, headed by Colonel Nunen, marched to King Payne's town, situated in what is now called Alachua County, where they attacked a party of about one hundred and fifty Indians, under King Payne and Bowlegs, two of the most prominent chiefs in the nation at that time. A long engagement ensued, during which the Indians sustained a considerable loss, and were finally defeated. King Payne, who, with Bowlegs, was a son of the celebrated Sacafaca, was among the killed.

About the same period, Florida was invaded by a Creek chief named McIntosh, also by a misguided gathering of men known to history as the Florida Revolutionists, or so-called "Patriots."* It is a curious coincidence that both of these invasions of Spanish territory were commanded by men—one Indian, the other white—who bore the same name. The Creek chief, with a band of his followers, waged damaging wars, at different times, on both Indians and whites. Of the "Patriot" war, J. A. Peniere,† the first United States' agent for the Florida Indians, reported to the Secretary of War in 1821, from Picolata, as follows:

"Seven years ago some self-styled patriots committed great ravages among the Europeans and friendly Indians, in this part of Florida. Almost all the houses were burnt; the domestic animals killed, and the slaves carried off."

In a correspondence between the Spanish Governor of St. Augustine and the Governor of Georgia, in December 1812, the former thus refers to some of the ex-

---

* These fanatics, residing principally in southern Georgia, had organized for the purpose of capturing Florida from the Spaniards and Indians. The United States Government sent word to the Governor of St. Augustine that the invasion was unauthorized.

† This highly respected gentleman died in the summer of 1821. He was a Frenchman, educated and refined, and was deeply attached to the Indians.

citing causes of the Indian outbreaks, and to the leading
object of the invasion of the whites :

" . . . But the Indians, you say—well, sir, why
wantonly provoke the Indians, if you dislike their rifle
and tomahawk? General Matthews told Payne, in the
square of Latchuo, that he intended to drive him from
his lands. McIntosh* sent a message to Bowlegs, another
Indian chief, that he intended to make him as a waiting
man; the Florida Convention (Patriots) partitioned
their (the Indians') lands amongst their volunteers, as
appears by a certificate in my possession signed by di-
rector McIntosh; the Indian trade was destroyed by
you and your friends, and they (the Indians) found
that, from the same cause, they were to be deprived of
their annual presents. These, sir, are the provocations
about which you are silent. . . . The Indians are to
be insulted, threatened, and driven from their homes; if
they resist, nothing less than extermination is to be
their fate. But you deceive yourself, sir, if you think
the world is blind to your motives; it is not long since
the State of Georgia had a slice of Indian lands, and
the fever is again at its height. . . ."

David B. Mitchell, twice Governor of Georgia, and
afterward (1817) Indian Agent, thus testified, regarding
the origin of the next trouble with the Seminoles, before
a committee of the United States Senate appointed in
1818 to investigate " the advance of the United States'
troops into West Florida," &c.:

" The peace of the frontier of Georgia has always
been exposed and disturbed more or less by acts of violence committed by whites as well as by Indians. . . .
These acts were increased by a set of lawless and

---

* Reference was had to General George Matthews and John H. McIntosh, leaders of the revolutionists.

abandoned characters (whites), who had taken refuge on both sides of the St. Mary's River, and living principally by plunder. . . . I believe the first outrage committed on the frontier of Georgia, after the treaty of Fort Jackson (1814), was by a party of these banditti, who plundered a party of Seminole Indians on their way to Georgia for the purpose of trade, killing one of them. This produced retaliation on the part of the Indians."*

Another factor, by some believed to be the primary cause of all the serious trouble that followed, was the determined refusal on the part of the Seminoles to deliver up the negro slaves who had fled from their masters in States north of the Florida line and taken refuge among the Indians.

There was still another cause, however. White residents in Georgia, becoming bold from the peaceful character of the Seminoles, crossed the boundary and settled upon their lands. A leading chief sent repeated notices to the trespassers that unless they departed there would be bloodshed. No heed was given to these warnings; on the contrary other settlers continued to arrive. The appropriation of the Indians' lands became so common, that Peter Early, Governor, and Commander-in-Chief of the army and navy of Georgia, fearing trouble, finally issued the following proclamation, dated Milledgeville, April 25th, 1814:

"Whereas, I have received repeated information that divers persons, citizens of this State, are making settlements on the Indian lands contiguous to our frontier by clearing ground and preparing to raise crops thereon. And whereas, such trespasses, in addition to the severe punishment annexed to them, are at this time peculiarly improper, I have therefore thought fit to issue

* Contained in the Committee's report.

this proclamation warning all persons against perseverance in or repetition of such unwarrantable procedures. And do hereby require all persons, citizens of this State, who have made any settlement . . . on the Indian lands, forthwith to abandon the same. . . ''

The Seminoles continued to be harassed, however, and finally took the law into their own hands.* For this, they were loudly denounced, as usual, and in this way the attention of the United States Government was secured. Instead of striking at the primary cause of this particular trouble, the latter perpetrated one of the most savage massacres against the Seminoles and their negro allies, of which any civilized or uncivilized people have ever been guilty.

Before giving an account of this wanton destruction of human life, it seems an appropriate place to notice the negroes who lived among the Indians. These people formed two distinct classes: the Maroons, and the more recent fugitive slaves. The former had been living with the Seminoles for so long a period that, although they had once been runaway slaves from Georgia and Alabama, or were descended from such, their identity had now become completely lost.† The title, ''Maroons,'' a Spanish word of West Indian origin, signifying ''free negroes,'' had been appropriately applied to them by the Spanish settlers in Florida. By the Indian agents and officers of our army they were usually referred to as ''Indian negroes,'' or ''Maroon negroes,'' while all others were called ''slaves'' or ''runaway slaves.''

* Article VI of a treaty between the United States and tho Creek nation, signed in tho city of New York, Aug. 7th, 1700, states that trespassers on the Indians' lands "shall forfeit the protection of the United Sta es, and the Creeks may punish him or not. as they please." Had the same law applied to the Seminoles and other tribes throughout the United States, in after years, millions of money and thousands of lives would have escaped sacrifice.

† Ex. Doc. 195, 2d Ses., 17th Cong. Also Ex. Doc. 1st Ses., 24th Cong.

The Maroons were thoroughly established among the Seminoles, had in a few cases intermarried with them, and were regarded more as brethren and allies. Most of them, however, were still held by the Indians in a mild form of servitude. Their happy and contented condition formed a striking contrast to the hard life of unrequited toil which was the usual lot of slaves under white overseers. J. A. Peniere, Indian agent, thus referred to these negroes in the year 1821:

"These negroes appeared to me to be far more intelligent than those who are in absolute slavery, and have great influence over the Indians. . . . . Their number is said to be upwards of three hundred. They fear being again made slaves, under the American Government."

In the same connection, a staff officer of General Gaines says:

"His life among the Indians is one, compared to that of negroes under overseers, of luxury and ease; the demands upon him are very trifling. . . The Indian loves his negro as much as one of his own children."*

This humane treatment of their slaves is in accord with the quiet domestic disposition and prevailing agricultural habits of the Seminoles, thus strongly contrasted with most of the Indian tribes.

The Seminoles positively refused to give up the Maroons, who had so long been their faithful allies, or even to assist in the capture of the runaway slaves. From this latter resolution, however, they receded, years afterward, as we shall see, for the sake of peace. The slave-catchers from adjoining States made extended forays across the Spanish lines into the Indian country, and in these expeditions frequently seized the Indians'

* War in Florida, 1836.

slaves as well as the fugitives for whom they were in pursuit. The slave-hunters also robbed a number of the Spanish settlers in Florida, carrying off their negroes and other property. Claims for indemnity for the loss of these latter slaves were before Congress as late as 1860.

The Spanish Governors of the province of Florida recognized both the Maroons and the fugitive slaves as subjects of the Spanish crown, entitled to the same pro·tection as the white citizens and Indians. Therefore, when the colonial government of South Carolina sent a messenger, in 1738, to demand a return of the fugitives, the Governor not only refused to deliver them up, but proclaimed protection and liberty to all such as would join his standard.* In 1742 the numbers of Maroons and fugitive slaves in Florida were so great that they were formed into military companies, officered by negroes adorned with gold lace, bearing the same rank as those commanding white companies.†

We will now take up the thread of our story. In the latter part of the year 1814, the British erected a fort on the left bank of the Apalachicola River, about twenty-five miles above its bay. On their departure from the country, they turned the fort over to the Indians and negroes of the neighborhood. From the official report of Col. Duncan L. Clinch, who took a prominent part in the assault on this fortress, we extract the following description:

"The parapet was about fifteen feet high and eighteen feet thick, and defended by one 32, three 24s, two 9s, two 6s, and an elegant 5 1-2 inch howitzer. It was situated on a beautiful and commanding bluff, with

---

* History of South Carolina, Vol II, Ramsey, 1858.

† Trumbull's History of the United States, 1810.

the river in front, a large creek just below, a swamp in the rear, a small creek just above, which rendered it difficult to be approached by artillery. . . . "

In an official report to the War Department under date of May 14th, 1815, Gen. E. P. Gaines, then commanding the army on the frontier of Georgia, first speaks of this fortress, referring to it as "Negro Fort,"* and stating that while the occupants were charged with no crimes, he would keep a watch on their movements. A year later plans were formed for attacking the fort, although it was on Spanish soil, about fifty miles from the United States line. On the 16th of May 1816, Gen. Andrew Jackson, commander of the Southern Military District, wrote General Gaines as follows:

"I have little doubt of the fact that this fort has been established by some villains for the purpose of rapine and plunder, and that it ought to be blown up regardless of the ground on which it stands; and if your mind shall have formed the same conclusion, destroy it and return the stolen negroes and property to their rightful owners."

General Gaines also received the following instructions from the Secretary of War:

"On receipt of this letter, should the Seminole Indians still refuse reparation for their outrages and depredations on the citizens of the United States, it is the wish of the President that you consider yourself at liberty to march across the Florida line and to attack them within its limits, should it be found necessary, unless they should shelter themselves under a Spanish post."†

In July 1816, General Gaines advanced to the attack upon the fort. His command consisted of a regiment of

---

* Fort Gadsden was afterward established on the site.

† House Doc. 122, 15th Cong., 2d Ses. Vol. 6.

regulars, under Col. Duncan L. Clinch, and five hundred Creek Indians. The latter had been secured by promises "that they should share in the plunder."* Two 18-pound cannon formed part of the equipment. Gunboats had previously been detailed and sent to Apalachicola Bay, via the Gulf. The land forces arrived at the place on the 20th of July, and the gunboats a few days later.

The Indians and Maroons had received intelligence of the proposed attack, and those living in the settlements near by, and in the surrounding country, repaired to the fortress with their families. The cultivated fields of the Indians and negroes "extended fifty miles up the river."†

Returning to the official report of General Clinch, that officer says:

" . . . I ordered Major McIntosh to keep one-third of his men constantly hovering around the fort, (on the 20th), and to keep up an irregular fire. . . On the 24th, I ordered Lieutenant Wilson to descend the river with a small party, to assist in getting up the vessels, and to inform the commanding officer that the fort was completely surrounded and that he might ascend the river in safety. On the 26th I went on board gun-vessel 149, about four miles below the fort. In the course of the evening, after consulting with the commanding officer of the convoy, I directed him to move up the two gunvessels at daylight next morning. About six o'clock in the morning they came up in handsome style, and made fast alongside of the intended battery.

"In a few moments we received a shot from a 32 pounder, which was returned in a gallant manner.

* Official statement of Sailing-Master Loomis, in charge of the gunboats used on the occasion,

† View of West Florida, John Lee Williams, 1827,

The contest was momentary. The fifth discharge (a
hot shot) from gun-vessel No. 154, commanded by sailing-master Basset, entered the magazine and blew up
the fort. The explosion was awful, and the scene horrible beyond description. Our first care on arriving at
the scene of destruction was to rescue and relieve the
unfortunate beings that had survived the explosion.

"The war yells of the Indians, the cries and lamentations of the wounded, compelled the soldier to pause
in the midst of victory, to drop a tear for the sufferings
of his fellow beings, and to acknowledge that the great
Ruler of the Universe must have used us as instruments
(!) in chastising the blood-thirsty and murderous
wretches that defended the fort."

> "The waves a moment backward bent—
> The hills that shake, although unrent,
> As if an earthquake passed—
> The thousand shapeless things are driven
> In cloud and flame athwart the heaven,
> By that tremendous blast."

"The property taken and destroyed," continues
General Clinch, "could not have amounted to less than
$200,000. From the best information I could obtain,
there was in the fort about three thousand stand of
arms, from five hundred to six hundred barrels of powder, and a great quantity of fixed ammunition, shot,
shells, etc. One magazine, containing one hundred and
sixty-three barrels of powder, was saved, which was a
valuable prize to the Indians. . . . The greater part of
the negroes belonged to the Spaniards and Indians. . ."

The Spanish Governor demanded the property saved,
but the United States refused to give it up, and Spain
not being in a position to enforce compliance with her
demand, was obliged to submit.

After the occurrence of this horrible massacre, the

border whites grew still more rapacious, and the red men suffered accordingly. Referring to one of the numerous depredations against them, *Niles Register*, April 12th, 1817, says: "The Seminole Indians, we are assured from high authority, have been plundered and one or two of them murdered." Another authority thus feelingly speaks in their behalf: "We believe they have been more 'sinned against than sinning;' and that if the truth was known it would appear that there never was a more oppressed race of men."

Again the Seminoles, unable to restrain their savage passions longer, tasted the revenge so dear to the Indian heart. A detachment of forty soldiers, together with seven women and children, were ascending the Apalach-icola River in a transport, when a large band of Indians and Maroons attacked them and killed all but six persons, four of whom were wounded. Other engagements followed, and our Government once more invaded Florida in pursuit of the Indians, and against the Spanish posts, which latter it was claimed furnished the red men with ammunition.

It must not be supposed that these invasions were made without at least a protest from the Spaniards. Their Government, through Don Jose Masot, Governor of Pensacola, protested to General Jackson in the following terms:

"It having come to my knowledge that you have passed the frontier with the troops under your command, and that you are within the territory of this province of West Florida, which is subject to my Government, I solemnly protest against this procedure as an offense against my sovereign, exhorting you and requiring you, in his name, to retire from it; as, if you do not, and continue your aggressions, I shall repel force by force. . . . .'' *

On the 6th of April, 1818,—soon after the above protest,—General Jackson again invaded Florida, and captured the fortress of St. Marks from the Spaniards. There was nothing to justify this hostile act against a friendly nation, and our Government disavowed it by immediately restoring the captured fort. The attack seemed to have been made solely in a spirit of bravado.

While at St. Marks, an act of barbarism was committed, with the approval of General Jackson, which indelibly stains the annals of our country. General Jackson had ordered Captain McEver, commander of the naval forces in the Gulf, to cruise along the coast and capture and make prisoners of all persons, together with all vessels, of whatever description. A friendly flag (British) was raised by Captain McEver, and by this means four Seminoles—two of the number being chiefs—were decoyed on board his vessel. They were afterward taken ashore and hanged in cold blood. The victims of this act of treachery and perfidy were on neutral soil, and not in arms against us, nor were they charged with any crimes; they were murdered merely as ''an example,''† as stated by General Jackson.

On the day following the above incident, General Jackson, in command of a large body of troops, commenced a march to the Indian settlements on the Suwanee River, where the last assaults of the so-called war were made by burning several Indian villages. A large number of women and children were captured, together with cattle and ponies. Scarcely any resistance was made by the Indians.

* Am. State Papers, Military Affairs, Vol. I.
† Letter of General Jackson, *Niles Register*, June 13, 1818.

Our army was now withdrawn and peace was at once restored. Several hundred lives—nearly all Indians and negroes—and a large amount of money had been sacrificed, while an established law of nations, as well as our Constitution, had been repeatedly violated and a friendly power subjected to gross indignities.

The President and General Jackson were severely criticised by the American people and others, for the invasions of Spanish territory, and for the wholesale bloodshed and destruction which followed. So great was the feeling against the last operations in Florida, which had been commenced and carried on by the General without previous authority, that an investigation was authorized by Congress in 1818, as before referred to. Each house reported by committee, censuring that officer. The Senate report was especially severe, among other things saying that "the weakness of the Spanish authorities is urged in justification of this outrage upon our Constitution."

After the appearance of the Congressional report, "A citizen of the State of Tennessee" published a volume of over one hundred pages, entitled, "A Vindication of the Measures of the President and his Commanding Generals in the Commencement and Termination of the Seminole War."

A curious circumstance occurred in the fall of 1819, as a result of the severe treatment received by the Seminoles at the hands of the frontier settlers. On the 29th of September in the above year, a party of twenty-eight Seminoles arrived at Nassau, N. P., in a wrecking vessel from the coast of Florida, for the purpose of seeking assistance from the commander-in-chief of the British troops, stationed on the island. The exiles were entirely destitute, and said they had been robbed and

driven from their homes. They were furnished with
rations and lodgings at the barracks, to relieve their
immediate distress.* The author is unable to learn
what became of this party.

* **Bahama** *Advertiser*, Oct. 2d, 1819.

CHAPTER III.

NEAMATHLA, THE PRINCIPAL CHIEF OF THE NATION—OTHER
DISTINGUISHED CHIEFS—JOHN HICKS AND MICKENOPAH,
SUCCESSORS TO NEAMATHLA—OSCEOLA AND HIS ASSO-
CIATE CHIEFS—EARLY LIFE AND PERSONAL APPEARANCE
OF OSCEOLA—HIS PEACEABLE CHARACTER—CESSION OF
FLORIDA TO THE UNITED STATES—EVENTS LEADING TO
THE SEMINOLE WAR—ACTS OF INJUSTICE—PROOF THAT
THE SEMINOLES WERE PEACEABLE.

Seventeen years elapsed after the close of General
Jackson's invasions, before open warfare again took
place. Before considering some of the events which
preceded and influenced the return to arms, it is appropriate to notice the principal chiefs and head-men of the
Seminole nation. We subjoin the full Indian names of
the more conspicuous men, with their English definitions
where known.*

The nation was divided into towns, as before mentioned, located in various parts of the country. Each
town was presided over by a head chief, but there was
one principal chief over all. The man who occupied this
responsible position, as early as 1820, was named Neamathla, and he resided in West Florida. This chief was
a remarkable character, and deserves more than passing
notice in these pages.

Colonel Gad Humphreys, who was appointed agent
for the Seminoles in 1822,—not long after the death of
Mr. Peniere,—thus speaks of Nea-mathla, in a letter

* According to the earliest authorities, treaties, official and private
letters of Indian agents and others.

written in April, 1824, to Wm. P. Duval, Governor of
the Territory:

"The promptitude with which Neamathla has uni-
formly, since the war, punished the offences of his
people, particularly those against the white inhabitants
of the country, has excited in the Indians an awe and
respect for his character, and gives him unbounded
influence over them, and, at the same time, furnishes the
surest proof of the strength of his desire to be on terms
of amity with the United States." *

Later in the same month, Governor Duval wrote the
Secretary of War regarding this chief, as follows:

"Neamathla is a most uncommon man; . . . This
chief you will find, perhaps, the greatest man you have
ever seen among the Indians.†   He can, if he chooses to
do so, control his warriors with as much ease as a colonel
could a regiment of regular soldiers; they love and fear
him . . . The hospitality and manly feelings of this
chief have always kept him in poverty . . . This chief
should be seen by you and then you can judge of the
force and energy of his mind and character."

The leading chiefs under Neamathla were: John
Hicks, Mulatto King, John Blunt, Cochran, Emath-lo-
chee, E-con-chatti-mico, and Tus-ki-hajo. Neamathla
was succeeded by John Hicks in 1825, and the latter by
Mick-e-no-pah (meaning a king over a king), some time
previous to 1832. Mickenopah was the owner of quite
a large number of slaves, also immense herds of cattle
and ponies. George Catlin, the celebrated artist in
Indian portraiture, who visited the Seminoles on two
different occasions, describes him as a "very lusty and
dignified man." His complexion was very dark, indicat-

---

* Am. State Papers, Vol. II, Indian Affairs, pp. 616–17.

† At the time this letter was written, Neamathla was contemplating a
visit to Washington, but the trip was finally given up.

ing the presence of Yamasee or negro blood in his veins.
The present town of Micanopy, Fla., preserves the name
of this warrior; in fact it was so-called long before the
seven years war, when Mickenopah himself occupied the
neighborhood with his followers.

The second chief under Mickenopah was Emathla,
or King Philip, as he was more commonly called. On
account of his advanced years he took only occasional
active part in the war. The other chiefs at this period
who became distinguished in one way or another, were
as follows:

Os-ce-o-la, or Rising Sun; Co-ee-hajo, or Hal-pat-ter
Tus-te-nug-gee, Alligator; Ye-ho-lo-gee, The Cloud;
Ho-lata-amathla, Jumper; Coo-e-coo-chee, or Co-wot-go-
chee, Wildcat; Thlock-lo Tustenuggee, Tiger Tail;
Charley Amathla; Ho-lata-mico, Blue King, more gen-
erally known as Billy Bowlegs; Ar-pe-i-ka, Sam Jones;
O-tal-ke-thlocko, The Prophet; Cha-ki-ka; Waxy-hajo;
Halleck Tustenuggee; Ya-ha-hajo, Mad Wolf; Hal-pa-
too-chee, and Ya-ho-la-hajo.

Wildcat was the son of King Philip. On the death
of Osceola he became the recognized leader of the war
party, and retained that distinction until he was transferred to Arkansas. Billy Bowlegs was a nephew of
Mickenopah; he possessed great influence in the last
hostilities (1855–58), and could speak English quite
well. His paternal ancestor was formerly called
"Boleck," but the whites soon corrupted this to Bowlegs.

Like the great Northwestern chief Black Hawk, and
many other noted chiefs, Osceola had more than one
name. His common name in the nation was As-se-ola,
and this was pronounced in different ways, as follows:
Yo-se-ola, As-se-he-ho-la, and Yo-se-ya-ho-la, by the

GROUP OF OSCEOLA'S WARRIORS.

1—MICKENOPAH. 2—KING PHILIP.
3—WILDCAT. 4—CLOUD.
5—ALLIGATOR. 6—ABRAHAM.

1, 2, 4 and 5 are from paintings by Catlin, in the Smithsonian Museum, Washington, D. C

Indians and Os-ce-o-la, or O-ce-o-la, by the whites. It is said that one of his names signified the "Black Drink," a dark-colored decoction of herbs, used freely by the Seminoles before important events, with the belief that it purified and invigorated the mind and body.* But the name by which he was commonly known signified "Rising Sun," according to the interpreters and to several of the army officers. The author of a little work relating to this famous Indian, states that he was also known as "The Sun," or "The Young Sun." †

It was a custom with certain Indian tribes, at the moment when a child was born among them, for the father or a medicine man present, to look out of the wigwam and to give the new-born infant the name of the first object, or impression, which happened to attract his notice. If, looking upward, he chanced to see a cloud driven before the wind, the child would receive the name "Flying Cloud." If the cry of a coyote happened to strike the ear, the name "Coyote" or "Howling Wolf" was given.

While the author has no positive knowledge that this custom was practiced by the Seminoles, still, in the case now under consideration, we may imagine that the infant first saw the light just as the sun was about to appear in the east, and therefore received the musical and auspicious name, "Osceola." If so, it was a most appropriate omen, for the babe then ushered into the world grew to be the brighest light of his nation, as well as one of the most world-famous of our American Indians.

To many of the whites Osceola was also known by the name of "Powell," and was believed to be the son

* Still used by the Florida Seminoles, at their annual Green Corn Festival.

† Osceola, By a Southerner, 1888.

of an English trader by that name. This was an error, however, perpetuated to the present day. The idea no doubt originated from the fact that an English trader by that name married Osceola's mother after the death of the boy's father.* Osceola himself repeatedly and scornfully repudiated the name "Powell." On one occasion he said to an army officer, in this connection: "No foreign blood runs in my veins; I am a pure-blood Muskogee." His own declarations were supported by those of other Indians, and many whites, who were well acquainted with him and his birthplace.

Dr. Welsh, an Englishman residing near Jacksonville at the time of Osceola's capture, became very much interested in the young chief. After returning to England, in July, 1841, this gentleman published a very interesting book, relating to his sojourn in America, part of which was devoted to Osceola's life.† In it he says:

"Judging from all I have been able to learn of the chief Osceola, from respectable white men who knew him from childhood, he was undoubtedly a thoroughbred Seminole."

George Catlin, than whom no man living or dead is more competent to give an opinion on this point, says:

"All his conversation is entirely in his own tongue; and his general appearance and actions those of a full-blood and wild Indian." ‡

A Florida editor, in an article entitled, "The Indian Chief Powell," also agrees with the authorities above quoted, as follows:

"It is proper to observe that he ought not to be

* Indian Tribes of the United States, McKinney & Hall, 1844.
† Osceola Nikkanochee, London, 1841. (See Appendix.)
‡ Eight Years' Travel Among the North American Indians, London, 1841.

called Powell, as that is only a nickname. His Indian name is Osceola, and by that he should be distinguished."*

In the official dispatches of the day this chief was usually referred to as "Powell," sometimes "Osceola or Powell;" and the cyclopedias and other works of the present time fall into the common error and declare in positive terms that Osceola was the half-blood son of an Englishman. If, however, we have established our position, we may safely infer that whatever intelligence and skill, or mercy and magnanimity this famous warrior possessed, was not due to the presence of a drop of white man's blood in his veins.

Osceola was born on the Chattahoochee River, in the State of Georgia, in the year 1804. After his father's death, his mother moved to Florida in 1808, and settled near the present site of Ocala, Marion County. As a youth, many testify to the fact that Osceola was a great favorite with his tribe, being uncommonly bright, accomplished and energetic. "Cudjoe," who was interpreter to our army for several years, and who had known Osceola from his childhood, said he was a very active youth, excelling in the chase, in running, leaping, ball-playing, and other Indian exercises.

When he attained manhood, his appearance was very prepossessing. He was of medium height, with a superb figure and a graceful elastic step. His black hair, as in after life, hung in tresses about his face, which was rendered attractive by a high, full forehead, large, luminous eyes, and a small, well-shaped mouth expressing indomitable firmness.

Army officers often spoke of Osceola's voice as being remarkably clear, shrill and far reaching. In

* St. Augustine *Herald*, Jan. 13th, 1836.

battle he was frequently heard above all others, urging his warriors on, or exhorting them to remain firm. The dreaded Seminole war-cry, "*Yo-ho-e-hee*," sounded from his lips, left a lasting impression on the memory of those who heard it.

Osceola evinced great pride of character, joined with no small share of self-esteem and vanity. He dressed with care and neatness, and decorated his person with a number of ornaments, chief among which was an ever-present plume of black and white ostrich feathers, doubtless purchased from some trader. In his intercourse with strangers he was reserved, but with those whom he believed to be his friends he often talked freely, though always through an interpreter.

Up to within a short period of the war, Osceola lived near Fort King, Marion County. When he first became known to the army officers at the fort, one of them said, "His deportment and appearance were such as to point him out as a person likely to become prominent." Another officer at the same fort thus paid him a higher tribute:

"He visited the fort frequently, and his services were always at the command of the officers to suppress the depredations of those lawless Indians who would sometimes cross the frontier to plunder." The same officer says that Osceola was continually engaged in some service, and that he became a favorite with many of the inmates of the fort.

Facts like these, and others to follow, clearly prove that Osceola was actuated by a sincere desire to deal justly by the whites and to live on friendly terms with them. Nor can we resist the conclusion that by this distinguished course he was entitled to very different treatment at their hands from that which he afterward received.

No great time was suffered to elapse after the close of
hostilities in 1818, before Southern statesmen, in the
interest of slave-owners and those who coveted the
lands, began to advocate the purchase of Florida from
Spain. One object of this was to deprive the Indians
and negroes of the protection of Spanish law and to
bring them under our own jurisdiction. The result
was, that partly by treaty and partly by force and
threats, Florida was finally ceded to the United States, for
the sum of $5,000,000. As soon as the transfer of the
territory became known to the Indian slaves and the
free negroes about St. Augustine, many of the former
and most of the latter transported themselves to Havana.*

The treaty of cession, however, did not mention the
particular rights of the Indians with respect to that
portion of the territory which they had occupied and
controlled for so long a period. This omission was soon
discovered by the Seminoles, through their interpreters,
and it caused them no little alarm. They finally forwarded a paper to St. Augustine for transmittal to the
President, in which they complained that the treaty
had been made without any notice of their claims or
stipulations as to their rights, and requested to be
informed of the views of the executive on these points.
Referring to their need of a larger territory than the
white people, and their ancient right to the soil, the
paper read :

"The Americans live in towns, where many thous-
and people busy themselves within a small space of
ground, but the Seminole is of a wild and scattered
race; he swims the streams, and leaps over the logs of
the wide forest in pursuit of game, and is like the

* Stroud's Sketches.

whooping crane that makes its nest at night far from the spot where it dashed the dew from the grass and flower in the morning. A hundred summers have seen the Seminole warrior reposing undisturbed,under the shade of his live oak, and the suns of a hundred winters have risen on his ardent pursuit of the buck and the bear, with none to question his bounds or dispute his range.''

A correspondent, writing from St. Augustine in September 1821, thus refers to the eloquence of the Seminole in the above letter:

"I had hitherto supposed with many others that the Indians were in general much indebted to the translators of their talks, but this does not appear to be the case in the present instance. I conversed with the gentleman who took down the letter from the mouth of the interpreter, and he informed me that he had given it verbatim as he had received it." *

The exchange of flags between the Spaniards and Americans took place in July, 1821. Under dates of September 2d and 17th, General Jackson, the newly appointed Governor, wrote the Secretary of War regarding the Indians, in which he assumed that the red men had no claim to Florida lands. In his first letter he says, "With a little trouble and expense, all the Indians in the Floridas could be removed up into the Creek nation (in Georgia), and at once consolidated with them. . . ." In his letter of the 17th, he thus refers to the same subject:

"The greater part of the Indians now in the Floridas consist of those who fled in the manner above mentioned; and why should we hesitate to order them up at once, when the Executive Government, with the

* *Gazette*, Charleston, S. C.

aid of Congress, can do ample justice, by law, if necessary, to those who deserve it, by giving such equivalent as will enable them to settle their families in the upper country, and to cultivate their farms. Unless the Indians be consolidated at one point, where is the country that can be brought into market, from which the five millions are to be raised, to meet the claims of our citizens under the late treaty with Spain?'' *

In order to justify his position, the General assumes that the Seminoles had no right to Florida soil because they had "fled," as he says, from the Creeks. The reader already knows the true reason for the emigration; also for how long a period the offshoot had retained possession of their adopted country,† after they had first secured control by conquest, according to their custom. But the last sentence in the foregoing quotation is the most significant, *as indicating the real object of the proposition at this and later periods, for removing the Indians to another country.* The ejection, however, was not attempted at this time; perhaps the rank injustice of such a scheme may have had some influence with the Government.‡

From the time that Florida became a possession of the United States, a certain element of the white settlers were disposed to look upon the territory as belonging wholly to us, ignoring entirely the claims of the Indians. Now began a series of the grossest acts of injustice toward the red men, including in many cases a bare-faced robbery of their fields, as well as their cattle and slaves.

We subjoin the evidence of a few impartial witnesses in this connection. Captain John T. Sprague,

* Am. State Papers, Vol II, Indian affairs.
† General Jackson is himself a witness on this latter point.

‡ This was the earliest proposition, at least of an official nature, to remove the Seminoles from Florida.

prominent throughout the war, and the author of the
best and latest history of the same from the white man's
stand-point, thus refers to the class who were almost
constantly harassing the Indians :

"It must be remembered that Florida, at the period referred to, was an Indian border, the resort of a
large number of persons, more properly temporary inhabitants of the Territory than citizens, who sought
the outskirts of civilization to perpetrate deeds which
would have been promptly and severely punished if
committed within the limits of a well regulated community. They provoked the Indians to aggressions,
and upon the breaking out of the war they ignominiously
fled or sought employment in the service of the General
Government, and clandestinely contributed to its continuance."*

It must not be inferred from the above that the
bona fide citizens of the country were *all* guiltless, for
they were not, as the reader will soon perceive.

Charles Vignoles, a United States Civil Engineer
who surveyed the Atlantic coast of the Territory, from
St. Marys River to Cape Florida, soon after the transfer,
gives some striking instances of these impositions upon
the Indians, among which is the following:

"A few worthless wretches from St. Augustine,
for the purpose of alarming the Indians and inducing
them to sell their slaves for almost nothing,—a piece of
imposition that had often before been practiced,—went
into the nation and spread reports that two thousand
American troops, under General Jackson, were coming
down to expel them from their lands and carry away
their slaves and cattle. The Indians upon this abandoned their crops and sold many of their slaves, by

*Origin, Progress and Conclusion of the Florida War, 1847.

which the avarice of the speculators was gratified."*

In corroboration of the above, we extract from a letter written by George Clarke, Esq., one of the most influential and highly respected residents of Florida, to Captain John R. Bell, commanding in the Territory. Captain Bell called on Mr. Clarke in 1821 for information regarding the section of country (northern border) in which he lived. In his reply, Mr. Clarke speaks of the "very grievous evil of parties of Floridians and Georgians combined, going frequently to the Indian country of Florida to plunder cattle; a lucrative practice that had been going on for years, and was carried to such excess that large gangs of cattle could be purchased along the river (St. Marys) at the low price of from two to three dollars per head."†

Woodbine Potter, a staff officer of General Gaines, who took copious notes during his stay in Florida and afterwards published a book, says of the depredations of white men:

"I am inclined to believe, from the mass of evidence furnished me, that the whites have not been backward in applying Indian property to their own uses, whenever it may have suited their convenience, and as the laws were alone favorable to the whites in consequence of the exclusion of Indian evidence in courts of justice,‡ they thought they had a doubtless right to do with the Indian or his property as they might think proper."‖

Another observer thus testifies:

*Observations Upon the Floridas, Vignoles, 1823.

†Contained in the Report of Rev. Jedidiah Morse to the Secretary of War, 1822. Also in Am. State Papers, Vol. 2, Indian Affairs.

‡"Every human being born upon our continent. or who comes here from any quarter of the world, whether savage or civilized can go to our courts for protection, except those who belong to the tribes who once owned this country."—Horatio Seymour.

‖The war in Florida, by a Late Staff Officer, 1836.

"Year after year the avaricious whites continued to advance farther and deeper into the peaceful country of the Seminoles, until they occupied the fairest portion of their soil. They corrupted the Indians by mean and petty traffic; degraded them with intoxicating and ruinous draughts; and contaminated their rude and simple virtues by frequent examples of deception and fraud, until, finally, by extortion and oppression, they roused the slumbering spirit of revenge, and drove the savages to madness and desperation."*

Perhaps the most convincing evidence, however, of the feeling and injustice toward the Seminole, is furnished in a statement made by a member of the Florida Legislative Council, in 1824, to Colonel Gad Humphreys, Indian Agent; after referring to the unwillingness of the nation to remove from the Territory, this representative of the people said:

"THE ONLY COURSE, THEREFORE, WHICH REMAINS FOR US TO RID OURSELVES OF THEM, IS TO ADOPT SUCH A MODE OF TREATMENT TOWARD THEM, AS WILL INDUCE THEM TO ACTS THAT WILL JUSTIFY THEIR EXPULSION BY FORCE."†

Reader, whoever you are, and whatever your views regarding the Indian in general, is not the above strong and conclusive evidence that the Seminoles were peaceably inclined? But let us clinch this with further proof, from a still higher source:

Judge Robert R. Reid, Governor of the Florida Territory in 1839, thus eloquently declared, in an oration delivered at St. Augustine July 4th, 1838:

*Osceola, by a Southerner, 1838.

†Official report of the agent to Thomas L. McKenney, Superintendent of Indian Affairs, under date of Aug. 9th, 1825.

"And cordially and quietly and prosperously were we moving on, fellow-citizens, when the Government sought to remove the Indians from our territory before the preparations for that purpose authorized the attempt. The Indians, stung by an indignity offered to Osceola, urged by his influence, and operated upon by their young men, who were panting for war, (?) gave a loose to their savage fury,—a fury which, notwithstanding the efforts of army and militia, remains yet to be subdued."*

What wonder then that such undeserved wrongs and accumulated outrages kindled in the bosom of the proud and revengeful Seminole an inextinguishable hatred for his white oppressor!

"Ye've trailed me through the forest; ye've tracked me
    o'er the stream;
And struggling through the Everglades your bristling bay-
    onets gleam;
But I stand as should the warrior, with rifle and with
    spear,—
The scalp of vengeance still is red and warns you, 'Come
    not here.'

"I loathe you in my bosom; I scorn you with mine eye;
I'll taunt you with my latest breath; I'll fight you till I die.
I ne'er will ask for quarter, and I ne'er will be your slave;
But I'll swim the sea of slaughter till I sink beneath its
    wave."

*Bench and Bar of Georgia, Miller, 1858.

CHATER IV.

Two years after the country was ceded to the
United States, it was proposed to remove the Seminoles
to the southern part of the peninsula. In order to consider a treaty to be drawn up for this purpose, seventy
of the principal chiefs and warriors were finally reluc-
tantly persuaded to visit Camp Moultrie, situated about
four miles south of St. Augustine, on Moultrie Creek.*
The first assemblage took place on the 6th of September,
1823, and the "talk" continued to the 18th. Neamathla was present, and the other Indians declared him
to be the principal chief of the nation.†

The treaty negotiated on this occasion, required
the Indians then living west of the Suwanee River, and
all others, to "relinquish all claim or title which they
have to the whole territory of Florida, with the exception of such district of country as shall herein be alloted
to them." They were to give up their old homes and
cultivated fields, where they had lived, in many cases,
for over a century, and remove to the wild country south

---

*This historic meeting place was on the south half of the southeast
quarter of Sec. 2, Tp. 8 South, Range 29 East.

†Am. State Papers, Vol. 2, Indian Affairs, p. 437.

of the Withlacoochee River. The tract selected for them was estimated to contain 5,000,000 acres.

The Indians were guaranteed "protection against all persons whomsoever, and to restrain and prevent all white persons from hunting, settling, or otherwise intruding upon said lands." The sum of $15,400 was to be divided among them as payment for their abandoned property. They were also to receive, among other things, an annuity of $5,000 for twenty years, the period during which the treaty was to remain in force. After much persuasion, thirty-three of the chiefs, including Neamathla, Mickenopah and King Philip, finally signed the document on the 18th of September.

Six of the old and prominent chiefs, who were present and had signed the treaty,—viz: Neamathla, John Blount, Mulatto King, Tuskihajo, Emathlochee, and Econchattimico,—earnestly requested that they be allowed to remain in West Florida. This request was finally granted—in consideration of the services they had rendered the United States, says the treaty—and they were allowed to select reservations along the Appalachicola and Chattahoochee Rivers, in what is now called Jackson County, and near the Ocklockney, in the present county of Gadsden. Neamathla's reservation was two miles square, and was situated in the latter locality, about four miles south of Quincy. It was afterwards thought that Neamathla was too far away from the bulk of the nation to properly govern them. This finally led to the election of John Hicks as principal chief.

At the request of the nation, a tract of land one mile square was reserved for their agent, Colonel Humphreys, as a token of the high regard in which he was held.

A prominent resident of the Territory at this time,

says that after the Indians removed to the south, "their improvements were immediately occupied by immigrants from different parts of the United States," and that "the land, to which they are legally banished, consists of dry sand ridges and interminable swamps, almost wh olly unfit for cultivation; . . . they are now in a starving condition."*

So miserable was the condition of the Seminoles in their new location, that in March 1826, President Adams addressed a message to Congress transmitting information on the subject, and asking for its favorable consideration.†

Referring to the former prosperous condition of the Seminoles in their old homes, Mr. Williams says:

"This tribe paid much attention to the raising of cattle and horses; and the women raised hogs and fowls. Indeed, their savage character was much broken; and had they continued to cultivate the rich fields of Mickasukey and Tallahassee, they would soon have attained a considerable degree of civilization."

"More than one hundred and sixty treaties with Indian tribes are on the statute books," says Thomas Donaldson, "as solemnly entered into as was a treaty with Great Britain. The effect was different, however. The Indian was powerless to enforce the treaty, and so the Indian suffered."‡

He suffered in this instance. Although the treaty expressly stipulated that white persons would be prevented from intruding on the Seminole reservation, many owners of slaves, as well as the piratical slave-catchers who only pretended to have lost such property,

*View of West Florida, Williams, 1827.
†Ex. Doc. 111, 1st Ses., 19th Cong.
‡The George Catlin Indian Gallery, 1885.

together with the cattle thieves, made forays into the new Indian settlements in every direction.

Notwithstanding the uneasy peace that prevailed, some of the wealthier Indians owned considerable numbers of negroes. E-con-chatti-mico, a chief highly respected by many white settlers, had as many as twenty, while others owned larger lots. These "Indian negroes," as mentioned in an earlier chapter, lived in a condition between servitude and freedom, usually having their own time and paying their masters an annual percentage of the crops they raised. Most of them lived apart from their masters, whom they never voluntarily left to join the whites. They were, however, frequently seized and carried off by the slave-hunters.

This practice became so common that a body of chiefs assembled at the agency, on April 17th, 1828, and protested against such outrages, declaring that "many of their negroes, horses and cattle were in the hands of the whites, for which they were unable to obtain compensation." At the same time, the Indians wanted to know "why the white people thus violated the treaty to rob them." Had the agent been frank in his reply, he would have admitted the disgraceful fact that United States citizens were ransacking their lands by permission of the Secretary of War.*

While the white settlers were allowed, on one pretext or another, to enter the country of the Indians, the latter were expressly forbidden, by an act of the Florida Legislative Council passed in 1824, to roam beyond the limits of the territory assigned them. The penalty for a violation of this act was thirty-nine stripes of the lash on the bare back of the offender, and the forfeiture of his gun. The act gave any person the right to arrest and take the Indian before a justice for sentence.

*Ex. Doc. 271, 1st Ses., 24th Cong.

There is abundant proof that the Seminoles adhered to their agreement with the Government. An officer of the 4th artillery, writing from Camp St. Johns, December 29th, 1837, pays them a glowing tribute on this point. He says, among other things, that the Treaty of Camp Moultrie "was maintained by the Seminoles with the greatest integrity," and that if an Indian passed the boundary lines without leave, "he was pursued by Indians, brought to the agency, and there, before the eyes of the agent, whipped by Indian hands."[*]

The chief Econchattimico, who with others lost all of his slaves by white robbers, finally petitioned Congress for indemnity, and called for protection according to the stipulations of Camp Moultrie Treaty, but without success.[†]

"During the nineteenth century," says the late Joshua R. Giddings, "perhaps no despotism has existed among civilized nations more unlimited or more unscrupulous than that exercised in Florida from 1823 to 1843."[‡] A vivid description of the barbarities practiced on the Seminoles, is contained in a letter from their agent, Col. Gad Humphreys, dated March 6th, 1827, to the Secretary of War.

Instead of adhering to the treaty and "preventing all white persons from hunting, settling, or otherwise intruding upon said lands," by which course peace would have been guaranteed for an indefinite period, our Government, with an avaricious eye upon the possession of the entire peninsula, now turned its attention to the removal of the Indians altogether.

In order to effect this object peaceably, a new treaty was proposed by the United States Government. The

[*] *Army and Navy Chronicle,* January 25th, 1838.
[†] Ex. Doc. 131, Vol. 2, 2d Ses., 24th Cong.
[‡] Exiles of Florida, 1858.

project, however, was not entirely new to either side. As early as 1825, George Walton, then acting as Governor of the Territory, had suggested the same plan to the Secretary of War. And again, two years later, Colonel Humphreys—whose long association with the Seminoles and full knowledge of the injustice and indignities to which they had been subjected, had enlisted his sympathies in their behalf—had assembled a number of prominent chiefs at the agency and advised them, as their friend, to avoid further trouble by emigrating west of the Mississippi. He also offered to accompany a delegation of their chiefs to inspect the new country. But the red men had refused to consider the proposition.

The usual mode of negotiating treaties with Indians, practiced from early times, with some exceptions, was to first secure the co-operation of one or more influential chiefs, by bribery and the free use of "fire-water," and then overcome the opposition of others in much the same manner. It was not always considered absolutely necessary that the signers thus secured should be representative men of the nation, qualified to act for the others; but our Government invariably declared them to be such, however.

After a like plan, no doubt, a new treaty was finally secured on the 9th of May, 1832. At that date a large body of chiefs was assembled at Payne's Landing, on the Ocklawaha River,* when fifteen of their number only, including Billy Bowlegs, Alligator, Jumper, and Charlie Amathla, could be induced to sign the articles. Neither Mickenopah nor King Philip, the first and second chiefs of the nation, (the former having succeeded John Hicks), nor indeed many others who were more

*Situated in Marion County, ten miles, following the course of the river, south of the mouth of Orange Lake Creek. The landing is now a rude affair, consisting of poles and logs, on which is a small building. For many years it has been used merely as a wood-landing for the river steamers.

prominent than most of the signers, would affix their
signatures.

An officer who afterwards served in the war, describes the scene at the signing of the Treaty of Payne's
Landing. He also speaks of the presence of Osceola,
and of his striking appearance; "his eye calm, serious,
fixed; his attitude manly, graceful, erect; his rather
thin and close-pressed lips, indicative of the 'mind made
up' of which he speaks; his firm, easy, yet restrained
tread, free from all stride or swagger; his dignified and
composed attitude; his perfect and solemn silence except
during his sententious talk; the head thrown backward
and the arms firmly folded on the protruding chest—
all instantly changed as by an electric touch whenever
the agent stated a proposition from which he (Powell)
dissented. . . . "*

· Osceola, who strongly opposed emigration, as may
be supposed, was not even a sub-chief at this time, and
therefore had no right to sign even had he desired to do
so.

By the new treaty, the Seminoles were promised
an equal amount of land in Arkansas,† west of the
Mississippi, in lieu of the five million acres which had
been granted them in Florida by the former treaty. They
were also to receive certain annuities, as well as $15,000
for the improvements to be relinquished and for the
slaves and livestock which had been stolen from them.
The Indians on their part bound themselves to pay the
sum of $7,000 as an indemnity for all fugitive slaves
then in their territory.

The fulfillment of the treaty on the part of the
Seminoles, was with this *proviso*: They agreed to send

---

*Notices of Florida and the Campaigns, Cohen, 1836.

†The country to which the tribes living east of the Mississippi River
were transferred, was formerly known as the "Indian Country," and finally as
Indian Territory.

seven of their chiefs to the West to examine the country and to bring back a report; if this should prove satisfactory *to the nation*, the removal was to be effected. This important and reasonable provision was clearly understood by all parties. The treaty itself is considered by some to be ambiguous on this point. A high authority, however, says "the fulfillment of the treaty was clearly conditional."* Seven chiefs were accordingly chosen and sent to Arkansas, accompanied by their agent, and their interpreter, "Abraham," a Maroon who acted in this capacity on nearly all important occasions.

As Abraham occupied a conspicuous place among the Seminoles, possessing great influence over them as well as over his own brethren, we will digress to briefly outline his history and character. Captain John C. Casey, an army officer of great prominence, writing his brother from Fort Brooke, Fla., under date of February 25th, 1837, says of this noted character:

"The negro Abraham is obviously a great man; though a black he has long been appointed 'sense-bearer' to the King (Mickenopah) to whom he formerly belonged. His master liberated him in consequence of his many and faithful services and great merits, and this paper is now in the possession of General Jesup, who captured it with a number of papers belonging to Abraham. Abraham is of ordinary stature, rather thin, with a slight inclination forward like a Frenchman of the old school. His countenance is one of great cunning and penetration. He always smiles, and his words flow like oil. His conversation is soft and low, but very distinct, with a most genteel emphasis. He is a full-

*Origin, Progress and Conclusion of the Florida War. Captain John T. Sprague, 1847.

blooded negro and has been all his life among the Indians.''*

General Jesup also speaks of Abraham as ''a good soldier and an intrepid leader. He is a chief, and the most cunning and intelligent negro we have here.''

Unfortunately, perhaps, for the Seminoles and the United States, Colonel Humphreys, the old and highly respected agent of the Indians, did not accompany the delegates on their journey to Arkansas. Major John Phagan, who had succeeded him in the spring of 1830, was in charge of the party. Colonel Humphreys was a man of sterling qualities of head and heart. He was thoroughly in sympathy with the Seminoles, and had labored hard and unceasingly to secure justice for them, at a time when they were oppressed by a horde of unprincipled men from all parts of the Union. He had been their agent for eight years, when he was removed from office through false representations of men who objected to the vigilance and fidelity which character- ized his every effort.†

While the delegation of chiefs were in the West, Commissioners appointed by the Government for the express purpose met them there and induced them to sign a so-called ''additional treaty.'' This piece of rascality was accomplished at Fort Gibson, Arkansas, on March 28th, 1833. The new ''treaty'' was signed by the seven delegates without the slightest authority from the nation, which at this time numbered upwards of 1,600 able bodied chiefs and warriors; in all probability, too, without a realization of the responsibility thus assumed or a suspicion of duplicity. In it they ''declare themselves well satisfied with the location provided for

*This letter and other valuable material was very kindly sent to the author by Maj. Wm. S. Beebe, a nephew of Captain Casey.

†See letter of Governor Duval, dated Jan. 2d, 1826, Am. State Papers, Vol. 2, Indian Affairs, p. 643. See also p. 685.

them by the commissioners, and agree that their nation shall commence removal to their new home as soon as the Government will make arrangements for their emigration satisfactory to the Seminole nation."

When the delegation returned and reported their action to the nation, the principal chiefs met and declared that the seven had no authority whatever to speak and act finally for the entire nation; that, in fact, neither the delegation nor the United States Commissioners were empowered to ratify any treaty. This action of the delegation and the reprehensible course of the Government in thus seeking to pledge the nation, excited great distrust in the minds even of those who were favorable to emigration.

Another reason why the Seminole nation, as a whole, strongly objected to removal, was that by the Treaty of Payne's Landing they were required to join the Creeks then in the West with whom, as we have heretofore stated, they had been at war for a long period. A provision in the "additional treaty" sought to remove this objection by assigning certain lands to the " separate use of the Seminoles forever." But the Indians were now so distrustful of the Government that no inducement whatever would influence them to give up their old homes.

Not until after a lapse of nearly two years did the United States approve the Treaty of Payne's Landing,* a delay which created additional doubt in the minds of many whites, as well as Indians, as to its validity. Nevertheless, preparations were made to carry it into effect, and on the 23d of October, 1834, General Wiley Thomson, who followed Major Phagan

*Ratified by the 23d Congress, 1st Session, and signed by Andrew Jackson, President, on the 12th of April, 1834.

as Indian agent, with headquarters at Fort King,* held
a meeting with some of the principal chiefs and sub-
chiefs of the nation, including Mickenopah and Osceola,
to secure their approval of the treaty.†   After the agent
had explained anew the provisions of the document, the
chiefs withdrew for private consultation. Osceola,
though only a sub-chief, took a prominent part in the
discussion. He begged the chiefs to remain firm,
reminding them that the nation had not approved of
the report and action of the delegation who had visited
the West. The council at length terminated with the
agreement to resist emigration at any cost; and, further,
to look upon any chief or warrior who dared to favor
the step as an enemy of the tribe. When the chiefs
returned to their conference with the agent, Osceola, acting as spokesman, stated that it was the desire of his
brethren to abide by the Treaty of Camp Moultrie, eight
years of which were still unexpired. The agent's official report shows that the council finally came to a close
with the following terse statement from Osceola:

"Powell said that the decision of the chiefs was
given, and that they did not intend to give any other
decision."‡

In the same official report General Thompson quotes
the remarks of a few other chiefs, as follows:

Mickenopah: "When we were at Camp Moultrie
we made a treaty, and we were to be paid our annuities
for twenty years. That is all I have to say."

Jumper: "At Camp Moultrie they told us that all
difficulties should be buried for twenty years, from the
date of the treaty made there."

---

*Fort King was situated about three miles east of the present town of
Ocala, Mari n County. The site only of the old fort remains to indicate
this famous old landmark.

†Ex. Doc. 638, 1st Ses., 24th Cong.

‡Ibid.

Charley Amathla: "The white people forced us into this treaty."

The person appointed by the Secretary of War to negotiate the Treaty of Payne's Landing was no other than the distinguished General James Gadsden, of South Carolina, who had acted in the same capacity at the former treaty. If the reader entertains any doubt as to the deceptive course pursued by our Government in its efforts to pledge the nation to this treaty, the subjoined statement of General Gadsden, written during the progress of the war, ought forever to remove such doubt. The St. Augustine *News* of July 13th, 1839, contained a long article over that General's signature on the subject of the Seminoles. The communication was dated at Suwanee Springs, July 6th. We extract the following:

"The chiefs went (to Arkansas) in good faith, examined, and were satisfied.* It is not to be doubted that, had they been permitted to return and make their report in council, ...the Seminoles would have been satisfied and fulfilled all the stipulations of Payne's Landing. Unfortunately the fatal mistake was made of meeting the deputation in the West with other commissioners. There the treaty was ratified by the chiefs instead of by the nation at home."

An army officer says of this transaction:

" A treaty thus obtained from an unfortunate and wretched people without means and reduced to the last extremity of distress . . . . could not—ought not to be ratified."

And the Treaty of Payne's Landing never *was* ratified by the Seminole nation.

*The delegates were satisfied with the country, but reported that the Indian inhabitants were in a deplorable condition,

CHAPTER V.

ANOTHER MEETING WITH THE CHIEFS—OSCEOLA "SIGNS" A
PAPER—THE CHIEF PLACED IN IRONS—THE AGENT'S
OPINION OF OSCEOLA—AGAIN IMPRISONED—OSCEOLA
GIVES THE WAR-CRY—SEMINOLES' RIGHT TO THEIR
HOMES—FIRST VICTIM OF THE NATION'S DECREE—OSCE-
OLA IS APPOINTED HEAD WAR-CHIEF—COMMENCEMENT
OF THE SEVEN YEARS' WAR.

We have seen that nothing was gained by the Government at the conference held at Fort King. But the
hope of reconciling the Indians to emigration had not
been relinquished, and six months later, on the 22nd of
April, 1835, General Thompson again prevailed upon a
number of chiefs and sub-chiefs to meet him at Fort
King for another "talk." He now assumed a somewhat
threatening attitude, warning them that if they should
refuse to emigrate peaceably they would be driven out
of the country with violence and bloodshed.

Fully resolved to make it appear that the entire
Seminole nation were pledged by the action of a few, the
agent concluded by inviting one after another of the
chiefs present to step forward and sign a paper acknowl-
edging the validity of the Treaty of Payne's Landing
and the so-called "additional treaty." A few complied,
but the majority simply shook their heads in refusal.
When it came Osceola's turn to be called, his companions were astonished to see him rise and walk forward in a deliberate manner, as though he was about to
affix his signature. When he reached the table he
paused, and, turning to the agent, said:

"The land is ours; we do not want an agent."

Then, before anyone could guess his intention, he quickly drew his long sheath-knife, and raising it high above his head thrust it through the paper and into the table, exclaiming in a loud voice,

"This is the only way I will sign!"*

"'And thus,' he cried, with the eye of flame,
'Thus Osceola signs your claim!'"

The meeting broke up in the greatest confusion, and Osceola, for thus asserting his independence, was at once arrested and placed in irons. He was confined in Fort King and told that he would be liberated if he would approve the treaty. At the end of four days, though still refusing to sign the paper, it is said that he gave his verbal consent to approval,† and was set free.

General Thompson's opinion of Osceola, as expressed at this period, may be of interest. In letters to the War Department, under different dates, he refers to this chief in the following style:

December 28th, 1834—"Powell, a bold, manly and determined young chief, who has perhaps been more violently opposed to removal than any other, ... "

June 3rd, 1835—"A few days since, Powell, one of the most bold, daring and intrepid chiefs in the nation, and one that has been more hostile to emigration and has thrown more embarrassments in my way than any other, ... "‡

Not long after his liberation, Osceola went to the fort and remonstrated with the agent for taking advantage of the action of a few of his brethren. After con-

*Or. "This is the only treaty I will execute!" This incident is given on the following authorities: Dr. Welch, then residing at Jacksonville; Sprague's History of the Florida War; Sketches of the Seminole War; Fairbank's History of Florida; and several newspapers of the day.

† There is no official confirmation of this report.

‡Ex. Doc. 638, 1st Ses., 24th Cong., contains both letters.

siderable excited talk, in the course of which Thompson intimated that Osceola lied, the young chief was again arrested and confined.   In his official report to the Commissioner of Indian Affairs, the agent simply said of this affair : " Powell used such language that I was compelled to order him into irons."

After a brief confinement, Osceola was once more set free.   But his proud spirit could not brook the insults he had repeatedly suffered.   The irons which had twice bound his limbs had burned deep into his soul, and only added to a fire that had been smouldering in his breast under the wrongs which he and his people had so long endured.

The author was told that the chief left the prison in silence, but that when well away he faced the fort and rent the air with the blood-curdling war-cry of the Seminoles, (*Yo-ho-e-he*), conveying eternal hatred and vengeance.   Even with this ominous warning sounded in his ears, the agent dreamed not of the terrible retribution that was so soon to overtake him!

From this moment the Seminole War may be said to have commenced, although General D. L. Clinch had long before been placed in command of troops in the territory,* and active preparations had been made for the open hostilities which must attend the forcible removal of the Indians from their rightful homes.

That the territory occupied by the Seminoles belonged to them by every consideration of justice and right, seems to the author to be indisputable.   Yet it has been claimed by some writers that the Indians, not being the original inhabitants of the peninsula, had no real right to any portion of the country.   The present

*There were 14 companies in Florida on the 30th of November, 1835, stationed principally at Fort King and Fort Brooke.

stage of our narrative would seem as appropriate a time as any other to consider this objection.

Those who maintain it, argue that the Spaniards had not recognized the Seminoles as owners of the soil; that in the cession of Florida by Spain to the United States, the Indians were not even mentioned in the treaty or recognized in any manner. We find that this plea was usually urged to excuse the general policy of the Government in its treatment of the Indians, or the acts of some of its public servants. The frontier settler, too, whom avarice often prompted to seize and occupy the Indians' clearings, justified his lawless acts by claiming that his right to the land was as good as that of the Indian.

Let us look into the equity of the Indian's claim. At a meeting between the English and the Seminoles, held at Pensacola, as early as the 18th of November, 1765, it was mutually agreed that the Indians should retain not only possession but ownership of all that portion of the province west of the St. Johns River, and between the Georgia line on the north and the Gulf. Their right was also acknowledged by the Spanish authorities, in a treaty signed at Pensacola in June 1784, as follows:

"Art. 13. As the generous feelings of his Catholic Majesty do not permit him to exact from the Indian nations any lands to form establishments to the prejudice of those who reap advantage therefrom, these motives, and a conviction of his paternal love for his people, induce us to offer you, in his royal name, the security and guarantee of those lands you actually hold, according to the rights of legitimacy, with which you possess them: that is to say, those lands comprised within the lines and limits belonging to his Catholic Majesty, our sovereign ; . . . ."

Some time after the conclusion of this treaty with Spain, the Seminoles sold Panton, Leslie and Co., English traders, a tract of land forty miles square, which sale was approved by the Spanish authorities.*

As to the failure of Spain to recognize the Indians in the treaty of cession, let the sixth article of the said treaty speak for itself.

"Art. 6. The *inhabitants* of the territories which his Catholic Majesty ceded to the United States by this treaty, shall be incorporated in the Union of the United States as soon as may be consistent with the principles of the federal Constitution, and admitted to the enjoyment of all the privileges and rights and immunities of the citizens of the United States."

The italics in the above quotation are the author's. That Spain included the Indians in the word "*inhabitants*," no one who is cognizant of the friendly relations existing between the two peoples at that period, can for a moment doubt.

In a report of the Committee on Indian Affairs, dated February 21st, 1828, to the House of Representatives, in which the rights of the Seminoles were considered, we find the following reference to the sixth article of the treaty of cession, above quoted:

". . . Hence it appears that, by treaty, we have solemnly bound ourselves to incorporate the *inhabitants* (the italics are the Committee's) of the territories of Florida into the Union. . . .The obligatory force of this treaty upon the Government, it is believed, is clear and conclusive."†

*Am. State Papers, Vol. 2, Indian Affairs.

†Am. State Papers, Vol. 2, Indian Affairs.

A Governor of the Florida Territory thus interpreted the treaty and the Constitution in the year 1838. . . .

"Sept. 1. Spain incorporated the Indians and made them subjects. Did she not pass them over to the United States by treaty, to be admitted into the Union? Yes, but according to the principles of the Constitution; and ours is a Constitution for white people, and not for red and black."*

The United States acknowledged the Seminoles' right to lands when it negotiated its first treaty with these people, at Camp Moultrie. This was in accordance with the settled opinion of the Supreme Court of the United States that "the Indian title is certainly to be respected until it be legitimately extinguished."† Therefore, the equity of the Seminoles' claim seems unquestionable, for the above treaty was *not* legitimately extinguished.

In November 1835, Osceola and the principal chiefs and warriors met in council and again resolved to resist removal. At this meeting they also decreed that the first chief who should make preparations for emigrating to the West, and who should refuse to abandon such intentions and to abide by the will of the nation, should suffer death. This action by the nation was deemed necessary on account of the number of their brethren who, preferring emigration to war, had been transported to the West previous to that time.‡

In spite of this warning, Charley Amathla (referred to by the agent as an "intelligent and honest chief") and a small party under him took their stand in favor of removal, and withdrew from the large majority. The

*Private diary of Judge Robert R. Reid. Bench and Bar of Georgia, 1858.

†Fletcher v. Peck, Cranch Vol. 6, p. 121.

‡According to the report of the Commissioner of Indian Affairs for 1836, 265 Seminoles had emigrated prior to September 30th, 1835.

nation, fearing that the influence of this chief might induce others to join him, decided to take measures to prevent such a possibility.

Accordingly, on the 26th of November, Osceola proceeded with a small party of warriors to Amathla's town and demanded that he and his followers should join the others in their fight for liberty and home. Two hours were allowed for his decision. At the end of that time Amathla still refused to join the majority, whereupon Osceola, acting by the authority of the nation, deliberately raised his rifle with the intention of killing the offender. At this moment, Abraham, the Maroon interpreter, interfered and suggested that they all retire and hold a council, which they did. Osceola and a few others, however, soon departed, and returning to the place where they had left Charley Amathla, Osceola shot him dead.

By this deliberate act, the latter justified the assertion of General Thompson that he was the most determined opponent of emigration among all the Seminole chiefs. The victim of this decree had sold a portion of his stock to the whites, preparatory to moving West, receiving his pay in gold. This money was found on his person after death, but Osceola refused to touch it or to allow any one present to do so, saying that it was the price of the red man's blood.* Soon after this event Osceola was appointed the " head war chief " of the nation.

The Seminoles now set about gathering their crops and making other preparations for the war which both Indians and whites knew to be inevitable. They removed their women and children to islands in the extensive swamps situated in the southern part of their territory;

---

*So stated by Sprague and others.

their cattle were driven to remote ranges in the same direction; they laid in large stores of ammunition. Their supplies were considerably increased by the capture of a baggage train, December 19th, (1835), which was on its way to Fort King under the escort of two hundred and fifty Florida volunteers.

If the War Department, its agents and its officers on the theater of action, had cherished any doubts as to the determined character of the people whom they had unjustly proposed to deprive of their homes, the day was now at hand when those doubts were to be dispelled. On the 28th of December, two tragic events took place which inaugurated the memorable Seminole War. Our people were now to learn that the Indians knew their rights and, knowing, dared to maintain them.

Osceola had been watching for an opportunity to revenge himself on Wiley Thompson, the Indian agent at Fort King, who, as he believed, had unjustly placed him in irons and otherwise insulted him. On the afternoon of the day above named, Osceola and a few chosen followers concealed themselves near the sutler's house, situated a few hundred yards from the fort. The agent, as fate determined, appeared within range of their rifles, accompanied by a friend, Lieutenant Constantine Smith, intent upon taking an after dinner walk.

Osceola's opportunity had now come, and he did not hesitate to strike the blow. At a signal from him the Indians fired, and both officers fell dead. Fifteen bullet holes were afterward discovered in the agent's body. The Indians then went to the sutler's house, killed the sutler and two other men, and set fire to the building. All this occurred within range of two six-pound cannon at the fort, but they could not be fired on account of an intervening structure.

After scalping their victims, Osceola and his band mounted their ponies and made all possible haste to another locality sóme sixty miles south, hoping to be in time to join Mickenopah and Alligator in a prearranged attack of far greater magnitude. In this hope Osceola was disappointed, not being able to arrive, as we shall see, until after victory had been won by his fellow warriors.

As this disastrous affair was the first, and in many respects the most memorable event of the entire war, it will be described in detail, with some particulars not heretofore published.

CHAPTER VI.

In anticipation of active hostilities, General Duncan
L. Clinch, commander of operations in Florida, had
early decided to increase the number of troops stationed
at Fort King.   For this purpose, on the 16th of December,
1835, he had ordered Major Francis L. Dade, then
stationed at Fort Brooke,* near Hillsborough Bay, to
proceed with his command to Fort King, 130 miles
distant in a northerly direction.   The route lay through
an unsettled wilderness of pine woods and hammocks,
cypress swamps and ponds.

On making inquiry for a guide and interpreter,
Major Dade was directed to a negro named Louis Pacheco,
who bore the surname of his owner, a Spanish woman,
living on the coast south of Tampa Bay.   Louis was
recommended as trustworthy and well acquainted with
the trails.   According to Captain John C. Casey, acting
quartermaster at Fort Brooke, this negro was very
intelligent, speaking four languages, and able to read
and write.   Although his condition was far better than
that of the ordinary plantation hands, he nevertheless

*Situated on the left bank of the Hillsborough River. The site only
remains, adjoining the city of Tampa on the south.

longed for freedom. He fully sympathized with the Maroons and runaway slaves in their efforts to elude the slave hunters, and he was at the same time friendly with the Indians.

While openly agreeing to the bargain between his mistress and Major Dade for his services as guide and interpreter, Louis secretly planned to inform the Indians and Maroons of the intended march through their country. He was hired on the day of Major Dade's departure, and it was afterward stated by General Jesup that Louis, according to positive proof, was in communication with the Indians from this time to the day of the massacre, keeping them posted as to the trail they would take and other facts.* The Indians had previously learned of the intended departure of the troops for Fort King, and had assembled near a certain point on the trail in order to waylay them.

At six o'clock on the morning of December 24th, Major Dade and his command, consisting of eight officers and one hundred and two non-commissioned officers and privates, commenced their ill-fated march. One of two six-pounders kept at Fort Brooke was drawn by four oxen. Owing to certain mishaps, they camped on the evening of the fourth day out only sixty-one miles from their starting point. The next morning, December 28th, the troops resumed their march at eight o'clock. When only four miles from camp they were suddenly attacked by a band of Indians.

The following account of the battle is condensed

*So stated in a letter accompanying a petition to Congress from Mrs. Pacheco, twelve years later, asking indemnity for the loss of her slave Louis, whom General Jesup had captured and sent West. (H. R. 18, 30th Cong., 1st Ses., Vol. I.) More than half a century afterward, this negro returned to Florida, and lived with his old mistress, then residing at Jacksonville. He died at this place in January 1895. (Seminoles of Florida, Willson, 1897.)

from the statements of the sole survivor of the massacre, Private Ransom Clarke :*

The battle took place in the open pine woods. The Indians lay concealed among saw palmettoes and tall grass which bordered the trail. Not a single foe had been seen nor a sign of warning received previous to the attack. At the very first fire, Major Dade and fully half of his command were killed. The rest of the troops were panic-stricken for a few moments, but soon returned the fire, and also brought the six-pounder to bear on the foe. At its first discharge the Indians withdrew out of range and did not return to the attack for about an hour. The brave soldiers took advantage of the lull and threw up rude breastworks of logs.

In the second attack, the Indians came on "like devils, yelling and whooping in such a manner that the reports of the rifles were scarcely perceptible." At one o'clock, two officers only survived. Speaking of the conduct of the troops under the second attack, Clarke says, "They were as cool as if they were in the woods shooting game." The battle lasted from about nine o'clock in the morning until four in the afternoon. The Indians numbered several hundred,† as near as Clarke could estimate in the excitement of the occasion. About half of them were mounted. They were accompanied by many Maroons, "who were more savage than the Seminoles."

Clarke was first wounded in the thigh and afterward in the arm and head. He lay inside of the breastworks, part of the time unconscious, until nine p. m. When he thought it was safe to do so, he made his way outside, and alternately limping and crawling, in constant agony

*Made to the editor of the Charleston (S. C.) *Courier,* and published in that paper Aug. 20th, 1836.

†See statement of Alligator, on a following page.

from his wounds, he managed to reach Fort Brooke on the third day after the massacre. Three other men, all privates, also left the battle-field alive. One of them was discovered at some distance from it, by an Indian, and killed; the other two made their way back to the fort, but both died later from their wounds.

Louis Pacheco, Major Dade's guide, had separated himself from the troops just before reaching the place which he well knew had been selected for the attack, and had joined the Indians and Maroons as soon as their position was disclosed.

Ransom Clarke remained at Fort Brooke, slowly recovering, until April 1836, when he was discharged for total disability. He afterward received a small pension of eight dollars per month, until his death, which event took place at York, New York, November 18th, 1840, from the effect of his wounds, at the age of only twenty-eight years. Thus the only survivor of the massacre passed away five years after it occurred.

Until the twentieth of February following, the victims of that terrible slaughter lay unburied. Major Belton, who had remained at Fort Brooke with a few troops, sent a dispatch to Fort King under date of January 1st, in which he gave an account of the massacre, as told by the survivors. He also stated that he expected an attack at any moment, and that his men were, at that writing, engaged in entrenching the place in every possible manner. The fact that Major Belton and his little command did not dare to leave the fort, accounts for the delay in the burial of the dead.

General Edmund L. Gaines, commander of the Western Military Department, with headquarters at New Orleans, was at Pensacola when he learned of the fate of Major Dade and his troops. He immediately proceeded to New Orleans, where he raised about 1,100 volunteers. With these he embarked at once for Tampa Bay, and arrived at Fort Brooke on the 10th of February. Three days later they set out for the scene of the massacre and Fort King, over the same road that Major Dade had taken. On the 20th, they arrived at the battleground,* which they found was seven miles northeast of the forks of the Withlacoochee River, near the west end of a large pond. We condense from General Gaines' official report, which was dated the 22nd of February, as follows:

"We came upon one of the most appalling scenes that can be imagined. We first saw some broken and scattered boxes; then a cart, the two oxen of which were lying dead as if they had fallen asleep, their yokes still on them; a little to the right one or two horses were seen." Those who fell at the first fire were found lying in and near the road, Major Dade and a few of his officers being in advance of the rest. On going to the rude breastworks, made by felling pine trees and forming a triangular inclosure, the partially decayed bodies of the unfortunate men who survived the first attack were found lying within. "They had evidently been shot dead, and the Indians had not disturbed them except by taking the scalps of most of them." All were recognized and accounted for. The bodies were buried on the spot, and the cannon, which had been thrown into the pond by the Indians, was planted upright at the head of the common grave.

Six years afterward, the remains were carefully exhumed and removed to St. Augustine, where the re-interment took place on the fifteenth of August, 1842.

*Situated in the northeastern part of Sec. 20, Tp. 21 South, Range 22 East, Sumter County. A bill was introduced in Congress in January 1898, by Hon. S. M. Sparkman, of Florida, for the purpose of purchasing and creating a National Military Reservation of this historic ground, with the idea of making it a National Park.

The graves are now marked by suitable monuments. The original graves at the battlefield, forming deep depresions in the sandy soil, will long remain visible as silent witnesses of the fearful struggle.

From an account given by Alligator to Captain Sprague, it seems that the attack upon Major Dade was delayed one day on account of the failure of Osceola and Mickenopah to join their brethren. The latter chief arrived on the twenty-seventh, and the attack was planned for the next morning. Mickenopah, Alligator and Jumper led the Indian forces, which numbered one hundred and eighty. Their entire loss was only three killed and five wounded. Osceola and his little party, hurrying from the scene of the tragic affair at Fort King, did not reach the camp of the victors until late in the evening.

Another account thus closes :

" Major Dade's uniform was not found. With this exception, not one of those brave but unfortunate men had been plundered. Silver, gold, jewelry and watches were untouched—nothing was taken but arms and ammunition. To what are we to ascribe conduct so singular? It was not the effect of hurry and fear of an attack by a stronger party, for they buried their own dead before leaving the field of battle. Osceola is a master spirit and must have gained a wonderful influence over the minds of his followers to induce them to forego the opportunity of gaining possession of articles of which they are notoriously fond. Our men were struck with awe and astonishment at the circumstances, and we fear that many a tragic event must be recorded before the close of this war with an enemy capable of such determination and such self-control."*

Let the reader consider that the Seminoles were far

* Editorial, *Niles' Register*, April 2d, 1836,

from being naturally a cruel and war-like people; that they had lived for many years on terms of peace with the white race, under both Spanish, English and American rule, and that all they desired—all they were fighting for now—were the simple rights which our Constitution guarantees to all men. Consider these things, and the forbearance exhibited on many occasions by the Seminoles throughout the heroic defense of their chosen homes, is fully explained. The final resort to the rifle and the scalping-knife was due to the injustice of the white man, and the intense patriotism of the Indian.

The next important incident of the war was a battle which took place on the thirty-first of December, only three days after Dade's Massacre, which event was entirely unknown to the white forces at the time of this second battle. The scene of the engagement was at a crossing of the Withlacoochee River, and the combatants were two hundred regulars and thirty volunteers, under General Clinch, on one side; on the other, two hundred warriors, fifty of whom were Maroons, under Osceola and Alligator. The conflict raged fiercely for one hour and twenty minutes, but Osceola was disabled early in the fight and his forces were finally compelled to retire. The killed and wounded of the troops numbered fifty-seven; on the other side only eight, although an official report says " about one hundred !"* Officers present said that the shrill voice of Osceola was continually heard, urging his men on.

After the engagement, Osceola sent the following characteristic communication to General Clinch:

" You have guns and so have we; you have powder and lead and so have we; you have men and so have we;

*It was a hard matter to form a correct estimate of Seminole losses, owing to the fact that the Indians almost invariably fought from the cover of dense hammocks or swamps, and quickly removed their dead and wounded to the rear.

your men will fight, and so will ours until the last drop of
the Seminoles' blood has moistened the dust of his hunt-
ing-grounds.''

Osceola also told General Clinch that with a little
longer time to secure his position, ''he could maintain
it for five years against the whole United States' forces.''

The truth of this bold prediction is strikingly shown
by the testimony of Judge Robert R. Reid, Governor of
Florida, who, in a message to the Legislature nearly a
year after Osceola's death, makes this statement:

'' The efforts of the General and Territorial governments to quell the Indian disturbances which have prevailed through four long years, have been unavailing;
and it would seem that the prophecy of the most saga-
cious leader of the Indians will be more than fulfilled;
the close of the fifth year will still find us struggling. . . .''

Indian depredations were more or less frequent all
along the border line during the war. The more reckless of the Seminoles and Maroons ventured to the
settlements and carried off such articles as would help
sustain them in resisting removal, more especially provisions and ammunition. In many instances buildings
were burned, and in a few cases whole families, who had
previously ill treated the red men, were ~~unharmed~~ *murdered*.

As an instance of the fact that the Indians did not
molest their known friends, we may mention that Colonel
John Lee Williams, from whose valuable works on Florida we have quoted in former chapters, lived alone
throughout the war on his place near Picolata.

We cannot forbear adding the testimony of Dr.
Welch, whom the reader will remember also resided on
the St. Johns River. He says that previous to the war
many of the Seminoles were in the habit of visiting him,

and that they were always treated with kindness and fairness by himself and his wife. They showed their appreciation by sparing the property of this gentleman, and it passed through the entire war without damage, while other places near by were devastated. The doctor also adds that his intimate acquaintance with the Seminoles "has inspired me with a high respect for their social and domestic character."*

Osceola's honorable and magnanimous character is well illustrated by the fact that he not only abstained personally from taking part in the violent border depredations during the war, but discouraged them in his followers. A negro interpreter named Sampson, formerly owned by Gad Humphreys, was captured by the Indians in 1835. He afterward gave the army officers an interesting account of his experience with the red men, in which he said :

"I lived with Osceola, who was my friend. He was a good Indian, and constantly urged the war parties to spare women and children."†

Sampson's statement is thus corroborated by Osceola himself :

"It is not upon them (referring to the women and children) that we make war and draw the scalping-kni'e; it is upon men ; let us act like men."‡

Regarding the Seminoles' treatment of their captives, we will introduce at this point the valued testimony of Mr. Andrew P. Canova, a life-long resident of Florida, who was engaged in the last hostilities against the red men :

"The fiendish instinct which led the wild tribes of the West to prolong the death of a captive over a slow

*Osceola Nikkanochee, Welch. London, 1841.
†"Narrative of Sampson," Savannah *Georgian*, Nov. 1841.
‡Captain Sprague.

fire, was totally lacking in the red men of Florida.
Through all the long and bloody strife which preceded the
settlement of Florida, no well-grounded tale was ever told
of a Seminole putting a captive to death in an unnatural
manner."*

Our knowledge of Osceola's chivalrous nature leaves
little room for doubt that so long as he remained head
war chief of his nation, his powerful influence would
have been exerted, had the policy of our Government
been different, to promote peace and amity between the
two races. But the white race would not have it so.
The alternative they offered the Seminoles was "banishment or extermination," and Osceola, from a
steadfast friend was transformed into a determined foe.

The able leadership and unflinching courage against
great odds in the fierce conflict on the Withlacoochee,
last described, as well as in other engagements, won for
Osceola the admiration of his enemies. This feeling was
plainly expressed by the editors of two of the most
prominent newspapers in Florida at this period, as
follows:

"The character of this chief is but little known and
not sufficiently appreciated. He is represented to be a
man of great tact, energy of character, and bold daring.
The skill with which he has for a long time managed to
frustrate the measures of our Government for the
removal of the Indians beyond the Mississippi, entitles
him to be considered as superior to Black Hawk."†

"Osceola or Powell, the head chief of the hostile
Seminoles, is likely to figure in history with Philip of
Pokanoket, or Tecumseh, possessing all their noble
daring and deep love of country, with more intelligence
and perhaps more ferocity."*

*Life and Adventures in South Florida, Canova, 1885.
†St. Augustine *Herald*, Jan. 13th, 1836.
Floridian, Tallahassee.

The latter journal also states that Osceola won his commanding rank by his superior talents, courage and ambition. The testimony of an army officer on the military talent of this chief, is worthy of note :

"He is allowed by all to be possessed of considerable military talent; in addition to his competent generalship and skill in the daring, rapid and subtle evolutions of active warfare, he has evinced what scarcely any other Indian chief has ever done, a considerable acquaintance with our tactics, as shown in the drill of his warriors."

Another army officer in describing the condition of affairs at this stage of the war, thus sympathizes with the foe he was obliged to face:

"If they (the Seminoles) have the courage of men, they will die with arms in their hands. The white man will not deny them the privilege of sleeping out their death sleep on the soil upon which he cannot endure their living presence."†

†Niles *Register*, Jan. 16th, 1836.

CHAPTER VII.

The Withlacoochee River, the scene of so many struggles in the Seminole War, was now to witness a more important engagement than any we have yet been called upon to describe, so far, at least, as numbers were concerned. On this occasion, General Gaines, who at the head of 1,025 regulars and volunteers was returning from Fort King to Fort Brooke, while seeking a place to ford the river, on the 27th of January, 1836, was fired upon by a force of 700 Indians and Maroons. The General was soon obliged to retire to the pine woods about half a mile from the river, where he erected a breastwork of logs. He then sent a messenger to General Clinch, at Fort Drane, calling for immediate reinforcements.

The Seminoles, with an inferior number, held General Gaines and his command in siege for nearly a week, toward the close of which time his men were compelled to kill horses to maintain their lives, their provisions having become exhausted. On the 5th of March General Clinch arrived with reinforcements, and the Indians withdrew.

Capt. John C. Casey, stationed at Fort Brooke, thus speaks of the Seminoles' part in this engagement, in a private letter* written to his mother a few days after it occurred:

"The Indians fought bravely, surpassing all previous Indian wars; they kept 1,100 choice troops seven days on the defensive."

During the interval from this stage until the end of August, six minor engagements took place, of which we shall mention only the two most important.

In April, a battalion of Georgia volunteers, commanded by Major A. Cooper, defended Cooper's Post, west of the Withlacoochee, against 250 Indians. After keeping the troops on the defensive from the 5th to the 18th, the Indians retired.

General Clinch owned a plantation eight miles from the town of Micanopy, which he occupied with his forces part of the time, and called Fort Drane. He abandoned it in July on account of depredations committed there by the enemy, and soon afterward Osceola and a hundred followers took possession of the place. On the 21st of August, Major Pierce and 110 mounted men, with one howitzer, sought to dislodge the chief. The engagement lasted an hour and a quarter, during which time Osceola and his men fell back to a hammock, where they fought with such desperation that Major Pierce retreated, leaving them in possession. In his report of the battle, the Major gives the Seminoles credit for determined bravery and skill.

On the 18th of November, the Seminoles suffered a great defeat in the hardest fought battle of the year (1836). They were assailed near the Great Wahoo Swamp, five miles north-west of Dade's old battleground,

*Sent to the author by Major Beebe.

by about 800 troops, under Governor Richard K. Call, who had assumed command of the Department upon the retirement of General Scott in the summer. The battle lasted more than two hours, when the Indians fled, leaving twenty-five of their number dead on the field.

Three days later, however, the red men retrieved their laurels on the same ground. With a large force, whose numbers were unknown, aided by many Maroons, they made an impetuous charge upon 1,800 soldiers under General Call. Twice that day the Indians were driven from their ground but returned to the attack each time. The second time, they crossed the Withlacoochee River, in their rear, and formed on its banks. The troops finally withdrew, leaving the Indians in possession of the field. Our loss was twenty-seven killed and wounded. The Indian loss was "supposed" by the General to be "not less than fifty."

In December, 1836, General Call was relieved of the command in Florida by General Thomas S. Jesup. At this time the principal part of the regular forces of the United States were concentrated in Florida; besides these, there were a large number of volunteers. Altogether General Jesup had at his disposal not far from 10,000 men* with whom to harass the Seminoles.

In the latter part of the following month, the new commander penetrated to the heart of the Indian country, and attacked a band of fifty Indians in their camp. On the following day they captured 100 ponies and 1,400 head of cattle belonging to the Seminoles. In his report of this affair, the General says:

"The enemy was found on the Hatcheelustee, in and near the Great Cypress Swamp, and gallantly attacked. Lieutenant Chambers, of the Alabama

*Annual Report, Secretary of War, 1837.

volunteers, by a rapid charge succeeded in capturing the horses and baggage of the enemy, with twenty-five Indians and negroes, principally women and children."

The "gallantry" of an attack with overpowering numbers and with such results may well be questioned.

On the day following this affair, General Jesup sent one of his captives in search of Alligator and Abraham, who had commanded the Indians in that action, with a message of peace and a request that they come in and have a talk with him. After much persuasion, these chiefs were induced to visit the General in his camp. The result of the interview gave him such confidence of success in obtaining the consent of the Indians to emigrate, that he ordered a general cessation of hostilities. At the same time, arrangements were made to meet the chiefs of the nation on the 7th of March, in a general council to be held at Fort Dade, situated on the left bank of the Withlacoochee, near its source.

A band of Indians under Wildcat, King Philip and Louis Pacheco, who had not learned of the cessation of hostilities by General Jesup and the chiefs, made a daring attack, on the 8th of February, on Camp Monroe (later Fort Mellon,*) situated on the south side of Lake Monroe. In the early part of the conflict, which lasted two hours, Capt. Charles Mellon was killed. Our forces had a cannon on a boat near the fort, and this was used with such effect that the Indians were finally compelled to retire, with a loss of several killed and wounded. Our loss was one killed and fifteen wounded.

Several months now passed without an engagement between the opposing forces. The Indians took advantage of this lull by harvesting their crops. During the earlier years of the war they depended for their subsist-

*The town of Mellonville was established near the site years afterward. Now absorbed by the city of Sanford.

ence nearly altogether on their crops and cattle. After their cattle had been captured, and they themselves had been driven to islands in the Everglades and the Big Cypress Swamp, they subsisted almost entirely on the koontee* or wild arrowroot, which was at that time very abundant in the southern part of the Territory, and on such game as they could secure. Fields were cultivated whenever a lull in hostilities admitted.

On the day appointed for the meeting with the chiefs at Fort Dade, a number of representatives of the nation assembled for a further hearing of what the Government, through its agents, might have to say upon the subject of removal. At the very commencement of the negotiations, the Indians refused their consent to any arrangement that would not secure to the Maroons, and other negroes claimed by them, equal protection and safety with themselves. General Jesup finally agreed to this demand, as shown in the fifth article of capitulation, as follows:

"Major General Jesup, in behalf of the United States, agrees that the Seminoles and their allies who come in and emigrate to the West, shall be secure in their lives and property; that their negroes, their *bona fide* property, shall also accompany them West; and their cattle and ponies shall be paid for by the United States."†

This and the remaining articles being satisfactory to the delegation of chiefs, the meeting closed with the understanding that those willing to emigrate would assemble near Fort Brooke. The reader is hereby in-

---

*The *Zamia integrifolia* of the botanist. The Indians made a fair quality of bread from a starch extracted from the root of the plant. For full information regarding this interesting plant, see "Koontee, the Seminole Bread Root," by the author in the *Scientific American Supplement*, August 20, 1898

†Ex. Doc. 225, 3d Ses., 25th Cong.

formed that this agreement was not a regular treaty negotiated by commissioners appointed for the purpose, but rather an "understanding" between General Jesup and the Indians.

In the course of the next few weeks, about eight hundred Seminoles, including quite a number of Maroons, visited Fort Brooke and registered their names for removal. It was believed that the nation would agree to emigrate according to their promise. Even Osceola, it was reported, went to Fort Mellon and signified his willingness to go West if the Government would do as General Jesup had agreed.* The consent of so many, among which were several chiefs, having thus been gained to the project of emigration, the commander of the army announced, on the 26th of March, that the war was at an end. He immediately commenced to discharge the volunteers, and asked leave to retire from active duty.

The War Department approved the agreement with the Indians, but the people of Florida and adjoining States objected to its ratification. They believed that under its stipulations many of the negroes whom they claimed as their property would be sent West along with the Indians. Certain families who had been obliged to leave the territory, also expressed their disapproval of the "Jesup treaty" in a memorial to Congress.† Many persons demanded the privilege of entering the Indian country for the ostensible purpose of capturing their fugitive slaves. These demands, as well as forays into the reservation, became so frequent that General Jesup finally issued an order to the commandant at Fort Armstrong,‡ on the Indian frontier, containing this sentence:

*The author is unable to confirm this rumor by any official report or record, and doubts its truth.
†Ex. Doc 225, 3d Ses 25th Cong.
‡On the site of Dade's Massacre.

"Hereafter no person, not in the employment of the Government, or express rider, must be allowed to pass your post."

In a letter to the commander of the Florida militia, under date of March 29th, General Jesup said:

"There is no disposition on the part of the great body of the Indians to renew hostilities, and they will, I am sure, faithfully fulfill their engagements if the people of Florida be prudent; but any attempt to seize their (the Indians') negroes or other property would be followed by an instant resort to arms."

A few days later, General Orders (No. 79) were issued to the same effect. This did not prevent many invasions of the Indians' territory, however. These repeated violations of the order, together with the discontented clamors of others, harassed General Jesup to such an extent that he finally signified his intention to amend the peace treaty, which not only himself but the Government was pledged to abide by, and make "an arrangement with the chiefs to deliver up the negroes, belonging to white men, *taken* by them during the war."

By the use of the word "taken," the General, following the example of others, intimates that the Indians were in the habit of taking or capturing the slaves of their white neighbors. The highest authorities, however, prove that negroes were never captured by the Seminoles except during open warfare; they were too anxious to remain at peace with the whites to interfere with their property. During the war negroes were sometimes taken prisoners, while at all times fugitive slaves fled to the red men for protection, as before stated. These could easily be distinguished from the Maroons and other negroes owned by the Indians, by the fact that the former did not understand the Seminole language, while the latter, with some exceptions, knew no other.

It is interesting to observe how firmly General Jesup resisted, for a time, the exactions of the claimants. In a report to the Secretary of War, the General stated that, in his opinion, the Treaty of Payne's Landing, under which the Government was trying to remove the Indians, exonerated them from all claims for slaves which had accrued prior to that date. This opinion was also sustained by the Secretary.

The arrangement which General Jesup said he had made "with the chiefs," consisted, as the reader will notice in the following chapter, of a promise secured from one chief only (Alligator) at Fort King, that such negroes would be brought in.

The United States Government had now taken the final step, through General Jesup, as was believed, for the removal of the Seminoles and their allies to the Western country. No less than twenty-six vessels were lying in Tampa Bay in readiness to transport them to New Orleans, and about eight hundred Indians and their slaves were on hand, waiting for the rest to join them.

But as might have been foreseen, the "arrangement" made with Alligator was justly considered by the nation to be a violation of the peace treaty agreed to at Fort Dade. Had the matter been proposed to the chiefs in council, the nation would in all probability have agreed to it. As it was, however, they refused to deliver the few negro prisoners taken by them during the war, or to capture and bring in fugitives who had taken refuge in their country. In the council held by them they decided that the promises of General Jesup could not be relied upon, and that his unauthorized addition to the treaty stipulations released them from their agreement to emigrate.

Exasperated by the failure of his plans, General Jesup, on May 25th, 1837, despatched to Colonel Harney, at Fort Mellon, the following instructions:

"If you see Powell again, I wish you to tell him that I intend to send exploring parties into every part of the country during the summer, and that I shall send out and take all negroes who belong to the white people, and that he must not allow the Indians or Indian negroes to mix with them.* Tell him I am sending to Cuba for bloodhounds to trail them, and I intend to hang every one of them who does not come in."†

When the Seminoles and Maroons learned of General Jesup's hostile intentions, as conveyed in his despatch to Colonel Harney, his menaces produced precisely the opposite effect from that intended. Most of those who had congregated at Fort Brooke for emigration, and others around the white settlements, again fled to their wild haunts, determined to cling to their old homes. Yet not all of them thus escaped from the grasp of the white man, for General Jesup managed to seize about ninety Indian negroes‡ and sent them to New Orleans, where they were confined in Fort Pike for nearly a year before they were finally taken to Arkansas.

These were the first Maroons sent to the West; but they did not reach their destination without great difficulty. While they were at New Orleans, various persons claimed them as their property, and the matter was finally taken to the courts. General Gaines now

---

*This demand informs the reader, through one of the highest authorities, how great was the influence possessed by this chief in the nation.

†H. R 225, 3d Ses., 25th Cong. The reference to bloodhounds was no idle threat, as will be seen later.

‡Letter of General Jesup to General James Gadsden, June 14th, 1837.

came forward and defended the rights of the Indians to
these negroes, stating in court that he had "never hes-
itated to assume the responsibility of doing his duty
or of doing justice." In the course of his convincing
argument, he said:

"The court appears to labor under the impression
that the negroes in question were captured by the Seminole Indians, in the course of their hostile incursions
upon our frontier inhabitants. Is this the fact? I will
assume for the learned council of the claimant, that he
will not have the temerity to assert that they are among
the number taken from our frontier inhabitants in the
present, or in any former war."

The General finally proved to the satisfaction of the
court that the negroes, "found in the service of the
Seminoles, and speaking the same language," had
never been captured from the whites, but were descendants of former slaves of the whites, who had been free
for upwards of a century. They were therefore released,
and soon after proceeded on their way in charge of one
of our army officers.

CHAPTER VIII.

CAPTURE OF KING PHILIP—SEIZURE AND IMPRISONMENT OF OSCEOLA—THE WHOLE TRANSACTION STRIPPED OF ITS DISGUISES—PUBLIC OPINION—GENERAL JESUP'S DEFENSE —ESCAPE OF WILDCAT.

On the tenth of September, 1837, General Joseph M. Hernandez, with regulars and volunteers, attacked a band of twenty-one Indians under King Philip at Dunlawton plantation, situated on the Halifax River, back of the present town of Port Orange. In this affair, one lieutenant was mortally wounded, and one Indian killed and three wounded. Seventeen Indians were captured, among them being the aged King Philip, second chief of the nation, and his son Cooacoochee (Wildcat). They were all taken to St. Augustine and confined in the old Spanish fort.

Although King Philip's advanced years had prevented his participation in most of the battles of the present war, he still possessed considerable influence in the nation, and his capture therefore caused great anxiety. The old chief soon applied for permission to communicate with his family and friends, and prevailed upon General Jesup, who was then at St. Augustine, to grant a temporary release to Wildcat for the purpose of bearing a message. This consisted of a request to his family, also to Osceola and others, to visit him and, if possible, to make arrangements for his release. Wildcat left St. Augustine with a promise to return in about ten days.

The reports of General Hernandez and other officers to General Jesup, under date of October 22d, state that Wildcat returned to St. Augustine on the 17th of that month, and reported that Osceola, with about a hundred followers, would be at Pellicers Creek, eighteen miles south of St. Augustine, on the following day.*

The next morning, General Hernandez with a small escort was despatched to the creek, where he found a part of the Indians already encamped. He learned from them that Osceola and others were expected to arrive that evening or the day after. Securing a promise from the Indians that they would move their camp to the neighborhood of Fort Peyton, seven miles southwest of St. Augustine,† General Hernandez returned to that town.

On the morning of the 21st of October, a messenger arrived at St. Augustine from the Indians with the information that Osceola and his retinue were in camp one mile from Fort Peyton, and that the chief desired an interview with General Jesup. That officer immediately gave General Hernandez his orders, including the following "memoranda of specific questions to be addressed to Osceola:"‡

"Ascertain the object of the Indians in coming in at this time. Also their expectations. Are they prepared to deliver up the negroes taken from the citizens at once? Why have they not surrendered them as promised by Coechajo (Alligator) at Fort King? Have the chiefs sent a messenger with the decision of the council? Have the principal chiefs, Mickenopah, Jumper, Cloud,

*H. R. 327, 2d Ses., 25th Cong.

†Situated on the south half of the northwest quarter of Sec. 11, Tp. 8 South, Range 29 East, near a branch of Moultrie Creek, and not far from the site of old Camp Moultrie. By the present road the distance from the city is about five miles.

‡H. R. 327, 2d Ses., 25th Cong.

and Alligator, sent a messenger, and if so, what is their message? Why have not those chiefs come themselves?"

General Hernandez also bore the following "secret order" from General Jesup to Lieut. R. H. Peyton, stationed at Fort Peyton:

"Should Powell and his warriors come within the fort, seize him and his whole party. It is important that he, Wildcat and others be secured. Hold him until you have my orders in relation to them." *

General Hernandez left St. Augustine at the head of about two hundred troops. On his way he met Captain Hanson and a small detachment, who had preceded the General with provisions for the Indians and were now returning. They were bringing with them under guard seventy-four negro prisoners, the property of white citizens, some of whom had been captured by the Indians during the war, but the greater part being "runaways." They had been secured by Osceola and brought in at this time, for delivery to General Jesup, no doubt as a peace offering, or to secure the release of King Philip.

This new concession to the demands of claimants of negro property would of itself indicate that Osceola and his people were acting in good faith. We are now to learn how this friendly act was rewarded.

General Hernandez, arriving at the Indian camp, found it located about a mile south of Fort Peyton, near a large cypress pond.† The chiefs in command were Osceola and Alligator, and their party consisted of

---

* This order, together with all of the official reports to General Jesup, in relation to the seizure of Osceola, and from that officer to the Secretary of War, may be consulted in the document last quoted.

† Nearly a mile and a half south of the fort, on the southwest one-quarter of the southwest one-quarter of Sec. 14, Tp. 8 South, Range 29 East, just west of the Old Kings Road.

seventy-one warriors, six women, and four Indian negroes. Among the women was the wife of King Philip.

General Hernandez arranged his men in such a manner, says that officer, that in about ten minutes after he reached the camp the Indians were completely surrounded. The latter, with no suspicion of treachery, and expecting to be received in the same peaceful spirit in which they had come, had laid their arms on the ground and were in readiness for the proposed "talk." After the usual opening of such meetings, General Hernandez, following his instructions, asked the Indians why they had come in. The reply was:

"We come for good. Philip sent us a message by Cooacoochee. We have done nothing all summer (meanng that they had engaged in no hostilities) and want to make peace."

When asked if they were ready to give up all the property they had captured, in compliance with the arrangement made by General Jesup with Alligator, they answered:

"We intend to do so, to bring in what is due to the white people; we have brought a good many negroes now."

Osceola stated that he and his band did not come in to deliver themselves up as prisoners, but to negotiate for the release of King Philip and a return to peace.

These replies are quoted from an official report made to General Hernandez, and may therefore be regarded as accurate, but that officer in his report to General Jesup, says:

"Their answers to the questions put to them in regard to the breach of their stipulations made with you at Fort King, I considered to be wholly evasive and unsatisfactory . . . . From these circumstances, and agreeably to your express orders conveyed to me during the talk, I gave a signal previously agreed on, and the troops closed in on them."

This whole transaction, stripped of its disguises, was only a new illustration of the old fable of the Wolf and the Lamb—a deliberate plot to seize the persons of Osceola and his followers, no matter what their replies might be. Thus, as stated by the editor of the St. Augustine *Herald*, on the day of the seizure:

"They were completely surrounded, and taken without bloodshed. The arms and baggage of the Indians, with fifty-two rifles and twenty-four ponies were collected, and the prisoners were marched to St. Augustine and closely confined in Fort Marion." *

Brief mention may be made at this point of Capt. John S. Masters, an interesting old gentleman still living at St. Augustine, Fla., who was one of a squad of soldiers who escorted Osceola and his party to that city. At the time of the chief's seizure Mr. Masters was thirty-one years of age, having been born in 1806. He is still hale and hearty, and recollects many of the details in connection with the seizure of Osceola. Speaking of this event, in a communication to the author, he said:

"I shall never forget that day, nor the sad, disappointed face of Chief Osceola and the other Indians. I thought it too unjust for anything." †

The dishonorable and wholly indefensible seizure of Osceola, made under a flag of truce and while a conference was in progress, was made known by General Jesup

---

* Supplement to the *Herald*, issued to announce the event.

† A few years since the St. Augustine Historical Society, with the aid of Mr. Masters, located the site of Osceola's seizure, and placed a sign-board on pine trees near by.

to the Secretary of War, under date of October 22d, in the following words:

"I have the satisfaction to inform you that Asseen Yoholo (Powell) is my prisoner, with nearly all the war spirits of the nation . . . . The sickly season being over, and there being no further necessity to temporize, I sent a party of mounted men and seized the entire party." He also says that he "had informed the chiefs at Fort King that he would hold no communication with the Seminoles unless they should determine to emigrate." The flag of truce, he says, "had been allowed for no other purpose than to enable them to communicate and come in without danger of attack from our parties." This being the case, the General adds, "it became my duty to secure them, on being satisfied that they intended to return to their fastnesses." *

A letter written by General Jesup to a friend in Washington, D. C., † dated at Picolata, Fla., Nov. 17th, is interesting reading. We quote and condense as follows:

"As I shall depart today for the interior, and, in the casualities of an active campaign, it is possible I may not return, I desire that the seizure of Powell and other chiefs and warriors may be understood by my friends."

After stating that part of those who accompanied Osceola probably intended to capture some of General Hernandez' men in order that he might thus secure the release of King Philip, the writer continues:

"The General (Hernandez) departed to Fort Peyton accompanied by a number of officers and citizens; among the former were the gentlemen of my staff.

* II. R. 327, 2d Ses., 25th Cong.

† Major Trueman Cross. Published in the *Army and Navy Chronicle* Dec. 14th, 1837.

Without communicating my intention to anyone, I followed to the neighborhood of Fort Peyton, sent in for Lieutenant Peyton, and ascertained from him the number and position of the Indians. I directed him to go forward and ascertain whether the answers of the Indians to the enquiries made by General Hernandez seemed satisfactory. In the mean-time I detached my aid, who had joined me, with orders to General Hernandez to seize all the party if the talk was not satisfactory."

In the interval, Lieutenant Peyton returned with the answers of the Indians to General Jesup, who had now left his hiding-place in the woods and repaired to Fort Peyton. As the General had resolved to seize Osceola and his party from the moment he had learned of their arrival, he found it convenient to consider their replies "evasive and unsatisfactory," to quote his own and General Hernandez' words. He therefore sent Lieutenant Peyton back in all haste to General Hernandez, bearing "Order No. 3," dated at Fort Peyton, in the following words:

"Order the whole party directly to town—you have force sufficient to compel obedience; they must be disarmed; they can talk in town and send any messengers out they please."*

General Hernandez says in his report that this "message was so promptly and judiciously executed by Major Ashby, of the Second Dragoons, that the Indians, though their rifles were loaded and primed, ready for action, had not an opportunity to fire a single gun."†

It has been claimed by some writers that Osceola was knocked down with the butt of a musket. In jus-

*The reader is again reminded that all of the official orders and reports in connection with Osceola's seizure may be found in H. R. 327, 2d Ses., 25th Cong.

†The weapons of the Indians were all on the ground, as before stated.

tice to the memory of General Hernandez, the reader is assured that this reported additional insult and injury did not take place; in fact, no violence was offered by either side. The author has abundant proof of this, including the testimony of Captain Masters.

Thus, disarmed and defenseless, defeated only by stratagem, Osceola, with true Indian stoicism, quietly submitted to the inevitable, and was soon a close prisoner behind the grim walls of Fort Marion.*

Such is the irony of fate! The eagle, proud king of the air, confined in a narrow cage; Napoleon, once master of the world, chained to the rock of St. Helena; Osceola, the free son of the forest and the ruling spirit of the Seminoles, eating out his heart in a murky dungeon of San Marco!

Throughout the civilized world, the flag of truce is recognized and respected as an emblem of peace, and its violation looked upon as an outrage. We do not find a single instance recorded in the long war with the Seminoles of a failure on their part to respect that flag. Indeed, George Catlin, who spent forty years of his life in studying Indian character and customs in every part of North and South America, says in this connection:

"Among all Indian tribes that I have yet visited in their primitive as well as improved state, the white flag is used as a flag of truce, as it is in the civilized parts of the world, and held to be sacred and inviolable."†

Abundant testimony shows that the Indian has a fine sense of honor. The late General John Gibbon, long familiar with Indian character, stated in a lecture delivered by him in Washington, D. C., in February

---

*This structure, once known as the Spanish Castle of San Marco, is one of the strongest, and by far the oldest of American fortifications.

†Illustrations of the Manners, Customs, and Conditions of the North American Indians, Catlin, 1857.

1895, that " the Indian has many qualities which make him a giant beside which the white man is a pigmy." To illustrate one of these qualities—the Indians' sense of honor—we offer the following reliable statement:

"When an Indian (a member of the Five Tribes) is condemned to death (in his nation) by shooting, he is given a period, thirty days usually, in which to go home and fix up his affairs. He goes without guard or control, arranges his earthly matters, bids his friends and family good-bye, returns at the appointed time, and is promptly shot. Not one man of the many so permitted to go home after conviction, up to 1890, has failed to appear for execution." *

We will now return to the captive chief. Public opinion throughout the United States sided with Osceola, denouncing his seizure as an outrage—a disgrace to the General who planned it, and to our Government which sanctioned it. Many officers and soldiers of the army who had borne their part in the efforts to subdue Osceola and his tribe in open warfare, now disclaimed all sympathy with the treachery which had entrapped him. Nor were the leading journals of the country less outspoken in their condemnation of the offense. The following is a mild expression of newspaper sentiment at the time:

"General Jesup has got possession of Osceola or Powell, and a large number of his warriors. The manner in which it was accomplished will be found under the proper head. We heartily rejoice if this event puts an end to the war . . . . but we disclaim all participation in the '*glory*' of this achievement of American generalship . . . . it must deepen the sense of wrong in the bosoms of the Indians . . . and produce more bloody and

*The Five Civilized Tribes, U. S. Census Bulletin, 1894.

signal vengeance than has yet marked their ruthless
doings. And besides, the capture will create distrust
among chiefs, and may shut the door to a satisfactory
treaty hereafter."*

An English writer, who resided in Florida at the
time, thus speaks of the seizure:

"Never was a more disgraceful piece of villainy
perpetrated in a civilized land. The Americans have
no plea by which they can justify such a violation of
the law of nations."†

Nearly two years after the event, with a knowledge
of the leading facts of the case, the New York *Herald*
referred to "the perfidious capture of Osceola, when
that chieftain was engaged in an honest parley with
General Hernandez—a parley which, it is believed,
would have terminated the war."‡

We find nothing that can palliate this treachery—
no circumstance or event that transpired previous to the
act lessens its enormity. General Jesup, on whom the
odium must rest, felt himself frequently compelled in
after years to justify, if possible, this and similar acts
of treachery to his Indian foes. After he had been relieved from duty in Florida, he made an official report
to the Secretary of War, dated July 6, 1838, covering
the period of his operations. In this he speaks of the
seizure of Osceola and his party, as follows :

"I deemed it proper to permit Wildcat to go with
the message of his father.   He promised to bring in all
the Seminoles of the St. Johns, but I authorized no one
to be invited to come in for any other purpose than to
remain. I promised, however, that all who should come
in and surrender should receive kind treatment.   Pre-

Niles' Register, November 4th. 1837.
†Osceola Nikkanoochee, Welch, London, 1841.
‡July 1839.

vious to his departure he (Wildcat) examined several sites, in company with General Hernandez, for the purpose of determining on a suitable point for an encampment."

In this statement, General Jesup evidently studies to convey the impression that Osceola came in to surrender, and that he was not seized under a flag of truce. The reader, however, already knows the truth of the matter. Osceola, as we have seen, distinctly stated that he and his band had not come in to deliver themselves up as prisoners, but to negotiate for a return to peace—in other words, to have a "talk" under a flag of truce.

Even twenty years after these events, we find the General defending his course in a long communication to a Washington newspaper,* in reply to certain published criticisms. In this article, General Jesup attempts to justify his action by saying that Osceola had killed one of his (Jesup's) messengers; also that he had violated the last truce made with the chiefs at Fort King, when they were to remain west of the St. Johns River. "By either of these acts," says the writer, "he had forfeited his life." The General also calls Osceola a spy, and asserts that he really came to capture the place and release the prisoners! Speaking of Osceola, he further says:

"But, although an intelligent and talented man, he belonged to a savage tribe not supposed to be acquainted with the laws of nations or the usages of war; and in place of punishing him I sent him out of the country, a prisoner. . . . . In my course on this occasion I was influenced alone by the high obligations of public duty."

* *Daily Intelligencer*, Oct. 13th, 1858.

In his letter to the *Army and Navy Chronicle* in 1837, General Jesup only claimed that Osceola intended to capture some of the soldiers at Fort Peyton, and to hold them as hostages for the release of King Philip and the other prisoners. Twenty years later he asserts that the chief came to capture St. Augustine and to release the prisoners! He had just referred to Osceola as "an intelligent man." He would surely be the reverse of an intelligent man who, with a force of seventy-two warriors and six women, would make a journey of over a hundred miles to undertake the capture of a town under the guns of an impregnable fortress and protected by several thousand citizens and soldiers!

It is related that Osceola refused to join certain of his companions who, as will be seen, succeeded in making their escape from Fort Marion. When questioned about this by one of the men who guarded his room, the chief proudly replied:

"I have done nothing to be ashamed of; it is for those to feel shame who entrapped me."

If the painter of the world-famed picture, "Christ before Pilate," should seek in American history a subject worthy of his brush, we would commend to him, "Osceola before General Jesup:" Osceola, the despised Seminole, a captive and in chains—Jesup, in all the pomp and circumstance of an American Major-General; Osceola, who had "done nothing to be ashamed of," calmly confronting his captor, who cowers under the steady gaze of a brave and honorable man!

Not long after the confinement of the Seminoles in Fort Marion, the chief Wildcat and a companion made their escape in a manner quite unexpected by their jailors. A prominent officer of our army* afterward

* Capt. John T. Sprague.

received a full account of the adventure from Wildcat.
The chief said that he and his companion were confined
in a small room lighted only by an embrasure, an opening in the wall about nine inches wide by eighteen long.
Through this they managed to squeeze with the greatest
difficulty, the sharp stones of the 'wall taking off skin
from their breasts and backs. Some strong bags furnished them material for a rope, by means of which
they reached the ground, and finally made their way to
the Tomoka, a small stream emptying into the Halifax
River, on the east coast, where Wildcat's band was
stationed.

Wildcat succeeded in convincing the nation that he
had not been the willing tool of General Jesup to betray
Osceola. He gave them a full account of the seizure,
and they resolved on vengeance.*

* "Recollections of Cooacoochee," were published in the Savannah
Georgian, February, 1842.

CHAPTER IX.

After the failure of General Jesup's "peace treaty"
of March 7th, 1837, by which agreement that officer announced the close of the war, the Government sought to
secure a settlement with the Seminoles through the influence of the Cherokees, then established in Arkansas,
with whom the Seminoles were on the most friendly
terms.

The plan was first proposed by Col. J. H. Sherburne, a special agent of the Government sent to the
West in September. But as the agent doubted his authority to enter into an agreement in the line proposed,
John Ross, principal chief of the Cherokee nation, visited Washington in October "to learn what the scope of
the proposed mission was to be."

The author feels that it is due to the memory of
this remarkable man, in view of his noble efforts in behalf of the Seminoles, to record in these pages an outline of his life and character. John Ross was born in
Tennessee, October 3d, 1790. His father, Daniel Ross,
was a Scotchman and an Indian trader; his mother was
a Cherokee. In the year 1812 he undertook the somewhat dangerous mission of endeavoring to prevent
Tecumseh from enlisting his followers in the war against
the United States. Returning from his mission he en-

tered the service of our Government, as an officer of the Cherokee regiment in the Creek war. He had received a good education at Kingston, Tennessee, and possessed great executive ability. He was strongly opposed to the removal of the Cherokees to the West, and spent much of his time for years in Washington, in the interest of his people, where he was well known to all the statesmen of that period.

His first wife was a Cherokee woman, who died in 1839. In 1845 he was again married, his bride being a Miss Mary B. Stapler, a prominent Quakeress, of Wilmington, Del. At the time of this marriage, the groom was fifty-five years of age, while the bride was but nineteen. John Ross died in Washington, D. C., August 1st, 1866, aged seventy-six years, after an illness of about five months. The *Washington Star* on the day following his death, contained a long obituary notice, from which we extract the following:

"John Ross was one of the most remarkable men of this country. He originated the written constitution of the Cherokee nation, and to his vigor and the intelligence of his administration must we attribute much of the civilization of the Cherokees.* The remains were taken to Wilmington, . . . and afterward removed for burial among his people."

George Catlin, who was well and familiarly acquainted with John Ross, characterizes him as a "civilized and highly accomplished gentleman," and says that he felt "bound to testify to the rigid temperance of his habits and the purity of his language, in which I never knew him to transgress for a moment, in public or private interviews."

*The New York *Herald* of Jan. 2nd, 1846, contained a model Thanksgiving Proclamation by John Ross, copied from a paper published by the Cherokees.

The Government finally approved of Colonel Sherburne's plan, and entered into an agreement with Ross by which he was to select delegates from among his chiefs and send them to Florida to mediate for a peaceful settlement with the Seminoles. Ross, who remained in Washington, accordingly appointed five of his principal chiefs, one of whom acted as interpreter, at the same time giving them a written appeal to be read "To the Chiefs, Head Men and Warriors of the Seminoles of Florida."*

This forcible appeal was addressed particularly to "Mickenopah, Osceola, and Alligator," as the leading men of the nation, and dated at Washington, Oct. 18th, 1837. (This, it will be observed, was three days before the date of the seizure of Osceola.)

The delegates, accompanied by the special agent, arrived in Florida early in November. They proceeded to the camp of Mickenopah, situated about sixty miles southeast of Fort Mellon, where they met that chief, also Cloud, Sam Jones, and many others. A council was held on November 30th, at Chickasawhatchee River, near Lake Poinsett, when the address of Ross was read and explained. It began thus:

"I address you in the name of the Cherokee nation, as its principal chief, and with feelings of a brother hold out to you the hand of friendship." He asks them to listen to his words, saying that "they emanate from the purest feelings of my own heart for your welfare." He advises them to lay down their arms and consent to removal under the Treaty of Payne's Landing, adding that they could depend on the United States doing them justice.

Soon after the conclusion of this council and its

*H. R. 285, 2d Ses., 25th Cong.

attendant ceremonies, Mickenopah, Cloud and eleven other chiefs, with a number of warriors, accompanied the Cherokee delegation to Fort Mellon, to confer with General Jesup, who had gone there to meet them. They arrived there December 3rd, and on the 5th the General held a meeting with them.

The Cherokees now went south once more, and on the 14th of December returned to Fort Mellon with an additional number of Seminoles. In the meantime, Wildcat had made his escape from the fort at St. Augustine, and this, together with an evident uneasiness among the Indians assembled at Fort Mellon, caused General Jesup to fear that his plans would again miscarry. With the probable intention to obviate this danger, the General, a day or two after the return of the last party, seized all the Indians at the fort, seventy-one in number, including Mickenopah, and made them prisoners, although all had come in under flags of truce.*

This fresh act of perfidy aroused the indignation of the Cherokee delegates, and at the same time excited a fear that the Seminoles might suspect them as traitors. The whole disgraceful transaction was ably and eloquently laid before the Secretary of War by John Ross, in a letter dated March 8th, 1838, in which he says:

"Perhaps you have forgotten the circumstances which arose at the very moment when Mickenopah and the chiefs with him were seized under a flag of truce. The Cherokee mediators, in whose presence this occurred, no sooner recovered from their astonishment, than they asked to clear themselves from the appearance of treachery in the minds of the Seminoles who had unhesitatingly come, through their means, into the lines of the army for negotiation, and lost their liberty."

*Ex. Docs. 285 and 327, 2d Ses., 25th Cong.

He thus explained the anxiety of his brethren to gain an interview with the prisoners and to remove from their minds all suspicion of treachery:

"Unless fully cleared from suspicion . . . how would they be viewed by the world at large, if any one could brand them as the willing tools to ensnare the confiding, under the sacredness of a flag of truce, which is respected by enemies the most ferocious, and by spirits the most untamable, throughout the peopled earth?"

General Jesup had refused to allow the Cherokees to converse with the Seminoles at the time of their seizure, and he even declined to make the explanation himself, as the delegates then requested; but he finally told them that they could have an interview with the prisoners in Fort Marion, whither they were at once taken.

The Cherokees, with their escort, Colonel Sherburne, accompanied the Seminoles to St. Augustine, a distance of more than two hundred miles, and saw them joined in confinement in the fort with Osceola and his party, who, as the reader knows, had been imprisoned there nearly two months before.

In order to see justice done in this matter, Colonel Sherburne at once requested an interview with the principal chiefs among the Seminole prisoners. Mickenopah and the other leaders seized at Fort Mellon, together with Osceola and the chiefs of his party, were ushered into the commandant's own room at the fort, and there the Cherokees at last had the satisfaction of explaining their position. After hearing all they had to say, the Seminoles stated that " they dismissed from their minds all suspicion of treachery on the part of their Cherokee brethren." *

General Jesup evidently experienced considerable

* Ibid.

remorse for his latest treacherous act, for at this meeting he requested Colonel Sherburne, on his (Jesup's) own responsibility, to lay before the assembled Indians the following entirely new proposition:

If the United States should set apart, for the exclusive use of the Seminoles, all that portion of Florida south of Tampa Bay, and bounded by the Gulf of Mexico and the Atlantic, would the Seminoles agree to guard that frontier for the United States from foreign invasion, and also to deliver up to their rightful owners all runaway negroes who might flee to their territory?

The General then inquired how many of the chiefs present would accompany him to Washington, in the event that such a proposition should be sanctioned by the Government. One by one each chief present replied that he would gladly agree to such an arrangement, and that he would go to Washington. * When the agent addressed Osceola, that chief plucked one of the white plumes from his turban, and handing it to the agent, replied:

"Give this to our white father† in token that Osceola will do as you have said."‡

It should be stated that Mickenopah alone qualified his assent to the proposition. He would only agree to it when thoroughly convinced that the word of the United States would not be broken. Osceola, on the contrary, notwithstanding the base treachery which had been practiced upon him, was more trusting. He displayed his magnanimity and his desire for peace by his willingness to overlook the past and to accede to terms which would allow his nation to remain in the land of their birth.

* Condensed from the documents last quoted.
† The President.
‡ Report of the delegates to John Ross, and quoted by him in his letter to the Secretary of War.

General Jesup forwarded the proposition, and the replies of the Seminoles, to the Secretary of War, but that official declined to consider it, stating that the settled policy of the Government must be adhered to and the tribe removed entirely from the Territory.

John Ross not only protested against the seizure of the Seminoles under a flag of truce, but he made a strong effort to secure their release from confinement, as will be seen from the following extract from one of his letters to the Secretary of War:

"I do most solemnly protest against this unprecedented violation of that sacred rule which has ever been recognized by every nation, civilized and uncivilized, of treating with due respect those who had ever presented themselves under a flag of truce before their enemy .... Moreover, I respectfully appeal to and submit for your decision, whether justice and policy do not require at your hands that these captives should be forthwith liberated, that they may go and confer with their people, and that whatever obstacles may have been thrown in the way of their coming in to make peace may be removed." *

Thus did this noble red man and staunch friend of the Seminoles appeal to the sense of justice and magnanimity of our Government through its official representative. But his manly and earnest words fell on deaf ears; the records do not even contain a reply to this last suggestion.

After the meeting at Fort Marion between the Cherokee delegation and the Seminoles, the former bade their unfortunate friends farewell, and left for Washington, to meet their chief. Soon after their arrival in the city, they called at the office of the *National*

* The entire correspondence between John Ross and the Secretary of War may be consulted in Ex. Docs. 285 and 327, 2d Ses., 25th Cong.

Intelligencer and made a plain statement with regard to Jesup's seizure of Mickenopah and those with him. Commenting upon this, the editor says, in his issue of Jan. 5th, 1838:

" . . . . But, whilst hopes were entertained that the rest of the chiefs would come in, and some were actually in motion for the purpose, circumstances occurred to produce a sudden change in the minds of those who were still in the hammocks and swamps . . . Those chiefs who had come in under the Cherokee flag of truce were made prisoners of war, and forthwith sent off to St. Augustine and imprisoned."

In defense of his course, General Jesup states in a letter addressed to the Cherokee delegation, dated Dec. 15th, 1837, that he sent Mickenopah and his party to St. Augustine on account of "the recent conduct of Arpeika (Sam Jones) and other chiefs and their people." He also claims that Mickenopah and Cloud were hostages under the treaty of Fort Dade.

Again, in a final report to the Secretary of War, under date of July 6th, 1838, presented after his retirement from the command of the army in Florida, General Jesup says he "authorized no assurance to be given to the Indians that they were to come to my camp and be permitted to return. I promised protection and kind treatment. If the Cherokees promised more it was on their own responsibility and without my authority."

It was perfectly understood that the Cherokee delegation was to visit the Seminoles in their fastnesses and induce them to come in and hold a council with General Jesup. The only way by which their presence could be secured was by assuring them protection under a flag of truce; and of this General Jesup was well aware. He knew full well, too, that the influence of their trusted friends, the Cherokees, would induce the Seminoles to do what probably no other means could have effected. His excuse, therefore, for seizing the persons of the Seminole chiefs was valueless and contemptible.

CHAPTER X.

TRANSFER OF OSCEOLA AND THE OTHERS TO FORT MOULTRIE—VISITORS FLOCK TO SEE THE FAMOUS CHIEF—OSCEOLA AND OTHER CHIEFS VISIT THE THEATER—DESCRIPTIVE POEM—SUICIDE OF AN INDIAN—GEORGE CATLIN PAINTS THE CHIEFS' PORTRAITS—PERSONAL APPEARANCE OF OSCEOLA IN CONFINEMENT.

After the seizure of Mickenopah and those with him, General Jesup no doubt feared a concentration of the Indian forces on the fort at St. Augustine, for he soon after decided to transfer all of his Indian prisoners to Fort Moultrie, situated on Sullivan's Island, opposite the city of Charleston, South Carolina. The number thus disposed of comprised the chiefs Mickenopah, King Philip, Osceola, Cloud and Alligator, together with one hundred and sixteen warriors and eighty-two women and children.

The party included no Maroons or other negroes, all of whom had been separated from the Indians and sent to Tampa Bay, in readiness for transportation to Arkansas. This arrangement General Jesup deemed necessary "for better protection," as he stated in a letter to General Arbuckle, and in order to prevent greater difficulty in carrying out his plans with the Indians,* who regarded the imprisonment of the Maroons, and their possible re-enslavement, as an outrage upon themselves.

The entire Seminole party, as numbered above, were embarked on the United States Steamer Poinsett, Captain

*House Ex. Doc. 219, Vol. 8, 2d Ses., 25th Cong.

Trathen, and arrived at Fort Moultrie January 1st, 1838, where they were all confined within the fortress. The officer in charge of their removal, Captain Morrison, testified to their good behavior on the passage, as well as throughout their confinement. Their arrival excited sympathy as well as curiosity, and many persons from various parts of the country visited them at the fort.

Osceola, although regarded as the most important of all the prisoners, was allowed to roam about the enclosure and to receive visitors in his room. The fearless bravery and manly qualities of this chief, his unusual knowledge of scientific warfare, and, above all else, his unswerving determination to defend to the last his chosen home, had spread his fame throughout the length and breadth of the country, and won for him respect and admiration even in the hearts of his bitterest enemies.

No wonder is it, then, that all who visited the fort found Osceola the center of attraction. The romantic interest which gathered around him was enhanced by sympathy; not alone on account of his treacherous seizure, however, for it was soon perceived that, although in the very prime of manhood, having hardly reached middle age, his health as well as his spirit, was broken.

To the visitor Osceola seemed always pining for the freedom of his native land. Though too proud to display this feeling by any unmanly manifestations, he sometimes talked, through the medium of an interpreter, with great spirit and even with fiery indignation, about the base manner in which he had been betrayed; nor did he cease to regret his inability to continue the fight in defense of his country. No one, at such times, could look upon the uncommonly attractive features and powerful yet supple form of this noble warrior, thus chafing in confinement, without mingled feelings of pity, admiration and respect.

On the evening of the 6th of January, Osceola and other chiefs were induced to attend the Charleston Theater as spectators. The public announcement in the newspapers of the previous day that these distinguished visitors were to appear, caused the building to be crowded to the doors. The play was "Honeymoon," with the admired actress, Miss Cooper, in the role of Juliana. The chiefs divided with her the honors of the occasion. The attractive scene and the bearing of the red men are graphically described in the following verses, entitled, "Osceola at the Charleston Theater," by James B. Ransom, a poet who happened to be sojourning in the city:

"The chandeliers sent forth a dazzling light,
And splendid lamps and paintings shone around;
The scenery was superb and all looked bright,
While not one vacant seat could there be found.
Indeed, a prince of high pretensions might
Have viewed the scene without a single frown,
For beauty, fashion, learning all combined
To form a crowd genteel, polite, refined.

Then Osceola with his warriors came—
A stern, unbending, stoic band they were—
Whose names, in truth, will long be known to fame
For deeds of valor and for love of war.
With earrings, trinkets, necklaces and bands,
Heads decked with feathers, rings upon their hands—
A group so wild, grotesque, and yet so sage,
Have very seldom looked upon the stage.

I marked the heavy thought upon his brow,
Which clung like mist around the mountain top,
And watched his listless mien and careless bow,
As though he saw the play but heard it not.
And then his lips would breathe some secret vow
To strike for injuries ne'er to be forgot,
And peril all, though life should be the cost,
To save his native home and country lost.

"The lovely glow of Juliana's face,
Her smiles and blushes, and the tears she shed,
Her splendid attitudes and native grace,
Were to his war-lit fancy stale and dead.
Yes, there he sat, subdued but still enraged,
As the fierce tiger, when he's caught and caged
Will lie composed, yet, when you pass him by,
You'll see a demon spirit in his eye.

The softest strains of music fell unheard,
And every sound seemed lost upon his ear,
While songs that spoke of love in every word
Nor made him sigh, nor smile, nor drop a tear;
For his wild thoughts, like some unfettered bird,
Flew swift as lightning to that home so dear, ·
Where his undaunted heart still longed to go,
To raise the savage yell and fight the treacherous foe."*

A singular incident occurred on the night of January 7th. On the previous night one of the Indian warriors, it was reported, had been concerned in depredations on a neighboring henroost. For this act the culprit was severely reprimanded by the chiefs, and was also threatened with punishment. The next morning he was found at the fort suspended by the neck with a piece of rawhide, his knees almost touching the ground. A coroner's jury was summoned and decided that the poor fellow had undoubtedly committed suicide, probably from mingled shame and fear of punishment.†

When George Catlin, the famous Indian portrait-painter, learned of the confinement of the Seminoles in Fort Moultrie, he at once decided to visit them and secure portraits of the most prominent prisoners. Our Government, also, made arrangements with him to paint the likenesses of four chiefs, for preservation in the War Department Collection. Arriving at Charleston, January 17th, Mr. Catlin went at once to Fort Moultrie and

---

*Charleston *Courier*, January 9th, 1838.

†Ibid. To the wild Indian, who never keeps anything under lock and key, stealing is regarded as a far greater crime than it is among the white people.

entered upon his congenial task.   He succeeded in transferring to canvas the portraits of eight prominent
chiefs, including two of Osceola—one of the head and
shoulders, (see frontispiece), the other a full length figure.
He also painted portraits of three of the Indian women.

When Mr. Catlin requested Osceola to sit for his
likeness, that chief readily consented, and immediately
prepared his person with the utmost care.   This was the
second portrait executed by the artist after his arrival,
the first being one of Mickenopah, chief of the nation.
This painting of Osceola is numbered three hundred and
one of the Catlin Collection, on exhibition at the United
States National Museum, Washington, D. C.

The artist was struck with admiration when he first
beheld the superb figure and fine countenance of Osceola.
In a letter written on the day of his arrival at the fort,
to a friend in New York, he refers to this chief as "a
fine, gentleman-like looking man, with a pleasant smile
that would become the face of the most refined and
delicate female."

That winning smile and those wonderful eyes drew
from an army officer who interviewed him, these glowing
words of admiration, addressed to Dr. Welch: ". . . But
the eye!—that 'herald of the soul'—was in itself constituted to command; when under excitement it flashed
firm and stern resolve; when smiling, it warmed the very
heart of the beholder with its beams of kindness."*

After seeing the Catlin portrait, the New York
Star spoke of the great contrast between the physiog-
nomy of Osceola and of the other chiefs—" the towering
forehead, the pensive, melancholy cast of expression,
the lurking fire of a noble black eye—as bearing the
very stamp of high mettled nobility and of commanding
genius."

*Osceola Nikkanoochee.

Mr. Catlin occupied a large room in the officers' quarters, "and every evening," says he, "after painting all day at their portraits, I have had Osceola, Mickenopah, Cloud, Coeehajo, King Philip, and others, in my room until a late hour at night, where they have taken great pains to give me an account of the war and the mode in which they were captured, of which they complain bitterly. I am fully convinced from all I have seen, and learned from the lips of Osceola and from the chiefs who are around him, that he is a most extraordinary man, and one entitled to a better fate."†

In his conversations with Mr. Catlin, Osceola made many inquiries about the West, its game animals, its wood, waters, and inhabitants, indicating that he had some hope of final release, and that he was debating in his mind, whether, in that event, it would not be better for him and his people to give up the unequal contest with the whites, and agree to removal. But his lingering hopes were never to be fulfilled.

Mr. Catlin painted another portrait of Osceola, a full length figure, (No. 308, Catlin Collection). In his great work on Indian life and character, the artist thus speaks of this portrait and the dress of the subject:

"I painted him precisely in the costume in which he stood for his picture, even to a string and a trinket. He wore three ostrich feathers on his head and a turban made of a varicolored cotton shawl, and his dress was chiefly of calicoes, with a handsome bead sash or belt around his waist, and his rifle in his hand."

The chief Mickenopah at first positively refused to be painted, but afterward consented, Mr. Catlin says, "if I could make a fair likeness of his legs, which he had very tastefully dressed in a handsome pair of red leggins,

†Catlin's "Eight Years," etc.

and upon which I at once began, as he sat cross-legged, by painting them upon the lower part of the canvas, leaving room for his body and head above."

A certificate dated at Fort Moultrie, January 26th, 1838, and signed by Captain Morrison and the other officers at the fort, including the surgeon, states "that the Indians sat or stood in the costumes precisely in which they are painted, and that the likenesses are remarkably good."

CHAPTER XI.

On the very day on which the last portrait of Osceola was painted, that chief was taken sick with an
alarming attack of quinsy. Previous to this illness, Dr.
Weedon, the assistant surgeon of the post, had expressed
his opinion that Osceola would not live many weeks in
confinement; and Mr. Catlin says he had observed a
" rapid decline in his face and his flesh " since his arrival
at the fort.

Several times during the attack, Mr. Catlin and the
officers of the garrison were called to Osceola's bedside,
as Dr. Weedon believed him to be dying. On the night of
January 27th, they all sat up with him until midnight,
expecting his death at any moment. On the morning
of the 29th, Mr. Catlin was obliged to leave, per steamer,
for New York. At that time the sick man's condition
had slightly improved, and it was thought that he might
recover.

Osceola, however, grew worse instead of better,
and Dr. Strobel, Professor of Anatomy in the College of
South Carolina, was called in consultation. But, on the
advice of one of the medicine men, who was among the
prison rs, the chief positively refused to take any of the
remedies which these gentlemen suggested, resisting to
the last their every effort to relieve him.

Perhaps the chief did not care to live; the faint hope of release which he evidently entertained previous to his illness may have fled; liberty to one of his nature was more than life.

The treatment given by the Indian doctor consisted mainly of poultices, and a wash or liniment, made from roots and herbs, which were freely applied to the throat and chest of the patient. Osceola's two wives were present and were most devoted in their attentions to the patient. One or the other of them was almost constantly trying something for his relief.

Finally, on the morning of the 30th of January, 1838, in the 34th year of his age, surrounded by his wives and children, by his brother chiefs and the officers of the garrison, Osceola, the Rising Sun—he who had been the very life-spirit of the Seminole War for home and country, passed peacefully away, his head resting in the lap of one of his devoted wives.

When Osceola realized that he would not recover and that death was near, he had requested Dr. Weedon to give Mr. Catlin—whom he, in common with nearly all Indians, knew to be his friend — an account of his last moments, which request was complied with as follows:

"About half an hour before he died, he seemed to be sensible that he was dying; and, although he could not speak, he signified by signs that he wished me (Dr. Weedon) to send for the chiefs and for the officers of the post, whom I called in. He made signs to his wives (of whom he had two, and also two fine little children) by his side, to go and bring his full dress which he wore in time of war; which having been brought in, he rose up in his bed, which was on the floor, and put on his shirt, his leggins and his moccasins, girded on his war belt, bullet-pouch and powder-horn, and laid his knife by the side of him on the floor.

"He then called for his red paint and looking-glass, which latter was held before him, when he deliberately painted one-half of his face, his neck and his throat with vermillion, a custom practiced when the irrevocable oath of war and destruction is taken. His knife he then placed in its sheath under his belt, and he carefully arranged his turban on his head and his three ostrich plumes that he was in the habit of wearing in it.

"Being thus prepared in full dress, he lay down a few moments to recover strength sufficient, when he rose up as before, and with most benignant and pleasing smiles, extended his hand to me and to all of the officers and chiefs that were around him, and shook hands with us all in dead silence, and with his wives and little children.

"He made a signal for them to lower him down upon his bed, which was done, and he then slowly drew from his war-belt his scalping-knife, which he firmly grasped in his right hand, laying it across the other on his breast, and in a moment smiled away his last breath without a struggle or a groan."*

The silent watchers in that rude chamber of death were acquainted with the manly character of the dead chief; they knew the intense love of home that had filled his being, and the indomitable courage he had displayed in its defense; they were aware of his treacherous seizure and cruel confinement. Therefore, when the Great Spirit came and claimed his own from further injustice, there were few dry eyes among those present, even the Indians being uncommonly affected.

*A footnote in Catlin's "Eight Years," etc.

The funeral of the Seminole chieftain was conducted with the honors and respect due to so distinguished a foeman. A detachment of the United States troops, followed by the medical men and many private citizens, together with all of the chiefs and warriors, women and children, in a body, escorted the remains to the grave, which was located near the main entrance to the fort. The coffin, with all the weapons and personal belongings of the deceased, was lowered, and a military salute fired over the grave. The Indians seemed to derive a melancholy satisfaction from the honors paid to their former leader.

One of the soldiers enclosed the grave with a neat paling, and a Mr. Patton, a generous and sympathizing resident of Charleston, erected a marble slab at the head, on which was cut this simple but expressive inscription :

OSCEOLA :

PATRIOT AND WARRIOR;

DIED, JAN. 30, 1838.

The wooden paling was afterwards replaced with an iron one, but the place has long been neglected; the stone now lies flat and is broken, while the inscription is deciphered with difficulty.

A few days after the burial, unknown persons opened the grave and decapitated the corpse, carrying off the head. Some time afterward, according to the New York *Star*, of that period, the head was on exhibition at Stuyvesant Institute, New York City. It was believed by many at the time that this infamous act was perpetrated with the full knowledge, if not the assistance, of one of the physicians in the neighborhood. Fortunately, a death-cast of the head and shoulders

OSCEOLA'S GRAVE.

(Near Fort Moultrie, Sullivan's Island, Charleston Harbor, South Carolina.)
Never before published.

the dead chief was taken before burial; this is now in the Smithsonian Museum, Washington, D. C.

After years of effort, the author at last learned that Dr. G. M. Vincent, of Braidentown, Fla., claimed to have the skull of Osceola in his possession. The following was received in reply to a request for a brief history of the relic:

"BRAIDENTOWN, FLA., March 24th, 1898.
"MR. CHARLES H. COE, Washington, D. C.
"DEAR SIR: Yours of the 21st to hand, and in regard to Osceola skull will say I will dispose of it for one hundred dollars and the history of same that I have certified to before a J. P.   Respectfully Yours,
                              "G. M. VINCENT."

A week after the death of Osceola, Doctors Weedon and Strobel, complying with a public desire or demand, each made a full statement in a Charleston newspaper regarding Osceola's sickness and death. Dr. Weedon states that soon after he commenced the treatment of his patient, the Indian doctor came into the room and "from the moment of his entrance there was a refusal to take anything" offered by the white physicians. Dr. Strobel said he agreed with Dr. Weedon's views and partial treatment, and that he was satisfied Osceola would have recovered from the attack if the surgeon had been permitted to put them into practice.*

The death of Osceola in confinement called forth renewed comments upon the manner of his seizure, many high testimonials to his greatness, as well as confident forecasts of his enduring fame.†

Courier, Feb. 6th, 1838.

†The memory of this hero is perpetuated in three counties and nineteen villages, in various parts of the United States, by the name of the chief. In Florida, a county. town, street, lake, a snake (*Osceola elapsoidea*, the handsomest serpent in the country), a newspaper, and a hotel. are so called. Among the white persons who bore the chief's name was the late Osceola C. Green. one of the most prominent and highly respected citizens of Washington, D. C.; Osceola Currier, a prominent business man of Newark, N. J.; and Osceola Lewis. author of a History of the 138th Penn. Reg. Vols , 1866. Several of the present Seminoles in Florida, and one in the West, are named after this famous warrior. The latest namesake is a United States torpedo boat destroyer.

The *Mercury*, of Charleston, South Carolina, commenting upon the death of the chief, said:

"When we saw him at the theater he looked sad and tired of the world. . .Is there not something in the character of this man not unworthy of the respect of the world? From a vagabond child he became the master-spirit of a long and desperate war. He made himself— no man owed less to accident. . .Such was Osceola, who will long be remembered as the man that with the feeblest means produced the most terrible effects."

Capt. John T. Sprague refers to Osceola as "a brave and generous enemy, and respected as he was by the country for his open, manly nature, he was too proud to be under the dominion of the white man."

Says Samuel G. Drake, author of several works on the Indians:

"He was a great man, and his name will go down to the latest posterity with as much renown as Philip of Pokanoket. Both by fatal errors were brought prematurely into the hands of their enemies. . .Osceola by a mistaken estimate of the character of his foes."

"In his narrow sphere," says Thomas W. Storrow, a prominent writer of his day, "Osceola displayed many heroic virtues; his life was engaged in a nobler cause than that which incites the actions of many whom the world calls great. If those who have devastated the earth to gratify their selfish ambition or thirst for conquest, have historians to record their deeds and poets to sing their praises, let us not withhold a token of applause to one who committed fewer wrongs, and during his life was a brave defender of his country."*

Various poems devoted to Osceola were published in newspapers and periodicals of the day. Perhaps the

***Knickerbocker Magazine*, November 1844.

most spirited and affecting was one by Alfred B. Street,
one of the leading minor poets of America, whose works
were praised for their realism and fidelity. We need
make no apology for reproducing it here.

OSCEOLA.

PART I.

The rich blue sky is o'er,
    Around are the tall green trees,
And the jessamine's breath from the Everglades
    Is borne on the wandering breeze.
On the mingled grass and flowers
    Is a fierce and threatening form
That looks like an eagle when pluming his wing
    To brave the gathering storm.

His rifle within his grasp,
    The bright plumes o'er his head,
His features are clothed with a warrior's pride
    And he moves with a monarch's tread.
He bends with listening ear,
    He peers through the tangled screen,
And he smiles with joy as the flash of steel
    Through the Everglade's grass is seen.

One wave of his stalwart arm,
    Wild forms around him stand,
And his eye glares bright with triumphant light
    As he looks at his swarthy band.
Nearer the bayonets gleam—
    At the edge of the hammock now,
The pale-face ranks are rallying,
    But they seek in vain the foe.

They see in that lovely dale
    But the humming-bird o'er the flower,
And the glit ering wing of the paroquet
    In the cool and fragrant bower.
But hark! from the cypress shade,
    From the bay-tree's glossy leaves,
And the nooks where the vine from bough to bough
    Its serpentine festoon weaves—

The loud. shrill war-whoops burst
    On the soft and s'eeping air,
And quick, bright darts of surrounding death
    Are fearfully glancing there.
The eagle with fierce delight
    Abroad his pinions cast,
And he shrieks as he bathes in the crimson rain
    And sweeps through the whizzing blast.

The battle-storm is o'er—
    The hammock is reeking red—
But who looks there with victorious smile
    On the heaps of the pale-face dead?
'Tis a tribe's young warrior-chief,
    The deeds of whose vengeful flame
Have filled the ear of a mighty land
    With the terror of his name.

PART II.

In a dark dungeon room
    Is stretched a mighty form,
And it shakes in its dreadful agony
    Like a leaf in the autumn storm.
No pillared palmetto hangs
    Its tuft in the clear bright air;
But a sorrowing group, and the narrow wall,
    And a smouldering hearth are there.

The white froth on his lips,
    His trembling, gasping breath,
And the hollow rattle in his throat,
    Proclaim the conqueror—Death!
'Tis the proud, victorious chief
    Who smiled 'mid the pale-face slain;
'Tis the eagle that swept through the whizzing blast
    And bathed in the crimson rain.

For his own sunny forest home
    He had struggled long and well,
But the soul hat breasted a nation's arms
    At the touch of a fetter fell.
He had worn wild freedom's crown
    On his bright, unconquered brow,
Since he first saw the light of his beautiful skies—
    It was gone forever now.

But still, in his last dread hours,
   Did not bright visions come—
Bright visions that shed a golden gleam
   On the darkness of his doom ?
They calmed his throbbing pulse,
   And they hung on his muttering breath—
The spray thrown up from life's frenzied flood
   That brightened the gulf of death.

The close walls shrank away—
   Above was the starless sky,
And the lakes with their floating isles of flowers,
   Spread glistening to his eye.
O'er his tent the live-oak spread
   Its branching, gigantic shade
With its dots of leaves and its robes of moss,
   Broad, blackening on the glade.

But a sterner sight is 'round.
   Battle's wild torrent is there—
The tomahawk gleams and the red blood streams,
   And the war-whoops rend the air.
At the head of his faithful band
   He peals forth his terrible cry,
As he fiercely leaps 'mid the slaughtered heaps
   Of the foe that but fought to die.

*   *   *   *   *   *   *

One gasp, and the eye is glazed,
   And still is the stiffening clay;
The eagle soul of the chief had passed
   On the battle's flood away!*

Mr. Street's graphic verses would seem to contradict the physician's account of Osceola's peaceful and painless death, but something may be pardoned to poetic license.

The fame of Osceola was well earned; not for that inhuman cruelty such as characterized most of our Western tribes, but for true patriotism and determined effort, against the combined armies of a great and pow-

*New York *Mirror*, March 1838; reprinted in the *Floridian*, Tallahassee Fla., April 28th.

erful nation, in one of the most remarkable struggles
known to history. His fame will never die; centuries
will come and go, but the name of Osceola will remain
as long as the earth is peopled.

CHAPTER XII.

Three weeks after the burial of Osceola, the Seminole prisoners remaining at Fort Moultrie were embarked on the brig Homer, Captain Nabb, for Arkansas, in charge of Lieutenant Reynolds, of the United States Marines. King Philip died on the passage up the Mississippi River, and was buried on Louisiana soil. The story of these banished unfortunates, who were never again to see their cherished Southern home, will be told in subsequent chapters.

It may as well be stated here that the author has been unable to trace the after movements of Osceola's immediate family; and the only reference to a connection of the chief's (with the exception noted in the Appendix), is contained in the following item, from the Van Buren, *Arkansas Intelligencer*, October 14, 1843:

"A Seminole Indian, Husti-colu-chee, half brother to Osceola, has recently been successfully preaching the doctrines of Christianity to the members of the tribe. He preached at Little Rock, Ark., on the 15th ult."

We now return to the theater of war in southern Florida, where hostilities were resumed in December 1837, by our army, still for a time under the command of General Jesup. After his treacherous seizure of Mickenopah and his party, the General had abandoned all hope of inducing the Seminoles to consent to peaceable removal to the Western country. The Cherokee mediators had very properly refused to have anything more to do with the matter of Seminole emigration, and, bidding goodbye to their unfortunate friends imprisoned at St. Augustine, had departed for Washington, as previously stated.

The body of the Seminole nation remaining on their reservation in the southern part of the peninsula, now under the leadership of Wildcat and Sam Jones (Arpeika), were determined to have revenge for the seizure of Osceola and the others. Sam Jones sent word to General Jesup that " he had never made a treaty and never would; he and his people would fight it out forever."*

The commander of the army now ordered into the field an officer who was at the head of a large force in the western and southern part of Florida, with headquarters at Fort Brooke, on Tampa Bay. This officer was General Zachary Taylor, who afterward became the hero of the Mexican War, and the twelfth President of the United States.

The clarion voice of Osceola no longer resounded on the battle-field, the waving plumes of his head-dress no longer flashed encouragement to his warriors, and from this time the fortunes of the Seminoles began to decline. Under a continuance of General Jesup's policy, however, the Seminoles would have defied our armies for an indefinite period. They still fought for several years with the courage of desperation, and the next battle, in which General Taylor commanded, (soon to receive attention), was the bloodiest of the war.

*Statement of Captain John C. Casey, in a private letter dated at Fort Brooke, January 14th, 1838.

The remainder of the campaign was fought around Lake Okeechobee and in the remote region of the Everglades. A brief description of this interesting and still partially unexplored wilderness, will greatly aid a proper understanding of the various contests which there took place.

Lake Okeechobee, an Indian name signifying "Big Water," is about thirty-five miles long by thirty in width, and covers a surface of more than 1,000 square miles, with an average depth of about twelve feet. Less was known of this lake prior to 1875 than of any body of water of equal area in the United States, owing to its remoteness and the extreme difficulty of reaching it. The lake is fed by numerous streams, the Kissimmee River being the most important. The principal outlet is the Caloosahatchee River, on the southwestern corner of the lake, while during seasons of high water the banks overflow into the Everglades on the south. The surrounding country is low, and much of it submerged after heavy and continuous rains. Cypress swamps and occasional growths of cabbage palmetto and ash, from a few hundred yards to several miles in width, extend around the lake. About eighteen miles of the eastern beach is hard white sand. In the southern part are several more or less wooded islands. Small steamers now traverse the lake and the entire course of the waterways to the north, also the Caloosahatchee River, which was made navigable in 1882.

South of this great body of water lies the remarkable region known as the Everglades. By the Indians it was appropriately called Pay-hah-o-kee, or Bi-ha-yo-kee, meaning "grass water." This tract is about one hundred and twenty miles long by sixty wide, and embraces a larger area than the State of Connecticut, or the combined States of Rhode Island and Delaware. It is best described as an inundated prairie, with water varying in depth from a few inches to several feet, according to the conformation of the bottom, and to the seasons. It is covered with a species of tall grass (the saw-grass of the south), and dotted, in places, with innumerable islands, on some of which pine and other trees grow. Some of the islands are several acres in extent, and capable of cultivation, but most of them are small and very low. A number of chiefs had their headquarters on islands remote from the borders of this desolate region, the most prominent being Chakika, Sam Jones, the Prophet, and Waxyhajo.

It is commonly believed that few white men have ever succeeded in crossing the Everglades, whereas no less than thirteen different expeditions, numbering from a few men to nearly three hundred each, have traversed the lower half in nearly every direction. With one exception the northern half has never been crossed, owing to the more continuous bodies of saw-grass, which render a passage next to impossible. The first expedition across the Glades was made by Lieut. Colonel W. S. Harney, in December 1840, a further notice of which will be given in another chapter. The latest expedition was undertaken by Lieut. Hugh L. Willoughby, who crossed in the winter of 1895, between Harney River and Miami. The hardships endured by those who have traversed this region cannot be exaggerated. *

One more remarkable formation claims description, the " Big Cypress Swamp," or Ah-shah-wa-yo-kee of the Indians, occupying as it did a prominent place in the Seminole war. Owing to its peculiar advantages

* A monograph entitled "The Florida Everglades: Their Character, Explorations, and Drainage," by the author, was read before the St. Augustine Historical Society in February 1898.

for concealment and defense, as well as the existence within its limits of many fertile spots for raising corn and other products, also to its natural food supply, this swamp was a favorite retreat of the Seminoles.* It occupies the southern and southwestern part of Lee County, and extends to the western border of the Everglades. It is composed of cypress and bay swamps, hammocks, ponds, and pine islands.† A statement made by an army officer in 1856, regarding the Big Cypress, is true to the present day. He says:

"To the Indian it possesses valuable resources. The means of subsistence are inexhaustible. If debarred from cultivating his garden or raising stock, the fish, game, and fruits supply abundant food. The cabbage palmetto trees alone would yield an unfailing support.‡ In case of hostilities and pursuit, the innumerable dense and tangled hammocks, thickets, and lily-ponds, where the whole tribe might baffle the pursuit of vastly superior numbers, render the Big Cypress, as a stronghold, almost impregnable."‖

With these explanations, we will now follow General Taylor, who, in obedience to the orders of his superior in command, commenced in December 1837, preparations for an active campaign in the Indian country. His first work was the opening of a road through the wilderness to Lake Kissimmee, almost due east of Fort Brooke. At the head of Peace Creek a post was established (Fort Fras·r), and on the Kissimmee River another (Fort Gardner).

* It is still occupied, with some other parts of the county, by the largest part of the remnant now living in he state

† Isolated tracts of pine woods or hammocks, sometimes acres in extent, surrounded by swamps or prairie.

‡ Reference is had to the undeveloped bud in the top of the tree, which furnishes a nutritive article of diet, resembling in flavor a delicate cabbage, hence the name. The edible part is about three inches in diameter by ten to fourteen in length.

‖ Florida South of Tampa Bay, 1856; published by order of Jefferson Davis, Secretary of War.

The General left the latter post on the 20th of December, and directed his course toward Lake Okeechobee. His force consisted of eight hundred regulars and volunteers, some of his officers being among the most valued in the service. He had prepared for rapid marching by leaving the artillery and all unnecessary baggage behind. Following the west bank of the river to a point about seventeen miles above the lake, he crossed over, after leaving a detail to construct a temporary fort (Basinger), and went around the head of the lake. On the third day's march, evidence of the presence of Indians in the neighborhood was discovered and it was soon apparent that they were retreating, keeping just far enough in the advance of the troops to be out of range.

On the morning of Christmas day, the enemy was traced to a large cypress swamp bordering the northeastern side of Lake Okeechobee. Fronting this swamp was an immense saw-grass "slough" three-quarters of a mile in width, through the center of which flowed a sluggish stream.* On the farther side of this tract the Indians had taken a stand, having purposely led our troops to this particular place, knowing the great advantage such ground would give them over an attacking party. General Taylor recognized the strength of the enemy's position, but he did not hesitate, and at once commenced preparations for an attack.† The slough before them was impassable for horses and nearly so for men. The animals were therefore abandoned, and, together with all of the baggage, left in charge of a guard stationed in the pine woods near by.

* Such tracts are common throughout the southern half of the peninsula. They are almost invariably boggy. and are crossed with extreme difficulty. The dense growth of saw-grass that covers these places is often as high as a man's head.

† The battle took place in Sec. 22, Tp. 37 South, Range 35 East.

The troops entered the slough in two lines, often up to their waists in mud and water, and crossed the stream in safety. Up to this time not a sign of the enemy was to be seen in the swamp before them; but no sooner were the volunteers, composing one line, within gunshot of the border, than a heavy fire met them from the Indians, causing them to break and retreat to the rear. They recrossed the slough and could not be induced to return.

The regulars, under Col. Alexander R. Thompson, moved steadily forward. General Taylor says in his report, (from which we are condensing), "they continued to advance until their gallant commander and his adjutant, Lieutenant Center, were killed; and every officer, with one exception, as well as most of the non-commissioned officers. . . . were killed or wounded."

Notwithstanding the fatal commencement of this memorable "Battle of the Okeechobee," our troops finally succeeded in entering the swamp and driving the enemy, which numbered about two hundred Indians and Maroons, from their position. The battle lasted about two and one-half hours. The leaders of the Seminoles were Wildcat and Sam Jones, and the loss on their side was thirteen killed and nineteen wounded. Of the United States' forces twenty-seven were killed and one hundred and eleven officers and soldiers wounded. No captures were made at this time, but on the following day three hundred head of cattle and one hundred ponies were secured.*

Let the reader imagine, if he can, the difficulties which confronted General Taylor and his brave command, in the midst of an unexplored wilderness, in places well-nigh impassable, over one hundred and fifty

---

* Some time after, our troops captured 1000 pounds of dried beef, packs of clothing, etc., from the Indians.

miles from their headquarters. The day after the battle
was occupied in the mournful and difficult duty of carrying the dead and wounded back across the slough. The
remains were buried in the pine woods near by, and the
balance of the day was spent in constructing litters to
convey the wounded out of the wilds. These litters
were made of poles over which were stretched dry hides,
large numbers of the latter having been found at abandoned Indian camps along the route.

The return march was commenced on the morning
of December 27th, and about noon on the following day
they arrived at Fort Basinger, where part of the heavy
baggage had been left on the march southward.   They
left this post on the morning of the 29th for Fort Gardner, where they arrived on the 31st.   General Taylor
sent forward the wounded to Fort Brooke, and remained
himself at Fort Gardner to prepare for another expedition against the Indians.

Capt. John C. Casey, writing from Fort Brooke
after the return of the command to that post, says that
the Battle of the Okeechobee "was the hardest yet
fought in Florida (since Dade's). So close were the
parties that two of our men were scalped during the
heat of the engagement! A short time before the battle
a palmetto leaf was found with a drawing of two rifles,
muzzle to muzzle, which had been left there to be picked
up, no doubt—a regular defiance."*

Although having gained a great victory in this last
battle, the Seminoles now retreated still farther into the
swamps. A long newspaper article relating to the
movements and condition of the Indians at this stage,
written by an officer of the 4th artillery, contains this
earnest appeal:

* From a private letter to his brother.

". . . . At length, after much suffering, they have been driven into the swamps and unwholesome places of their country, and they are now clinging with the last efforts of desperation to their beloved home. Can any Christian in this republic know this and still pray for the continuance of blessings, when he is about to wrest from the unhappy Seminole all that the Great Spirit ever conferred upon him?"*

Our army contained many such officers and privates as the above writer, who, though always faithful in the discharge of their duty to their country , nevertheless felt a deep sympathy for their oppressed and outraged foe.

Not only was the army of the United States employed against the Seminoles, but the naval forces as well took part in various ways, at times, during the years 1838 to 1842 (both inclusive). This branch of the service was known as the "Florida squadron," and was commanded by Lieut. John T. McLaughlin. As many as nine sailing-vessels and two barges, with several hundred sailors and marines, were stationed at Indian Key, off the southern coast. From this rendezvous detachments explored the greater part of the country south of Okeechobee, in search of the Indians.

An engagement took place near Jupiter Inlet, in January, 1838, between eighty men from the squadron and an equal number of red men. Our loss, before the latter withdrew, numbered five killed and twenty-two wounded; Indian loss unknown.

In the forepart of January, General Jesup marched southward in command of about 1,200 men, in search of the enemy. On the 24th of the month, nine days after the naval affair, he encountered a band of about one hun-

---

* *Courier*, Charleston, S. C., January 1838.

dred and fifty Seminoles and Maroons, at a crossing of the Lockahatchee, a branch of Jupiter River, about six miles from the inlet by that name. A short but severe conflict ensued, during which General Jesup received a slight wound, and seven of our men were killed and thirty-one wounded. The Indians displayed great determination and skill in this affair, and withdrew with little if any loss. The day after this battle an enclosure was erected and named Fort Jupiter, at which place the troops remained for over a week, when they moved forward a day's march and camped.

CHAPTER XIII.

GENERAL JESUP AGAIN NEGOTIATES FOR PEACE—RECOMMENDS ALLOWING THE SEMINOLES TO REMAIN IN THE COUNTRY—REPLY OF THE SECRETARY OF WAR—EDITORIAL OPPOSITION—SEMINOLES SUSPECT TREACHERY—SEIZURE OF SEVEN HUNDRED INDIANS AND MAROONS—OFFICERS PRESENT DESCRIBE THE " GRAB "—SIGHT RESTORED TO A BLIND SEMINOLE WOMAN.

While our troops were encamped one day's march from Fort Jupiter, conferences were held between General Jesup and his staff, including such prominent officers as Generals Eustis and Eaton, and Colonel Twiggs, looking to a peace settlement with the Seminole nation. These officers being on the ground and comprehending the true position of affairs far better than those at a distance, were impressed with the fact that the best interests of the Government, if not in justice and humanity to the Indians, required that they should be permitted to occupy in peace their homes in the southern part of the peninsula.

Finding that this was a very general desire on the part of his officers, General Jesup determined to send a messenger to the Indians and offer them peace, pending a submission of the question to the Department at Washington. Accordingly, on the 8th of February, some of the principal chiefs in those parts were persuaded to visit the camp of their opponents for another "talk." At this meeting General Jesup offered to recommend to the authorities at Washington that the Seminoles be allowed to remain in the country, and occupy the territory granted them by the Treaty of Camp Moultrie.

(In his final report to the Secretary of War, dated July 6th, 1838, after he had been relieved from the command of the army in Florida, General Jesup thus refers to this action: "Though the arrangement for allowing the Indians to remain in the country was urged upon me by General Eustis, Colonel Twiggs and other officers, I admitted it on my own responsibility.")

General Jesup also agreed at this council that a certain tract near his camp should be set apart, and occupied by the Indians and their families in safety, until he could learn the views of the Government as to his proposed recommendations.* Runners were sent out with the news, and several hundred Indians and negroes gathered at the place designated, pleased with the thought that their Great Father might do as was proposed.

On the 11th, the General wrote the Secretary of War from Ft. Jupiter advising the Department to terminate hostilities by allowing the Seminoles and Maroons to remain in the region they were now occupying. His mind was freely expressed in regard to the matter, as the reader will see by the following extracts from the official correspondence:

"In regard to the Seminoles we have committed the error of attempting to remove them when their lands were not required for agricultural purposes; when they were not in the way of the white inhabitants, and when the greater portion of their country was an unexplored wilderness, of the interior of which we were as ignorant as of the interior of China. We exhibit in our present contest the first instance, perhaps, since the commence-

* Ex. Doc. 219, Vol. 8, 2d Ses., 25th Cong.

ment of authentic history, of a Nation employing an
army to explore a country (for we can do little more
than explore it), or attempting to remove a band
of savages from one unexplored wilderness to another."

The General then apologizes for commenting upon
the policy of the Government, and, continuing, says
that the prospect of terminating the war within a
reasonable time is anything but flattering. "My
decided opinion is," says he, "that unless immediate
emigration be abandoned, the war will continue for
years to come, and at constantly accumulating expense.
Is it not, then, well worthy the serious consideration of
an enlightened Government, whether, even if the wilderness we are traversing could be inhabited by the white
man (which is not the fact), the object we are contending for would be worth the cost? I do not certainly
think it would; indeed, I do not consider the country
south of Chickasawhatchee worth the *medicines* we shall
expend in driving the Indians from it. If I were permitted (and it is with great diffidence I venture the
suggestion), I would allow them to remain." *

(This was not the first time that General Jesup had
advised this course, or that he had doubted the success
of any other. Before the seizure of Osceola, he had
written the Secretary of War to the same effect. The
latter official replied at great length, informing the
General that the original plan must be adhered to. The
Secretary's letter commenced as follows:

"Sir: As you have in several of your letters
expressed an opinion of the impossibility of removing
the Seminoles, and a doubt of the policy . . . . it be-
comes necessary to explain to you the views of the
Executive . . . . ")

* Ibid.

General Jesup's letter to the Secretary of War, written from Fort Jupiter, clearly indicates the leading object of the Seminole War, viz: the avaricious possession of the land. This view is supported by the reply of the Secretary, which was received by the General on the 17th of February, and from which we make the following extracts:

"In the present stage of our relations with the Indians residing within the States and Territories east of the Mississippi River, including the Seminoles, it is useless to recur to the principles and motives which induced the Government to determine their removal to the West. The acts of the Executive and the laws of Congress evince a determination to carry out the measure, and it is to be regarded as the settled policy of the country . . . .

"Whether the Government ought not to have waited until the Seminoles were pressed upon by the white population, and their lands become necessary to the agricultural wants of the community, is not a question for the Executive now to consider . . . . I cannot, therefore, authorize any arrangement with the Seminoles by which they will be permitted to remain, or assign them any portion of the Territory of Florida as their future residence.

"The Department indulged the hope that, with the extensive means placed at your disposal, the war by a vigorous effort might be brought to a close this campaign. If, however, you are of the opinion that, from the nature of the country and the character of the enemy, such a result is impracticable, and that it is advisable to make a temporary arrangement with the Seminoles by which the safety of the settlements and the posts will be secured throughout the summer, you are at liberty to do so." *

The Secretary's reply no doubt caused General Jesup considerable chagrin at the cool reception of his recommendation, especially since, just previous to his taking command of the army in Florida, he had criticized the policy of General Scott, in a letter, dated June 20th, 1836, to a friend in Washington,† and had stated that with proper management the removal of the Seminoles could be easily accomplished. It was this letter, shown to President Jackson soon after its receipt by Mr. Blair, that caused Scott's removal and Jesup's appointment to his place.‡

In authorizing "a temporary arrangement with the Seminoles," the head of the War Department virtually acknowledges the fact that it was the desire of the Seminole nation to live at peace with their white neighbors. The old settlers in Florida were also well aware of this desire, as the author has learned from the lips of more than one survivor of the war. The newspapers of the day likewise admitted the fact, of which the following is an illustration :

"Thus the case stands—if the Indians are to be allowed to remain in the Territory, and we accede to their conditions, we could without doubt have peace to-morrow." ‖

The simple "conditions" demanded by the Seminoles are well known to the reader. When one considers the situation calmly and without prejudice, he must acknowledge that the bloodshed and devastation which marked the Seminole War were directly chargeable to the

---

* Ibid.

† Francis P. Blair, editor of the *Globe*.

‡ Ex. Doc. 78, 2d Ses., 25th Cong.

‖ Extract from an editorial under the head "Prospects of Peace," St Augustine *News*, May 18th, 1839.

selfish policy of our enlightened Government, and not to the " blood-thirsty savages," who were simply defending their rights like the true patriots they were.

We have said that the leading sentiment of a majority of the American people favored a discontinuance of the Seminole War and a settlement on the basis of justice to the red men. But it must be remembered that Florida, in general, and to some extent adjoining States, formed an exception to this rule. General Jesup was therefore severely censured for his efforts to terminate the war by allowing the Seminoles to remain in the Territory. In a long editorial relating to the correspondence between the General and the Secretary of War, the leading newspaper in the Territory thus expresses the sentiments of its readers:

" From the confidence with which General Jesup expresses his views of the policy to be pursued toward the Indians, we should suppose he had entirely mistaken the nature of his mission to Florida. We presume the General Government will feel under no obligations to him for spending their money in constant negotiations with the enemy whom he is sent to subdue, whilst an army of 10,000 men is kept in pay merely to witness his rare talents for diplomacy. And we are sure the people of Florida will not thank him for his assiduous efforts to barter away their lands to their savage enemies . . . . In whatever light the proposition is received, it is abhorrent to every man endowed with the common feelings of humanity." *

General Jesup's suggestions were opposed by many on the ground that the national " honor and dignity " were involved. On this point another journal says: " The people of Florida will not submit to it . . . . The

* *Tallahassee Floridian*, Mar. 31st, 1838.

national honor and dignity are too deeply concerned for it to listen for one moment to the proposed arrangement." *

It did not seem to occur to these writers that, in truth and justice, the lands occupied by the Seminoles belonged to them; or that thousands of American citizens in other sections of the country could also claim "the common feelings of humanity." Clearly, in the opinion of such editors and of many of their readers, the red man had "no rights which the white man was bound to respect." Before the war was over, however, the majority of the genuine settlers in the Territory were ready for peace on any terms.

The expression of General Jesup's views in his recommendations to the Secretary of War, do greater credit to his head than his heart. He argues on the ground of governmental policy and economy, but has nothing to say of the *rights* of the Indians as human beings. In all his dealings with these unfortunate people, he seems to have regarded them as *savages*, not as fellowmen to whom the Golden Rule applies.

> " We call them savage. O, be just!
>   Their outraged feelings scan;
> A voice comes forth—'tis from the dust,—
>   The savage was a man! "

It was reserved for others associated with General Jesup to view the question from the standpoint of sympathy and justice. Thus an army officer, who was with him at Fort Jupiter, wrote the *Political Arena:*

" It is no cause for triumph to beat and drive the poor miserable Indians, who are desperately and obstinately contending for their natural rights and possessions, against most unequal numbers." †

* St. Augustine *Herald*, Feb. 17th, 1838.
† February, 1838.

The same journal had said editorially, the previous month:

"It is too late in the day to contemn an enemy, who, seconded by the peculiar characteristics of the country, has baffled the military operations of successful generals, and virtually defeated our troops in every skirmish. The fact is, we are inclined to believe that the Seminoles are impregnable in their fastnesses, and are not to be subdued by military force. Soft words and the pursuasive force of gold, may induce them to emigrate. Otherwise, we believe that they will maintain their footing, in spite of all the efforts we can make to dislodge them. The country to which they might be confined is uninhabitable for the white man, and the question seriously presents itself, whether the design of forcibly expelling them had not better be relinquished. It is idle to suppose that the national honor requires their subjugation. No credit will accrue from the most successful termination of the war."

The last sentence of this judicious editorial expressed the sentiments of a great majority of the people throughout the Union.

Two days after the receipt of the decision of the Secretary of War, or on the 19th of February, General Jesup sent word for the chiefs to assemble at his camp the following day, to agree to a temporary arrangement, in accordance with the suggestion of the Department. The chiefs, however, who were not in favor of such a plan, and probably fearing the same treachery that had been practiced upon Osceola and others, on former occasions, refused to comply with the General's invitation. Instead, the Indians and Maroons, to the number of nearly seven hundred, who had assembled in the neighborhood, as before stated, to await the reply to

General Jesup's recommendation, began making preparations to depart.

Upon learning the intentions of the Indians, General Jesup resolved upon another bold stroke, and immediately ordered Colonel Twiggs (whom the reader will recognize as the officer who executed the former's orders for the seizure of Osceola) to seize the whole party. This step was easily accomplished, with the large number of troops on hand, on the 21st of February, and all were made prisoners with the exception of fifteen Indians, who managed to escape from the grasp of our forces.

In his report to the War Department, General Jesup says of this transaction, "Five hundred and thirteen Indians and one hundred and sixty-five negroes were secured," not one of whom, does he claim, voluntarily surrendered.* One hundred and fifty-one of the negroes thus seized are recorded in the official document as Maroons or the property of the Indians. These were sent to Tampa and the Indians to Fort Moultrie, S. C.

An army officer who was on the spot at the time, thus describes the seizure:

"General Jesup had arranged with the chiefs in camp near Jupiter to meet him on the 20th of February, but they failed to attend, and from driving in of ponies and other indications, he believed they were preparing to fly to the swamps. The General determined they should not escape, and ordered Colonel Twiggs to secure them. The Colonel arranged matters so admirably that he succeeded in taking every individual on the morning of the 21st." †

Another correspondent of the same paper, writing

* Ex. Doc. 3rd Ses., 25th Cong,

† Savannah *Georgian* April 10th, 1838.

from Fort Jupiter a few weeks later, refers to the "late 'grab' of five hundred Indians."

That General Jesup had entertained some idea of this seizure from the first,—although he had induced the confiding Indians to come in and remain under a flag of truce, and had assured their safety,—is evidenced by the fact that in his letter of February 11th to the Secretary of War, he had cautioned that officer to keep the matter as confidential at Washington as possible, so that letter-writers would not be the first to make known the decision of the Department; for, says the General, "there can be little doubt of their flying to the swamps again and renewing the war, should the decision be to remove them."

It is probable that the Indians had received secret information of the Secretary's decision. Many an officer and private sympathized with them, and perhaps from this source the red men received hints of intended treachery, but too late, unfortunately, to enable them to escape.

Among this last lot of prisoners secured by General Jesup, and finally forwarded to New Orleans, was a young Seminole woman who had been born blind. While at the Crescent City, awaiting removal to Arkansas, her relatives were told that her blindness could be removed by a certain surgeon. After consulting together, however, the Indians refused to allow the operation to be performed, saying, "What the Great Spirit has denied, pale-face cannot give; what He has ordained, it would be bad in His children to wish to change."

Their consent was finally gained, nevertheless, and the operation was successfully performed, in the presence of several chiefs. The operation was watched with great interest by Cloud, one of the chiefs who had been confined with Osceola. In those days anæsthetics were not employed, and the surgery was so painful that at one stage the woman refused to allow it to proceed; but when Cloud told her he had " observed the pale-face closely and was satisfied he could give her sight," she submitted. The woman had a child which was also born blind, and the sympathizing surgeon expressed his wish to restore its sight also.*

* **New Orleans** *Bulletin*, **April 1838.**

CHAPTER XIV.

GENERAL JESUP RETIRES FROM COMMAND OF THE ARMY—AN
IMPROVED POLICY UNDER GENERAL TAYLOR—OVER A
YEAR OF PEACE—JESUP VOLUNTEERS ADVICE—THE
MACOMB "TREATY"—END OF THE WAR ANNOUNCED—
DOUBLE DEALING APPARENT—FLORIDA PRESS AND PEOPLE
CONDEMN THE DECEPTION.

Over a year now passed without active hostilities,
with the exception of a slight affair near Newnansville.
This outlook for the better was largely owing to a change
of commanders in Florida, and to an improvement in
the policy of carrying on the campaign of removal. On
the 15th of May, 1838, General Jesup retired from the
field, and General Zachary Taylor was promoted to the
chief command.

This officer, as we have seen, had led in the bloody
conflict of Lake Okeechobee, and had followed the
enemy further into their fastnesses than any other commander. He had disapproved of the policy of forcible
removal, but, like a good soldier, had abstained from
meddling with the affairs of his superior.

When, however, General Taylor became the responsible head of the army in Florida, he discarded that policy
altogether. He refused to use his forces for the benefit
of the owners of fugitive slaves, nor would he allow the
piratical slave-catchers, or even the bona fide owners of
lost slaves, to inspect the negroes who were captured by
him or who voluntarily came into his camp for emigration. The negro he regarded as truly a prisoner of war
as the Indian.

From the first, the General strove to make it clear to the Seminoles that he favored their removal to the West for their own good. Under his pacific policy, parties of Indians and Maroons occasionally came in and expressed their willingness to emigrate, until in less than a year more than four hundred joined the others, now numbering about 1,700, in Arkansas. Strange to say, the women forming part of an emigration of 250 Indians sent West by General Taylor, "were very reluctant to go, and upbraided the men with cowardice in refusing to die upon their native soil. The vessels departed amid their lamentations and taunts and reproaches upon the conduct of the warriors."*

It is interesting to note that after the irrepressible General Jesup had retired from Florida, he again volunteered his advice as to the best method of removing the Seminoles. In a letter to the Chairman of the Senate Military Committee, he suggests: "Let them be crowded by white settlers, and that which has invariably occurred throughout the whole history of our settlements will occur again."†

Let us enquire, for a moment, what light "the history of our settlements" will shed upon the methods thus recommended. It discloses a regular system of persecution of the Indian—settling within his boundary, and various other acts of lawlessness and indignities, not infrequently including murder itself—for the purpose of compelling him to sell his land and "move on." When the Indian stood his ground, and defended his own after his own custom, a great cry would be raised against the "treacherous savages," our army would be called to the scene, and the work of extermination and

<hr>

*St. Augustine *News*, March 16th, 1839.

†Ex. Doc. 163, 3rd Ses., 25th Cong.

expatriation commenced by border whites, or "white savages" as they have been called, would be continued under the auspices of "our Christian government."

But the darkness of this picture was somewhat alleviated by the presence and control of a more humane and judicious leader. General Taylor, so long as he remained at the head of affairs, reversed the policy of his predecessor, and studied to temper justice with mercy. Under his management very little blood was shed.

About a year after General Taylor assumed command in Florida, General Alexander Macomb, Commander-in-Chief of the Army of the United States, arrived in the Territory with instructions to negotiate a new "peace treaty" with the Seminoles, by allowing them to remain in possession of their homes. Referring to this policy, Joshua R. Giddings says:

"General Scott, a veteran officer of our army, had exhausted his utmost science; had put forth all his efforts to conquer this indomitable people, or rather to subdue their love of liberty, the independence o thought and of feeling which stimulated them to effort—but he had failed. The power of our army, aided by deception, fraud and perfidy, had been tried in vain. General Jesup, the most successful officer who had commanded in Florida, had advised peace upon the precise terms which the Seminoles had demanded at the commencement of the war; and General Macomb was now commissioned to negotiate peace on those terms."*

General Macomb arrived at Fort King, April 27th, 1839, and messengers were soon after sent to different parts of the Territory with friendly dispatches to the chiefs requesting them to assemble at the fort on the

*Exiles of Florida, 1858. Strange to say, Mr. Giddings does not once mention the deceptive character of General Macomb's negotiations.

18th of May. The messengers were instructed to say
that the Government had concluded to allow the Indians
to remain in the country, which news was of course received with delight by all those who had any faith left
in the white man's promises.

About one hundred and fifty Indians, including
chiefs, sub-chiefs and warriors, were present at the appointed time and place, twenty of whom came with
Colonel Harney from far-off Biscayne Bay. No regular
treaty was drawn up at this meeting, nor werë signatures
affixed to a paper of any kind, the promises and con-
cessions on both sides being made verbally.

From a graphic account of the assembly, by a
surgeon of the army who was present, we extract as
follows:

"On that day (May 18th) General Macomb said:
'To your Great Father at Washington his red children
were as dear as his white; he loved them both alike; he
regretted what had taken place. Let the Indians lay
down the scalping-knife, rifle and the tomahawk; let
them go south of Little Peace Creek, and their Great
Father would see that they were left tranquil and undisturbed. He would establish a neutral ground and shield
them from disturbance by the protection of his troops.'

"The Indians said: 'They were alike desirous of
peace; the war had originated from a misunderstanding
with their white brethren; they would gladly lay down
their rifles, but wanted some time to gather their crops
before crossing the line; they would in the mean time
cease all hostilities and send runners to all their people
to let them know the treaty.'

"The General replied that they would be allowed
sixty days in which to gather their corn. The treaty
was explained by the General as follows: 'The Indians

are to remain within a boundary drawn from Charlotte Harbor up Peace Creek to Little Peace Creek, thence in a straight line, from west to east, to the Kissimmee, thence down to Okeechobee Lake, and from thence in a straight line, from north to south, to a small river which empties into the gulf near Cape Sable.* The neutral ground is to be from Tampa Bay to Fort Mellon, thence along the St. Johns to its source, and from thence to the coast.' "†

The council took place in the open air, and over the speaker's stand a large American flag floated in the breeze. We learn from the same correspondent that, at a second meeting, the Indians "were all fed, clothed, tobaccoed, and *whiskied* extensively," and that they sent out runners soon after to promulgate the "peace news" in all directions.

The reader's especial attention is called to the following quotation, as it offers further strong proof in support of the present writer's claim that the Seminoles were peaceably inclined, and that our Government did not attempt their removal from the country on account of any misdeeds on their part. Referring to the latest negotiations, a prominent newspaper says editorially:

"General Macomb had an interview with the enemy, and the people of Florida would again live in security and quiet. All this amount of obligation is entailed upon them by the noble interference of Major General Alexander Macomb. The services of Generals Clinch, Scott, Gaines, Call, Jesup and Taylor, sink into insignificance when compared with this masterly movement. The condition now accorded them would, in the outset, have spared this waste of life and treasure . . . . The Indian interpreter who was here said that 'the Indians

*Shark River.
†St. Augustine *News*, May 23d, 1839.

would sell us, for the next twenty years, skins and venison; that peace would be again, and the whites and
Indians live as they had done.' This is likely to be
realized so far as the allowance for the Indians to remain
in the country is a part of the treaty.''*

It will be seen presently that the above editor's opinion of General Macomb's services as a peacemaker was
exactly reversed. For the time, however, he was so
tickled at the prospects ahead that he fell into rhyme,
in the same issue, as follows:

> "The war is ended, past a doubt;
>   Each breechless urchin's shouting frisky;
> The General's had a battle?—no,
>   But bought a peace with knives and whisky!''

The contemptible trickery of the Government in its
dealings with the Seminoles at this period is once more
illustrated by the fact that this so-called '' peace-treaty ''
was conceived and negotiated with the secret intention
of violating it and holding further negotiations in the
autumn looking toward the entire removal of the Seminoles from the Territory.

But the victim of this systematic deception,—the
simple child of the forest,—delighted with the concession which he had long fought to secure, and too completely under the influence of Government "firewater"
to raise any doubts, was easily hoodwinked and persuaded to believe that the arrangement was intended to
be permanent.

That we are dealing with substantial facts, and
doing no injustice to early administrations or to
army officers, let the following quotations bear witness:

Under date of May 30th, the *News* correspondent,
previously quoted, says: '' The chiefs never *asked* General Macomb whether they would be permitted to perma-

News, St. Augustine, Fla., May 23rd, 1839.

nently remain south of Peace Creek, and he never *told*
them they would."

Another public print declares editorially: "No
definite information is given them that this arrangement
is temporary, and that in a few months a new negotiation
will be opened with them, in order to buy up their consent
to removal."*

And in his report to the Secretary of War, dated
on the 22nd of May, General Macomb is a witness to his
own perfidy, as follows: " . . . .Nor did I think it politic
at this time to say anything about their emigration,
leaving that subject open. . . ."†

This double-dealing was also approved by the Secretary of War, as the reader will soon notice. The only
part of the General's agreement with the Indians which
could possibly be construed as a reference to removal,
was the following:

" 'Should any of them wish to go and visit their
friends in Arkansas, the United States would furnish
them with the necessary means.' To this," says the
army surgeon whom we are again quoting, "the Indians
strongly expressed their dissent. The General then told
them that ' their friends West would be allowed to visit
them in Florida.' "

The Commander-in-Chief now confidently announced
the termination of the war in the following General
Orders, issued from Fort King on the day of the council,
and published in the newspapers:

" The Major-General, commanding in chief, has the
satisfaction of announcing to the army in Florida, to
the authorities of the Territory, and to the citizens

____

*_Herald_, St. Augustine, Fla., June 1st, 1839.

†In a report to the Secretary of War six months later, General Macomb
stated that he told the Indians that " he or some other p rson would in the
autumn meet them on Peace Creek, when the whole nation would be assembled and *further arrangements* entered into with them."

generally, that he has this day terminated the war with the Seminole Indians by an agreement entered into with Chitto Tustenuggee, principal chief of the Seminoles and successor to Arpeika, commonly called Sam Jones, brought to this post by Lieutenant-Colonel Harney, 2d Dragoons, from the southern part of the peninsula. The terms of the agreement are: that hostilities immediately cease between the parties; that the troops of the United States, and the Seminole and Mickasukey chiefs and warriors, now at a distance, be made acquainted with the fact that peace exists, and that all hostilities are henceforth to cease on both sides, the Indians agreeing to retire into a district of country in Florida below Peace Creek."

Then follows a detailed description of the country assigned them, after which the orders continue: "That sixty days be allowed the Indians, north and east of that boundary, to remove their families and effects into said district, where they are to remain until further arrangements are made under the protection of the troops of the United States, who are to see that they are not molested by intruders, citizens or foreigners; and that said Indians do not pass the limits assigned them. All persons are therefore forbidden to enter the district assigned to the Indians without written permission of some commanding officer of a military post."

A Down-East paper refers to this latest announcement of the termination of the war, as follows:

> " And yet 'tis not an endless war,
> As ' facts ' will plainly show,
> Having been ' ended ' forty times
> In twenty months or so."

So deceptive was General Macomb's " treaty " with the Indians, and also his announcement of the end of

the war, that the merely temporary force of the agreement was not yet apparent to the general Florida public.
At a meeting held by the citizens of St. Augustine in
the latter part of May, a strong protest was made against
the ratification of the treaty, on the ground that it
secured peace by allowing the Indians to remain in the
country. The resolutions passed were forwarded to
President Van Buren, and by him referred to his Secretary of War, who replied, in part, as follows:

"I am of the opinion that the arrangement made
by General Macomb will lead to the pacification of the
country and enable me to remove the Indians from the
Territory much sooner than can be done by force."

The Florida people soon discovered that the arrangement on the part of the Government was only temporary,
and to their credit be it said many of them—perhaps *all*
of the bona fide citizens—condemned its duplicity in no
uncertain terms. Thus we see that even in Florida, by
no means all of the leaders of public sentiment allowed
their hearts to be hardened against their red brethren by
self-interest.

After General Macomb had returned to Washington,
the Florida newspapers contained numerous editorials in
derision and arraignment of that official, and his deceptive course. The following passages, from editorials of
different dates, are illustrative:

" But the most discreditable part of the proceeding
is his studied silence with regard to the Seminoles
remaining in the country, and leaving the Indians
with the impression that they are to be its (permanent)
. occupants." *

Again, in the same paper, one week later:

" It is a splendid triumph of the achievements of

* St. Augustine *News*, June 8th, 1839.

military diplomacy, and one upon which the country must look as the most humiliating in character which has yet marked the history of her arms."

> "Oh! what a tangled web we weave,
> When first we practice to deceive!"

CHAPTER XV.

It was not long before the Seminoles, through their
shrewd interpreters, became aware of the deception that
had been practiced upon them: As a natural consequence they were greatly enraged, war was again
declared, and the lives and property of the border
settlers once more became insecure. Every act of depre-
dation and lawlessness that now occurred was, as
usual, charged to the Indians, in many cases quite
undeservedly.

Shortly after the promulgation of the Macomb
"treaty," a well known white man was found murdered.
The Indians were at once charged with the crime, but
they stoutly protested their innocence. Certain Florida
newspapers printed scathing editorials denouncing them
as the cu prits, and calling upon their readers not to
trust them, and to show them no mercy. It finally came

to light, however, that a white man had committed the murder, on account of an old grudge.*

Throughout the Seminole War fake stories of Indian massacres and depredations were frequently disseminated by the newspapers of Florida and adjacent States. Their origin could seldom be traced, but all had the same obj ct, viz: the injury of the Indian in the eyes of the public and his speedy removal from the country. One editor thus apologizes for the appearance of these false reports in his columns:

"It is a matter of regret to us that we so often impose upon our readers (after being ourselves duped) reported Indian inc'dents, that are frequently sheer fabrications, or at least so exaggerated and highly colored that their identity with the facts is barely perceptible. Such is the faculty of invention at the present day, that to gratify a morbid appetite for excitement, Indian fights, horrid massacres, and hair-breadth escapes, are spoken into existence with all the appearance of reality, upon the mere hazard of possibility." †

On the 23d of July, 1839, a band of two hundred and fifty Indians, under the leadership of Chakika, attacked a detachment of nineteen soldiers and seven citizens, commanded by Lieutenant-Colonel Harney, at a point on the Caloosahatchee River, where the party had gone to establish a trading-post in accordance with the Macomb treaty. The men were encamped on the river without defense of any kind, and the attack was made just before daylight. Eleven of the soldiers and five of the citizens were killed; the remaining ten persons, including Colonel Harney, managed to escape.

From the standpoint of the Seminole, mocked as he had been by a pretended treaty of perpetual peace, his

* St. Augustine *News*, August, 1839.
† Ibid, March 12th, 1841.

renewal of hostilities was only honorable warfare, in retaliation for the trick and disappointment. In the opinion of the white man, their attack on Colonel Harney was an unjustifiable outrage, perpetrated in time of peace. Whichever view we take of it, it was a direct fruit of the Government's latest attempt to impose upon the Indians. Yet the Secretary of War said, in part, of this assault, "Our people fell a sacrifice to their confidence in the good faith and promises of the Indians." And the President, in a message to Congress, the following December, takes the same view, as follows: "But, after entering into solemn engagements with the Commanding General, the Indians, without any provocation, recommenced their acts of treachery and murder." Even the Governor of Florida, in a message to the Territorial Legislature, speaks of "a contest remarkable for magnanimity, forbearance and credulity on one side, and ferocity and *bad faith* on the other!"*

These officials entirely ignored the deception that had been practiced upon the Indians by General Macomb, with the approval of the Secretary of War, for the purpose of securing a temporary cessation of hostilities until the deep-laid schemes of the Government could be perfected. Overlooking all this, and more—the repeated treachery of Jesup, the depredations of the lawless whites, and even the well known desire of the Seminoles to occupy a remote section of the country in peace— they raised the common cry against the red men. Thus were the minds of these public officials warped to a sense of impartial justice toward the red men.

> "There's good and bad in Indian,
>   And there's good and bad in white;
> But, somehow, they are always wrong,
>   And we are always right!"

*December 1839.

After the bloody affair on the Caloosahatchee, no battles of importance occurred for more than a year; but in the uneasy state of feeling that existed between the two races, several assaults took place at intervals in various parts of the Territory. The more timid settlers were kept in almost constant alarm, very often, however, by false reports. The author will cite an instance of the latter kind, related to him by an estimable old lady still living, in Volusia County.

During the war, the lady referred to was living at Picolata, on the St. Johns River. She was sitting alone one evening with a baby in her arms, when a man rode up on horseback and warned her to "flee with all haste to a place of safety, for the Indians are coming." She instantly left the house with her child, not even stopping to extinguish a light which was burning on the table. The next morning she returned to the house and found everything as she had left it, including the burning light!

It was proved in several instances that white guer-illas, dressed and painted as Indians, went about the country, robbing and murdering mail and express riders, driving off stock, and committing other lawless deeds.* Such depredations were well known to the officers of our army.

The state of affairs that existed at this time was extremely perplexing to the Government. Although several thousand troops were stationed in Florida, and the number of Indians and Maroons had been reduced by emigration and death to less than a thousand, the War Department was unable to exterminate the remnant, or even to fully protect the settlers, except by agreeing to the simple and just terms of the red men.

* So stated by Captain Sprague and others.

Finally the policy was again changed. General Taylor was relieved from command, at his own request, in the spring of 1840, upon which he retired from the State. His successor was General Armistead, who, by direction of the Secretary of War, sent to the West and secured the services of twelve Seminoles, who had emigrated some time previously with their families. These men were induced to repair to Florida and act as mediators for the emigration of the remainder of the tribe.

But the move proved to be an unwise one, defeating, as it did, the very end which the Government had in view. The so called mediators were not slow in informing their brethren of the failure of the United States authorities to set apart a separate territory in the West for their use, as had been expressly agreed, thus leaving them without a home which they could call their own.

Nothing was therefore accomplished; the delegates returned to their Western home, and the others to their strongholds.

One of the most memorable incidents of the war may be called the Indian Key Massacre. This island lies east of Lower Matacumbe Key, about twenty miles from the southern mainland, and is about seven acres in extent. At the time of the massacre, the population numbered about forty persons. Early one morning in August, 1840, seventeen canoe-loads of Indians, under the leadership of Chakika, landed on Indian Key, and immediately commenced an attack on the village. Six persons were killed, and the others, with one exception, escaped to a neighboring island, or took refuge on a small revenue vessel belonging to the Florida squadron, then lying in the harbor. Nearly every building was burned to the ground.

During their stay on the island, the Indians found a six-pounder, belonging to one of the residents, and exchanged shots with a detachment of marines from the vesssel. After firing two shots from swivel-guns, the whites were compelled to retire. This was partly owing to the loss of the guns overboard at the second fire. The red men held possession of the Key for twelve hours, when they departed with a large quantity of merchandise, taken from a store kept by one of the residents.

Among the lives lost in this massacre (not included in the above number) was that of Dr. Henry Perrine, an educated gentleman, an experienced botanist, and withal a remarkable man. His charred remains were found among the ruins of his own building. Dr. Perrine had represented the United States as consul at Campeachy, Mexico, some years before, and had also rendered valuable service by introducing many rare and desirable plants into our country. After his return, he proposed to establish a botanical garden in the southern part of Flor da, for the cultivation of tropical plants, and Congress granted him a township of land for that purpose. Dr. Perrine's untimely death, however, prevented the commencement of his enterprise.

Before the war about two hundred Indians were in the habit of trading at Indian Key, and the massacre was afterward attributed by some to unfair treatment of the red man by the trader. The old saying that "the Indian never forgets a kindness or a wrong," was clearly illustrated in this case. While the stock of the trader was carried away and his buildings burned, the property of Charles Howe, Esq.. a prominent resident, who had always treated the Indians with fairness, was unharmed.

Early in December 1840, an expedition consisting
of about a hundred troops, commanded by Lieutenant
Colonel Harney, went into the Everglades and attacked
several camps of the Seminoles, located on islands in the
southern part.   Four warriors were killed and six more,
with thirty women and children, were taken prisoners.
Five of the captured warriors were hung a few days
afterward from the tops of tall trees.   Chakika, one of
the most dreaded of the Seminoles, (sometimes referred
to as a Spanish Indian), was among the first killed.   A
member of this expedition recorded in his diary* at the
time, that the slayer of the chief took his scalp, also that
his dead body was run up alongside of the others.   These
ghastly objects, swaying in the wind, were discovered
by Sam Jones some days later and given burial †   Chakika was said to have been the largest Indian in Florida;
as he was six feet tall and weighed over two hundred
pounds.   A large quantity of ready-made clothing,
hardware, ammunition, and provisions were found on
Chakika's island, and identified as part of the property
taken from Indian Key in August.

It was at this particular stage of the war that the
authorities, with a desperate determination to attack
the Seminoles in their secret hiding-places, called to their
aid the Cuban bloodhounds, referred to in Chapter VII.
The Florida Legislature first authorized the purchase of
these brutes.   A messenger was finally sent to Havana
to secure a supply of them, and a pack arrived in Florida
in January 1840.   Thirty-three hounds were obtained,
at a cost of a little over one hundred and fifty dollars
each.

General Jesup had intended to employ the hounds

*Consulted by the present writer.

†No act ever recorded against the Seminole even approaches this one
of Colonel Harney's in barbaric features.

for trailing negroes, for which purpose they were especially trained, but considerable objection being made to this by some, the animals were finally led out by the army (after Jesup had retired from command) for tracking the Seminoles to their remote fastnesses. A very few trials, however, proved their utter worthlessness for the purpose; as might have been expected, the hounds would not follow an Indian's scent. The army was therefore compelled to abandon this wild scheme, amid general ridicule.

In May 1841, General Wm. J. Worth rose to the command of the army, and his policy and zeal proved successful in speedily bringing the long war to a close. Discarding the methods of Jesup and Armistead, he returned to the more enlightened policy of General Taylor, and in fact improved upon it. One of General Worth's first acts was to make friends with the chief Wildcat, the most intelligent, and one of the most influential leaders of the remaining Seminoles, and through him to secure the good will of other chiefs. By his evident good faith and interest in their welfare he won the confidence of many Seminoles. Like General Taylor, he recognized the Maroons, no less than the Indians, as prisoners of war, and sent to the West all who came into his hands. Wildcat's followers, numbering one hundred and eighty persons, including women and children, finally came in and gave themselves up for emigration; and in a short time, through the potent influence of this chief, about three hundred Seminoles and Maroons were assembled at Tampa Bay awaiting transportation to a new home in Arkansas. Most of these were finally sent off, a few, however, remaining to induce others to come in.

In November 1841, Captain R. D. A. Wade, with a

company of sixty men, surprised two camps of the
Indians near Lake Worth, at which time eight Indians
were killed and forty-eight taken prisoners. Twenty
canoes and a large quantity of provisions were destroyed.
(The immense amount of Indian supplies found by our
troops was something remarkable. Two months before,
Major Childs had demolished about forty acres of grow-
ing crops while scouting in the Everglades.)

On the 9th of April 1842, the last battle of the
Seminole War was fought. The conflict took place at
Pilaklakaha, chief Mickenopah's old town, near the
Great Wahoo Swamp. General Worth commanded in
person, with about four hundred troops. The attack
was made against the stronghold of Haleck Tustenuggee,
an inveterate opponent of emigration, and his band of
forty warriors. After a prolonged and cautious fight,
the Indians scattered and escaped, with the loss of two
killed, three wounded and one taken prisoner. One of
our men was killed and four wounded. A few days
afterward, the chief entered General Worth's camp, with
his warriors, in an almost starving condition, when the
entire band were made prisoners.

The scene of this closing conflict was only a short
distance east of the Dade massacre battle-ground. Thus,
by a strange coincidence, the long and stubborn Seminole War ended almost on the very spot where it had
begun.

Shortly before active hostilities were brought to a
termination, General Worth reported to the War Department that, as near as he could estimate, only about three
hundred Seminoles remained in Florida. These, he said,
could not be captured, as they were hiding in various
remote sections of the country. He advised that they

be allowed to remain in the Territory, and that the greater part of the troops be withdrawn.*

The Department did not at first agree to these suggestions, but when the Governor of Florida and many of her leading citizens wrote to the Secretary, making precisely the same request, it was thought best to comply.

Accordingly, after considerable delay and extended search, representatives of the remnant were found and were induced to visit the headquarters of General Worth, August 14th, 1842, at which time a final "talk" was held and peace terms agreed to. The Indians were allowed to remain in the territory on condition that they would cease all hostilities and never renew them, and that they would retire to a certain designated part of the southern extremity of the peninsula.

Considerable doubt was expressed by many at the time as to whether these terms were temporary or permanent; but the government had no intention to depart from its original policy, and the Indians were this time fully informed as to the temporary character of the arrangement.

General Orders (No. 28) were now issued, under date of August 14th, announcing the war at an end, and a large number of troops were withdrawn. General Worth retired for a time from the command, and went to Washington, where he received promotion as a reward for his zealous and successful efforts to terminate the war.

In November 1842, General Worth returned to Florida and re-umed command of the troops, for the purpose of establishing the boundaries of the reservation assigned to the Indians, and directing them to occupy it. Four

---

* Report to Secretary of War, Feb. 17th, 1842.

months later, the troops were still further reduced in numbers, one regiment of infantry being left to guard the frontier and to see that peace was kept by all parties. Captain Sprague, who was afterward left in charge of Indian affairs, with headquarters at Fort Brooke, says of the remaining Indians, and others:

"Idle reports were constantly in circulation of their contemplating or having made hostile movements. There was a large class of hangers-on with the army at all times, who saw with regret the close of the war, for on its continuance depended their livelihood."

General Worth finally retired from Florida in November, 1843, when he testified to the excellent behavior of the Seminole remnant.*

The number of Seminoles and Maroons who were transferred from Florida to the West during the war, between April 1836 and February 1842, was 3,930.† They left the country in fifteen different lots, the smallest number going together being seven and the largest 1,160. With one or two exceptions, each lot was accompanied by a conductor, in most cases an army officer being detailed for the purpose. The passage from New Orleans was made in about one month. Many never lived to reach their new home, for almost every lot was reduced in numbers en route by death, resulting from disease induced by their confinement, change of food, and homesickness. One party which numbered three hundred and seventy when they left Florida, was reduced by fifty before their destination was reached. The largest party who emigrated at one time sustained a loss of ninety-one.‡   To the above total number should

* See Chapter I, Part II.
† The exact number of Maroons cannot be ascertained, as they were generally listed as Seminoles, but it was not far from 400.
‡ Official records, Indian Office.

be added two hundred and sixty-five, comprising a lot who emigrated prior to the war, and two hundred and twenty-five, who departed after hostilities had ceased, in the fore part of 1843; making a grand total of 4,420 persons.

In the removal of the bulk of the Seminoles to the territory west of the Mississippi River, the object of our Government had finally been attained, but at what a loss of life, treasure, and national honor! The last item can never be estimated, but we may briefly sum up the two former. The number of deaths in the army and navy, as a direct result of the war was 1,555. The loss among citizens, Indians and negroes, is unknown, but it surely greatly exceeded the above number.

Up to the close of hostilities, the war had cost our Government no less than $19,480,000 for the employment of *militia* and *volunteers,** and for losses claimed by settlers. When the expenses of the regular army and navy were added, the aggregate amounted to nearly forty million dollars.† Great as this sum is, it is nevertheless far from the total expenditures, to date, as a direct result of the forcible removal of the Seminoles from their lands. Millions of dollars, in addition to the above amount, have been paid in pensions to survivors and their widows.‡ Claims for losses alleged to have been sustained by settlers, are also before Congress at this writing.

No sooner had the war been terminated than the

---

* The number of volunteers called into the field from the different States, between Dec. 20th, 1835, and Dec. 31st, 1840, was 20,026. Of this number Florida furnished 6,854.

† According to one of our standard histories, and also to one of the latest standard cyclopædias, the war cost $10,000,000!

‡ The Pension Bureau informs the author that the exact sum cannot be furnished, for the reason that for some years past all claims resulting from the Seminole War have been grouped with those of the Black Hawk War, Creek War and Cherokee Disturbances.

great object of its prosecution was made manifest; settlers began to crowd into the Territory, and its growth was very rapid from this period, as the following figures demonstrate. In 1840, according to the United States Census and the Territorial enumeration, the population of Florida was 27,943; in 1850, 47,203. Only eighty-eight permits had been granted to settlers under the "armed occupation law" (which gave 160 acres to every settler capable of bearing arms) up to May 1st, 1843, six months before General Worth left the Territory. One month later, however, six hundred and thirty-six permits had been granted from the land offices at St. Augustine and Newnansville, while more than two hundred were on file awaiting their turn.   Among the first applicants at St. Augustine, says the *News* of April 7, 1843, were a party of eighteen gentlemen, "all men of wealth," accompanied by twenty slaves, bound for distant Lake Worth.

Such was the eagerness manifested for the lands of which their Indian owners had been deprived. Referring to this greed, the Hon. Theodore Frelinghuysen, United States Senator, and President of Rutgers College, New Jersey, had said some time before:

"We have added purchase to purchase; the confiding Indian listened to our profession of friendship. We called him brother, and he believed us. Million after million of acres he has yielded to our importunity, until we have acquired more than can be cultivated in centuries, and yet we crave more. We have crowded the tribes upon a few miserable acres on our Southern frontier; it is all that is left to them of their once boundless forests, and still, like the horse-leech, our insatiable cupidity cries, 'Give, give.'"

Speaking of the close of the war, a prominent writer of the day truly says:

" There is not to be found on the page of history, in any country, an instance of a scattered remnant of a tribe, so few in number, defending themselves against the assaults of a disciplined and numerous army, with the same heroism and triumphant results, with those of the Seminoles in resisting the American troops." *

* Henry Trumbull, 1846.

CHAPTER XVI.

In the negotiations for the removal of the Seminoles
from Florida, it was agreed that they should receive a
tract of land in the West for their separate use. This
was demanded by them, and it operated more effectually
toward their final peaceable removal than any other
inducements held forth.

But this pledge, constantly referred to by the officers
and agents of the Government, was violated, and on the
arrival of the Indians, instead of assigning them a
separate territory of their own, the Government sought
to settle them with the Creeks, a plan which was earnestly desired by the latter tribe, for reasons which will
presently be stated.

A large body of these deluded people, however,
flatly refused their consent to the arrangement, and the
Cherokees, seeing the trying situation of their friends,
showed their sympathy by generously offering them a
tract of land upon which they could remain until the
Government should fulfill its obligations, or other means
should be provided for them. Those who took advantage
of this offer, says their agent in 1844, "numbered, it is

believed, about one thousand souls, headed by two
formidable chiefs, Alligator and Wildcat, the latter a
reckless spirit, and, in the opinion of the undersigned, a
man of no ordinary mould."

About one year after the bulk of the tribe arrived
in the West, Wildcat addressed a letter to the editor of
the Arkansas *Intelligencer*, in which he set forth in
pathetic words, the hardships which his people were
compelled to endure, living as they were without lands
of their own. The editor published the letter entire
(March 30, 1844,) with the following prefatory
remarks:

" . . . . No one sympathizes with him (Wildcat)
more than we do for the pitiable condition to which he
and his people are reduced by their invincible conquerors
and false friends."

Under such auspices were the Seminoles introduced
to the new country to which they had been persuaded
to emigrate by the most flattering promises. Upon their
arrival, utter disappointment awaited them, as we have
seen. They not only found themselves without a home
they could call their own, but with no means of subsistence except the promises of the United States Government to supply them with rations for a year. To *any*
race of people such a prospect would have been a sore
trial—to the Seminoles, whose intense love of home
may well be called their master passion, it was simply an
outrage.

Accepting the hospitable offer of the Cherokees, the
party of Seminoles above mentioned, with many
Maroons, continued to live with them until the summer
of 1845. For a long time previous to that date much
dissatisfaction was expressed by the emigrants at the
manner in which they had been deluded by the Govern-

ment.   The Cherokees and Creeks also shared the
discontent, but for very different reasons.   The former
having repeatedly assured the Seminoles that the
Government would abide by its promises, fully sympathized, as we have related, in their bitter dis ppoint-
ment.   The Creeks, on the other hand, were exasperated
because the entire body of Seminoles were not compelled
to settle with them, in accordance with the original
treaty of Payne's Landing, and to submit to Creek
laws.

The main object of the Creeks in thus insisting that
the other tribe should be compelled to settle with them,
was that they had long desired to secure possession or
control of the Maroons and other negroes owned by the
Seminoles.*

The agents among the Indians vainly endeavored to
quell the constantly threatened outbreak, and finally the
Government sought to accomplish its original plan by
further negotiation.   With this object, on the 25th of
January, 1845, a treaty was entered into between the
United States, the Creeks, and the Seminoles, by which
the latter—as a last resort of a discouraged people—all
agreed, under certain conditions, to settle with the
former tribe.

One of the conditions was that they should be
allowed to settle in a body, or otherwise, in any part of
the Creek territory.   They were also to make their own
town regulations and to manage their own pecuniary
affairs, but were to be under the control of the Creek
Council, in which they were to be represented.

The Seminoles removed to the Creek territory, but
it was not long before the previous unfriendly relations
were renewed.   The former refused to give up their

* Senate Doc. 271, 1st Ses., 24th Cong.

nationality or to submit to Creek despotism. As a tribute
to the character of the Seminoles at this period in their
history, we quote the following words of their agent,
written in the year 1849:

"Among the poor, neglected and despised Seminoles, there is as much honor and integrity as among
any other tribe, though the others may be far in advance
of them in the habits of civilized life . . . . They have
great affection for their children, pay much deference to
their wives . . . . I admit, however, with all their good
qualities, they have some bad ones; but if left to themselves, and not instigated by bad white men, they would
have fewer of these."

Again, writing in the same year, this agent says:
"The great cause of dissatisfaction to the Seminoles
is that they have no country that they can call their
own. This has a tendency to depress their feelings and
is a constant source of uneasiness; and, until removed,
it need not be expected that they will become content.
They utterly repudiate the idea of becoming a constitu-
ent part of the Creek nation."

In illustration of the truth of the agent's words
last quoted, within a year from that time a strange and
romantic episode in Seminole history was revealed,
greatly to the surprise of the Indian agents and higher
officials. In 1850, a band of several hundred members
of the tribe, including a smaller number of Maroons
headed by Abraham, with a few other Indians, all under
the leadership of the famous chief Cooacoochee, or
Wildcat, resolved to emigrate to Mexico, in order to escape entirely from the jurisdiction of the United States
Government, and to enjoy the rights and liberties denied
them here. As some account of the fortunes of this heroic and freedom-loving band cannot fail to interest the

reader, we here insert the following particulars, extracted from a Mexican publication :*

"Shortly after the establishment of military colonies in Mexico, in 1850, certain Seminoles, Kickapoos, and Muskogees presented themselves in the district of Rio Grande, in the State of Coahuila, soliciting lands on which to settle, since they truly affirmed that the Americans had appropriated their own lands."

The Indians composing this band received from the Mexican Government, on the 26th of July, 1851, lands on the San Rodrigo and San Antonio rivers, which flow into the Rio Grande in the northern part of the country. As a recompense for this gift, they had signed a treaty on the 16th of the previous October, in which they promised their services against the incursions of the warlike savages of that region.

Actual trial of this location, however, proved to the Seminoles and the others that they could not remain there in peace and safety, owing to the dangers encountered on the United States border. They were therefore persuaded by the Mexican authorities to remove to the mountains of Santa Rosa, thirty leagues to the southwest. They asked for and received agricultural implements from the Government, while in this location, and were industrious, and also desirous of instruction for their families.

The Seminoles undoubtedly found their new location a good one, for in July 1852, Wildcat and another Indian presented themselves in the City of Mexico and solicited additional reservations. One was granted them in the State of Durango, and another in a locality known as Nacimiento, "*in recompense for the good service they had already begun to render against the savages.*"

<hr>

* "A translation, ordered by the Mexican Government, of the Reports presented by the Commissioners whom it sent to the Frontier, to Investigate the Depredations Committed on both sides of the Rio Grande." 1875.

After one of the campaigns waged by the Seminoles against the Comanches, they received the formal thanks of the Mexican officials. Several expeditions were made by them in the years 1856-7 against warlike tribes, with good results, but in the latter year many Seminoles died of small-pox. Among the victims was the chief Wildcat.

It was intimated in a publication of the United States Government that the Seminoles, among other Indians, were probably responsible for certain depredations on the Texas side of the Rio Grande. These depredations were thoroughly investigated by the Mexican Government, who found that white men, disguised as Indians, were the culprits. Speaking of the raids into Texas between the years 1848 and 1856, the Commission reported that *"no voice was ever raised to attribute them to the Seminoles*, who then resided (since 1850) in Mexico with a few Kickapoos, although they traversed all this region, according to their custom, in quest of game."

In 1857, an American named Bernard, residing at Corpus Christi, made a contract with the government of Nuevo and Coahuila for bringing the Florida Seminoles to Mexico.* Agents of the American Government, however, prevented the accomplishment of this purpose.

Early in the year 1858, two Seminole chiefs visited their kinsmen in the United States. On their return to Mexico they endeavored to persuade their people to emigrate to their former homes in Indian Territory. "This action," says the Commission, " was regretted by the Mexican authorities, on account of the good services they (the Seminoles) were rendering against the savages."

* Reference is had to that portion of the tribe who finally emigrated to Indian Territory, under the leadership of Billy Bowlegs, in 1858.

The Mexican Government induced the Seminoles to temporarily postpone their departure, but most of them finally removed to the United States, mainly through the efforts of two Americans who resided at Santa Rosa, until, on the 26th of February, 1859, only sixty Seminoles remained at this place. On August 25th, 1861, the remainder of the band went to Texas, on their way to Indian Territory. The removal took place, says the official report of the Mexican Government, "*to the general regret of the inhabitants of Santa Rosa.*"

"To understand fully the causes of the return of the Seminoles to the United States, it will be expedient to remember that. . .on the 12th of March, 1859, a representative of the United States' agent for the Seminoles came to Villa Guerrero and informed Colonel Blanco that his object was to bring about the removal of the two tribes in question (Seminoles and Muskogees) to their reservations (in the United States). This person was given a passport and an escort to Monterey, and was accompanied by the Seminole 'Tiger,' this mission leading to the removal which took place two years later, as above mentioned.

"The measures taken at this time for the return of the Seminoles to the United States did not spring from any misdeeds committed by them. No accusation of the kind was brought against them. The motive may have been to unite the dispersed members of the tribe, or the fear that the Mexican portion would attract their American brethren, and thus leave the agents without the gains of their official posts. At all events, the action was not a just one, for it damaged legitimate Mexican interests, on which considerable sums had been spent."

The Mexican Government characterized the Seminoles as peaceable, law-abiding and industrious, but stated that they did "not undertake the defense of the Kickapoos, for it is true that some individuals may have committed robberies."

This official report forms a document of several hundred pages, but the above extracts and condensation contain the substance of the portion relating to Wildcat's band. From the unbiased statements of the Mexican Government, it is plainly evident that the people whom the Floridians and the United States military powers drove from their former and rightful homes, departed from Mexico with the sincere regrets of her citizens.

> " Then just believe me, once for all,
> To those that treat him fair,
> The Indian mostly always was,
> And is, and will be, 'square.' "

Let us now return to the Seminoles who had remained in Indian Territory, and who had recently been joined by the band returning from Mexico. The climate of the Western country was far different from that of semi-tropical Florida, and the change proved very trying especially to the older Indians. From this cause, and also by reason of the trouble and discouragement they had encountered since leaving their former home, their numbers had decreased from the first. About 4,500 had settled in the West up to the year 1844. In 1851, the agent of the Seminoles reported that "their numbers continue to decrease, as shown by the pay-rolls." Three years later their population was estimated at 2,500. After making due allowance for those who emigrated to Mexico, the above figures indicated an alarming decadence.

In the year 1852, a special agent of the Government persuaded a delegation of the Seminoles to visit Florida for the purpose of influencing their brethren there to join the nation in the West.* On the return of the

*Due notice of their efforts will be given in its proper place, in Part II

former to their homes, the nation addressed President Pierce the following letter:

"SEMINOLE AGENCY, July 1, 1853.

"*To the President of the United States:*

"We, the chiefs, head men and warriors of the Seminole nation, having this day met in council, and after due deliberation had, would most respectfully represent to our Great Father, the President of the United States, as we have heretofore done through our former agent, that we are situated in the Far West; . . . At the same time we are desirous that you should make us a separate nation from that of the Creek nation. . . .

"We left our land and the graves of our fathers at the request of our Great Father, the President of the United States, and removed to the Far West. At the time of our removal we were assured by our Great Father through his officers that things should be right. When we undertook this matter we were young and knew nothing of the country. But we moved here; we find the land here. But at the same time we are laboring under many disadvantages, which have heretofore been represented.

"When we left our homes, or at least a part of us, and went to Florida to induce our friends to remove West, we failed in a great measure to do anything. But if a father has two sons and one of them is bad it is no good reason why the other should be cut off from everything. We therefore think it but right that we should have a country of our own. We will at all times render our influence to get our brothers to remove and settle with us. . . . All in Council.

"Very respectfully,

"JAMES AND JOHN JUMPER,

"Principal Chief."

In manly defense of these deceived people, their agent, J. W. Washbourne, thus writes to the Indian Commissioner, in April 1855:

"There have been many slurs cast upon the Seminoles, as being savage, cruel, improvident, and lawless, ...It is true that they fought for their country, and savagely, too, as was their custom. It is also true that they have made scarcely any improvement since their removal West.

"And what have been their inducements? Their nationality swept away, their country under the control of another tribe, their annuity miserably small, no provision for schools or any other species of improvement; no incentive of any character whatever—how could they improve? Why, then, should they be blamed for not doing what is morally impossible under the circumstances? Why have slurs been hurled upon them for indulgence, to a less extent, in the vices peculiar to Indians, and more especially to those for whom the Government has done the most?

"To rebut this slur I will simply mention two facts: Among the Seminoles there has not been perpetrated a murder, one upon another, for the past seven years. Neither, though styled troublesome and dangerous neighbors in the treaty (Creek) of 1845, have they in any manner participated in the (vaporing and harmless) forays which other tribes make, and boast about, against the prairie tribes. These facts speak volumes for them when their discontented state is remembered."

Four months later, the agent wrote: "It seems palpably prominent to my mind that the Seminoles, no matter how provocative their wars in Florida were, have been treated with neglect and injustice." During the same month it was suggested by another agent that, in view of the unfriendly relations that existed between the Seminoles and Creeks, the former be given the separate country which they had been promised.

The Government was at last compelled to acknowledge that its pet scheme of amalgamating two distinct nations, which had been living apart as such for a long period of time, had proved an utter failure.* Being thoroughly assured of this at last, and also for the accomplishment of another object, † the Government now proposed a new treaty. After considerable trouble and delay, the consent of the Creeks was finally secured to convey to the Seminoles a portion of their territory. The negotiation was known as the "Treaty of Washington," and was consummated in that city, August 7th, 1856.

By this treaty, a tract of 2,169,080 acres, lying within the Creek lines, was sold to the Seminoles, who at once settled on it. With their nationality preserved and a home of their own, these people found at last their wishes gratified. Their life with the Creeks had been felt as a degredation by a proud-spirited people, nor had any appreciable progress been made by them during that gloomy period. Now, however, the bright star of Hope was once more in the ascendant. Referring to this happy state of affairs, Mr. Washbourne, their agent, wrote in January, 1857:

"The Seminoles continue to manifest increasing desire for schools and improvement. Even Alligator, an aged chief, and former foe not only of the white man but of all his ways, so much desires schools now, that he sends his (the band's) young children to the mission school . . . . and is himself learning the alphabet!"

In a later letter, the agent says, in reference to the

*The first proposition to settle the Seminoles among the Creeks, was made by General Jackson in 1821, to the Secretary of War. See pp. 32-3.

†See Chapter III, Part II.

treaty, "by it the unhappy differences between the Seminoles and Creeks are ended." He also stated that the population of the former tribe at that time numbered 1,907 souls, all told; that they live by tilling the soil; that they hunt for pastime only, or for furs and peltries; and again states that "they desire very much the establishment of schools."

We have briefly referred to the extreme change of climate from the balmy airs of Florida to the wintry blasts of the Western highlands. In illustration of this and other physical trials which this suffering nation was called on to endure, we may quote again from agent Washbourne. In one of his letters, written in the year last mentioned, to the Indian Office, he says:

" One day, especially, before a fire (built in a hut) the ink froze in my pen ere I could write across the page! In such weather, with very few tents, not much provisions, the Seminoles were encamped ten or twelve days, exposed, thinly clad, to the searching severity of the northwestern blasts icy from the tops of the Rocky Mountains.

"One widow, with a young child, whose horse had been stolen from her by the prairie thieves (Osages), walked over seventy miles to the agency in moccasins, through ice and snow, with scarce a mouthful to eat. But in all this inclemency the Seminoles did not murmur . . . . One party of Seminoles while examining their new country lost all of their horses, twenty-two head in all, which had been stolen by the Osages. They were consequently unable to make such examinations, and were compelled to return on foot in the severest part of winter." *

* The material for the last few pages was mainly extracted from unpublished official records in the Indian Office.

If these ill-fated exiles could have anticipated the severe exposures and other trials which they would be called on to endure, they would perhaps have fought still more desperately to retain possession of their sunny Florida homes.

CHAPTER XVII.

THE SEMINOLE IN THE CIVIL WAR—BORNE UPON PAY-ROLLS OF
BOTH ARMIES—DRIVEN FROM THEIR HOMES BY CONFED-
ERATES—ENLIST IN THE UNION ARMY—ENGAGED IN
TWENTY-EIGHT BATTLES—SERVE THROUGHOUT THE WAR
—BITTER FEELING BETWEEN THE TWO FACTIONS—UNION
SEMINOLES ARE REIMBURSED FOR LOSSES—ODD APPEAR-
ANCE IN REGULATION UNIFORMS.

Among the Five Civilized Tribes in Indian Territory, namely: the Cherokees, Creeks, Seminoles, Choc-
taws, and Chickasaws, twenty-four organizations of red
men were raised during the Civil War. These comprised three regiments of Home Guards on the Federal
side, numbering 5,238 persons, and twenty-one smaller
organizations with the Confederates.

The Seminoles, as well as the other tribes, were
represented on both sides of the conflict; in the Union
army, principally in the Second and Third Regiments of
Home Guards, with Creeks, Cherokees and other Indians;
on the Confederate side in the First Seminole Cavalry
Battalion (afterward First Seminole Regiment), under
Colonel John Jumper, a prominent member of the
nation.

At the beginning of the war, the Confederate
authorities showed their characteristic promptness by
sending agents among the different tribes in Indian
Territory for the purpose of winning them over to the
Southern cause. When these agents approached the
Creek and Cherokee nations, especially, on the subject

of severing their relations with the United States, the majority expressed themselves as having made up their minds to remain neutral. Comparatively few among the Five Tribes held slaves, and it was natural that the majority should take little interest in the question that had long been agitating the country; moreover, they regarded the trouble as belonging to the whites to settle among themselves.

An ex-chief of the Creeks named McIntosh had been won over to the Confederacy by an appointment as Colonel. This flattering offer had been made in view of the following he was supposed to be able to influence. Failing to enlist all of the Indians on their side, the Confederates finally determined to attack the neutrals as well as those sympathizing with the Union cause.

The Confederate force consisted of white soldiers as well as of Indians from all of the Five Tribes, under the command of Colonel Cooper and others. The opposing party was led by an old and highly respected Creek chief, rejoicing in the formidable name of Ho-po-eith-le-yo-ho-la, a most determined opponent of the Confederate plans. When this chief had discovered that the Confederates intended to make war on him and his followers, he determined to resist to the utmost. He was certain of the support of more than half of his own tribe and a large number of Seminoles and Cherokees. He was confident that he could hold his ground against Indian foes, but doubted his ability to do so if they were aided by white soldiers. It was his intention, if he should be overpowered, to make his way to Kansas, where he believed he would find friends and allies. His second in command was Halleck Tustenuggee, prominent in the latter part of the Seminole War.

Several engagements took place between these

opposing forces, in two of which, in 1861, the Union Indians were victorious. In one engagement the old chief defeated his enemy by setting fire to the prairie grass which separated him from the others, causing them to flee for their lives. The principal battle, however, was fought on the 26th of December, 1861. It was a severe conflict, lasting from noon to four in the afternoon, in which the Federal forces contested every in·h of ground, but the superior numbers against them finally compelled a retreat.

The Creek chief, carrying out his premeditated plan, now set out for Kansas, with all the warriors, women and children of his nation who had stood by him, and a large number of Seminoles and Cherokees. followed later by another band of Creeks, who preferred to share the hardships of a winter march rather than submit to Confederate dictation. They carried with them only such property as could be gathered hastily. This retreat was made in mid-winter through snow and ice. So severe was the cold that. according to the commander of the Confederate troops, a soldier in the pursuing force was frozen to death.

The total number on the Federal s'de who fled to Kansas was estimated at from six to ten thousand. Within two months after their arrival two hundred and forty of the Creeks alone died from exposure to the severe weather.*

In the summer of 1862, the Indians who had thus been driven from their homes, enlisted in the service of the United States, with an especial desire to be led against those who had expelled them. They were accordingly regularly mustered in and borne upon the

*Annual Report Commissioner of Indian Affairs, 1863.

payrolls of the army, forming the three regiments before mentioned, and serving throughout the war.*

These regiments were engaged in twenty-eight regular battles of greater or less magnitude, and in numerous skirmishes. A large number of those who had at first joined the Confederates afterward went over to the Union side. The author has been unable to ascertain the losses sustained by the Seminole regiments separately (from their allies) during the war, but the total number of deaths, from all causes, among the Union organizations of Indian troops, was 1,018.†

A division of the Seminole nation took place almost from the beginning of the war, and bitter feeling was engendered between the Federal and Confederate sympathizers, the former constituting about two-thirds of the nation.‡ This feeling continued to exist until a short time after the war, when all differences were finally settled between them and the two factions were again united.

The Seminoles who had been compelled to leave their homes and take refuge in Kansas, afterward settled at Neosho Falls, in that State. While there in 1863 their number was estimated at 672. Most of these were women and children, the able-bodied men having joined the forces on the Union side. These were known as "Southern" Seminoles, while those who had remained neutral at home, in Indian Territory, or who had sided with the Confederates, were styled "Northern" Seminoles. ‖

*The foregoing account has been gleaned principally from Civil War on the Border, by Wiley Britton, (1890), who served on the Union Side in Kansas throughout the war.

†Official records, War Department.

‡Annual Report Commissioner of Indian Affairs, 1863.

‖The reader will please note that these terms do not refer to the different sides taken in the war.

Shortly after the conclusion of the war the "Southern" Seminoles returned to Indian Territory. They did not settle on their vacated lands, says their agent in 1866, but were temporarily located with the Cherokees, on account of the proximity of supplies. Both sides suffered severely by the war, not only in considerable loss of life, as before referred to, but in devastated lands and the loss of buildings and stock, of which latter they possessed large herds of both cattle and horses.

By a treaty, ratified March 21st, 1866, the Seminoles who had remained steadfast to the Union received the sum of $50,000 to reimburse them for their losses. The money thus appropriated was derived from the sale of lands by the nation to the United States, under the same treaty. Thus it came about that the part of the nation that sympathized with the South, were compelled to contribute directly from their own pockets for the benefit of the others.

The following account of the odd appearance of the Union Indian soldiers in the regulation uniform, is extracted from Wiley Britton's book, from which we have previously quoted :

"It was quite amusing to the white soldiers to see the Indians dressed in the Federal uniforms and equipped for service. Everything seemed out of proportion. Nearly every warrior got a suit that, to critical tastes, lacked a good deal in fitting him. It was in a marked degree either too large or too small. In some cases the sleeves of a coat or jacket were too short, coming down about two-thirds the distance from the elbows to the wrists. In other cases the sleeves were too long, coming down over the hands.

"At the time these Indian troops were organized, the Government was furnishing its soldiers a high-crowned stiff wool hat for the service. When, therefore, fully equipped as a warrior, one might have seen an Indian soldier dressed as described, wearing a high-crowned, stiff wool hat, with long black hair falling over his shoulders, and riding an Indian pony so small that his feet appeared to almost touch the ground, with a long squirrel rifle thrown across the pommel of his saddle. When starting out on the march every morning any one with this command might have seen the warrior in full paint, and he might have also heard the war-whoop commence at the head of the column and run back to the rear, repeated several times.''

CHAPTER XVIII.

Treaty of 1866—Government's serious blunder—General Grant's Indian policy—Present condition in the West—Government of the tribe—Governor John F. Brown—Seminoles free from intruders—Efforts of the Dawes' commission—Seminoles and the United States sign a new agreement—Seminoles first to embrace citizenship.

After the close of the Civil War, another treaty was concluded with the Seminoles, as referred to in the preceding chapter. The nation thereby ceded to the United States the entire tract of 2,169,080 acres, which they had purchased from the Creeks ten years before. For this the Seminoles now received the sum of $325,362, being at the rate of fifteen cents per acre. The Government next secured by treaty with the Creeks, June 14th, 1866, the west half of their territory for thirty cents per acre, and sold 200,000 acres of this to the Seminoles for fifty cents per acre.*

It may interest the reader to know how the balance of the money received by the Seminoles was expended. The amount of $30,000 was used to establish them on their new land; $20,000 for purchase of stock, tools, seeds, etc,; $15,000 for a mill; $50,000 invested in a school fund; $20,000 as a national fund; $40,362 for subsistence; and $50,000 for losses of loyal Seminoles during the war, as previously explained. The nation granted by this treaty 640 acres of their land to each society that would erect mission or school buildings.

* The land was patented, and the sale is recorded at the General Land Office.

By this treaty all slavery among the Indians was abolished, and henceforth the negro enjoyed equal rights with his former master. This equality was more easily accomplished in the case of the Seminoles, who had always treated their slaves with much consideration, as we have recorded in previous chapters. Delegates from the Seminole and Creek nations remained in Washington from January 1866, to late in the summer, attending to the negotiation of these treaties and sales.

All went well for several years. But the "Great Father"* at Washington, while constantly expressing the warmest feelings for the welfare of his "dear children," nevertheless seemed to be the cause of nearly all of their troubles. He was responsible for another cloud that commenced to gather in 1871. About this time it was discovered by the Seminoles and Creeks that the former, instead of being located, as they were told by the Government, on lands of their own, were actually over the boundary on Creek land! By some it was believed that this was only another effort to unite the two tribes.

The agent for the Seminoles reported in 1872 that they were troubled and discouraged, and that they looked to the government to right the wrong. He says, also, that the Seminoles had improved the disputed lands "with more assiduity and care than their neighbors." Referring to this latest blunder (to call it by no harsher name,) the Commissioner of Indian Affairs had this to say :

"A cause of discontent and just complaint on the part of this people is found in the fact that the Government, in providing them a new home after the cession of their reservation under the treaty of 1866, misled

* We use this term in an impersonal sense.

them as to their boundary lines, so that many"
(afterward discovered nearly all) " have settled beyond
the line upon territory still belonging to the Creeks,
and have there established themselves in comfortable
homes and upon lands which they have much
improved."*

A commission was appointed in 1873 to settle all
differences, but the Creeks refused to sell the Seminoles
the land, and again proposed that they merge their
nationality with them. To this proposition the latter
nation strongly objected, in fact positively refused to
consider it. Two years later another special commission
was appointed, but the desired object was not attained.
Nothing was accomplished until 1881 when, by treaty
of February 14th of that year, the Creeks finally sold to
the Seminoles 175,000 acres, on which the latter had
been living since 1866.

One of the brightest chapters in General Grant's
administration as President of the United States, is
found in the new policy which he inaugurated in our
national treatment of the Indian tribes. Up to the
year 1869 nearly three hundred and seventy treaties
between the United States and Indian tribes had been
entered on our national records. Under this old system
of treaties, perpetually made and perpetually broken, both
the Indians and the Government were systematically
robbed, and disturbances and collisions were frequent.
Under the new policy a reorganization in all the departments of the service took place. Among the many reforms
in the system, was an act passed by Congress making
it unlawful for the Government to enter into treaties with
the Indians as nations. This in itself was a long step
in the desired direction.

* Annual Report 1872.

The Seminoles are still located at the present time on lands purchased of the Creeks in 1866 and 1881, forming a tract of 375,000 acres. The total population of the nation is now about 3,000 souls. This includes several hundred negroes, most of them descendants of the famous Maroons, who are recognized as Seminoles by the tribe, and who enjoy all rights of the others except intermarriage with the Indians, although there are some admixtures.

Generally speaking, the Seminoles are considered the least civilized of the Five Tribes, but it must not be forgotten that they were the last to be conquered, the final emigration from Florida not taking place until 1858. Let it be remembered, also, that they have had more to discourage them and fewer advantages placed within their reach than the other tribes, until within the last fifteen years.

Indians are phlegmatic in temperament and slow to change. They must have abundant time to alter their fixed habits. Constituted as they are it is unreasonable to expect otherwise; the wonder is that they have made such progress as they have. Regarding this radical and too commonly overlooked element in their nature, let one of their race speak:

"Consider the primitive but fair English in the fields of their ancient isle; consider the Germanic tribes on their vast prairies and in their primeval forests; consider that it has taken them twenty centuries to reach the wonders of this magic age; and then ask whether or not it is reasonable to expect Indians to attain even a measure of it in a few short years."[*]

Nevertheless, the Seminoles have made wonderful strides toward civilization, as the reader may judge for

[*]The Indian of To-day, by a native Arapahoe, *Colorado Magazine*, May 1893.

himself. Their government consists of one principal chief or Governor, a second chief, a superintendent of schools—elected by the people, a treasurer, and a council of fourteen "band chiefs," (with two sub-chiefs to each band), which acts as legislature and judiciary. All hold offices for a term of four years. They have neither printed laws nor records, but the chief holds a set of written laws, regarding crimes, penalties, etc.

The agent or superintendent for the Five Tribes reported in 1889 that the Seminoles were "the most peaceful and law-observing of the five nations, and it is seldom that there is any clash in their affairs."* He attributed this favorable condition principally to the almost entire absence of "boomers" or intruders. Three years later they were free from this class, as they are at the present time.

"The Seminoles recognize the value of an education," says their agent in 1891, "and by liberal appropriations judiciously expended have placed its attainments within the reach of every one of their young men and women."

There are now six public and two large mission schools in the nation; twelve church organizations, divided among the Baptist, Presbyterian, and Methodist denominations, with several church edifices. Their postoffice towns are four in number, the principal one being Wewoka. Two of the public school buildings cost $60,000 each, and would prove creditable to any city in the land.

The lands occupied by the Seminoles, and purchased by them as before stated, are held by the nation in common. No assessments are made on either real or personal property, and no taxes of any kind are collected.

* Annual Report Commissioner of Indian Affairs, 1889.

The inhabitants are generally engaged in farming and stock raising. Most of them live in small cabins built of logs. All wear citizens clothing. Many are fairly educated, some of whom are fully competent to fill positions of responsibility and trust.

The author is indebted to John F. Brown, the present principal chief or Governor of the nation, for most of the foregoing information relating to the present condition of the Seminoles. This was conveyed in several very interesting conversations. Mr. Brown is an educated gentleman, in fact one of the best examples of a self-made man. He was born in the Cherokee nation, October 23d, 1843, during the temporary stay of the Seminoles with the former, and is related to the famous Wildcat. He has served his nation in various capacities: as band-chief, Superintendent of Schools, frequently as a delegate to Washington, and is now serving his third consecutive term as principal chief.

In the spring of 1894, a conference was held with the Seminoles, in common with all of the Five Civilized Tribes, by the Dawes Commission, which was appointed by Congress in 1893, to enter into negotiations with these tribes for an allotment of their lands in severalty and a substitution of territorial for tribal government. After the meeting, the Seminoles met and passed resolutions condemning a change, and declining to take any action whatever with a view of negotiating with the Commission.* It should be stated that they were not alone in objecting to any interference with their affairs; the feeling was shared by the other tribes.

The argument advanced by the Dawes Commission that the tribes are unable to govern themselves and to control the crime which is so rampant, will not apply to

*Senate Mis. Doc. 24, 3rd Ses., 53rd Cong.

JOHN F. BROWN.
Chief of the Western Seminoles.

the Seminoles ; for the class who commit eighty percent
of the murders,* and other crimes in nearly like proportion, are unknown by their presence in this nation, as
before stated.

The Commission continued their efforts, however,
with the result that the Seminole nation finally concluded
it would be to their advantage to do as the former proposed, in part at least. Accordingly, an agreement was
signed on the 16th of December 1897, by the Dawes,
and Seminole, Commissions, and ratified by the general
council of the Seminole nation on the 29th of the same
month.† The instrument provides, among other things,
that the lands owned by the nation in common shall be
divided equally among the members of the tribe, who
shall have the sole right of occupancy during the existence of the tribal government. When the latter ceases to
exist, the occupant is to receive a guarantee deed to the
land which was allotted to him. This will also include
a tract of forty acres, which is to be made inalienable
and nontaxable as a homestead in perpetuity. A division
of the tribe's moneys will be made among the members
after the extinguishment of tribal government. $500,000
of the funds belonging to the nation, now held by the
United States, are set apart for a permanent school fund.
A prominent stipulation on the part of the United States,
is that the latter agrees to " maintain strict laws in the
Seminole country against the introduction, sale, barter,
or giving away of intoxicants of any kind or quality."

The plan of making citizens of the Indians seems to
be a good one, and it is creditable to the Seminoles that

* The Five Civilized Tribes. U. S. Census Bulletin, 1894.

† Sen. Doc. 78, 2d Ses., 55th Cong. (A delegation of the Western Seminoles, headed by Governor Brown, remained in Washington during the winter
and spring of 1897-98, awaiting the dilatory action of Congress in ratifying
the agreement.

they were the first (and only one of the Five Tribes at this writing) to take advantage of the new proposition. It remains to be seen how well, and for how long a time, our Christian Government will live up to its pledges.

END OF PART I

PART II.

THE REMNANT IN FLORIDA.

PART II.

THE REMNANT IN FLORIDA—LAST HOSTILITIES—FINAL EMI-
GRATION—THE FLOWER OF THE NATION—
APPENDIX.

CHAPTER I.

GENERAL WORTH'S TRIBUTE—MURDER OF THREE WHITES—
EXCITEMENT AND ALARM OF THE SETTLERS—CAPTAIN
JOHN C. CASEY, THE SEMINOLES' FRIEND—GENERAL
GIBBON'S TESTIMONY REGARDING INDIAN AGENTS—TRIB-
UTES TO CAPTAIN CASEY—THE BOWLEGS' PEACE TOKEN
—CAPTAIN CASEY MEETS THE INDIANS—NATION DISA-
VOWS THE MURDERS AND DELIVERS THE CRIMINALS—
GENERAL TWIGGS' HIGH TRIBUTE—SUICIDE OF PRISONERS.

The first part of our story has followed the fortunes of the Seminoles to their Western home, and has glanced at their present condition there. Leaving them for the future historian, we now return to the sunny land whence they emigrated a half century ago, while we attempt to narrate the adventures of the little band whom neither military force could compel, nor bogus "treaties" persuade, to leave their birthplace and the graves of their fathers.

A few days after General Worth's final departure from Florida, he wrote the Secretary of War, under date of November 17th, 1843, as follows:

"Since the pacification of August 14th, 1842, these people have observed perfect good faith, and strictly fulfilled their engagements; not an instance of rudeness against the whites has yet occurred."

191

This desirable state of affairs continued for seven years after the General's words were written. But in the month of July 1849, the white settlers throughout Florida were thrown into a feverish state of excitement and alarm by the reported murder of three white men, one on Indian River, and two on Pea (Peace) River, on the Gulf.

The long period of peace was now suddenly terminated; plantations were again deserted for blockhouses and other places of safety to the northward, until, as was reported soon after, only one white man dared to remain on the east coast south of New Smyrna. It was believed by some that general hostilities had again commenced, and that another war was inevitable.

General D. E. Twiggs, with several companies of regulars, was sent to investigate the murders, and, if necessary, to quell further outbreaks. The Governor of Florida, now a State of the Union, also ordered out volunteers. The former official reported in August, that owing to conflicting rumors he could not secure reliable intelligence regarding the outrages supposed to have been committed by the Seminole nation. But the desired information, with full particulars, was soon after voluntarily furnished by the Indians themselves.

Our work would be far from complete without some notice of Captain John C. Casey, the zealous and efficient agent of the Seminoles at this time, and with one exception, perhaps, the most trusted white friend these red men ever had. We may best introduce him to the reader by quoting from his own account of his second arrival in Florida some years after the war.*

"I came here in 1848, as an invalid, and found that all confidence in the Government was lost, and no

*He had served throughout the war.

chief would trust himself in the power of the commanding officer of the regular troops! Partly, I fear, from
errors of some commanders, and partly from the bad
influence of the traders. At great risk and exposure of
life and health, during three years, I restored their confidence, so that every chief but Sam Jones would come
when I called, and he met me in the woods. They
trusted commanding officers; they gave up six men for
execution—killed one—and enacted every severe law I
could recommend (to prepare them for emigration).
The frontier was quiet—any cracker cow-driver would
go across the line without fear, when I told them it was
safe, and they drove cattle through to Fort Myers without fear or danger.''*

The late General John Gibbon, U. S. Army, whose
long and honorable experience with the Indian had
commenced with Captain Casey in 1849, among the Seminoles, and afterward continued in the Yellowstone and
other campaigns in the West, makes the following perti-
nent statements regarding Indians and their agents:

" There are no human beings on earth possessed of
a quicker faculty for (in Western phraseology) ' sizing
up' a man placed in authority over them, than Indians.
Innately honest themselves, they will detect in a very
few days whether or not their agent is honest and disposed to fairness in conducting their affairs. He speedily finds out by observation, not only the honesty or
dishonesty of an agent, but as to whether he is just,
fair and zealous in his conduct of affairs.

"When once his confidence is gained, he is as truth-
ful and faithful as a little child. On the contrary, if
the agent is not one calculated to inspire this kind of
confidence, he can never gain it, and will always be

<hr>

*From a private letter to a friend in 1854; sent to the author by Major
Wm. S. Beebe, nephew of Captain Casey.

looked upon with suspicion and fear; and when despairing of getting their rights in any other way, the Indians conclude to go to war, the first one on whom they wreak their vengeance will, in all probability, be the agent himself."*

In the same article, General Gibbon thus explains the manner in which Captain Casey gained the confidence of the Seminoles:

"He early made it a matter of principle *never* to deceive them, never to promise a thing he was not able to fulfil, or never to allow them to first discover his inability to carry out a promise when circumstances took out of his hands the power to do so, but to warn them beforehand of his inability to do what he had promised. In this way he won their unbounded confidence in his honesty and integrity."

Captain Casey was appointed a special Commissioner or Agent for the Florida Indians in October 1850, and continued to act in that capacity, with the exception of a few months, until his death, which took place at Fort Brooke, Florida, December 25th, 1856, at the age of forty-nine years.† Many testified to the noble character and work of one whose chief desire had been to faithfully and conscientiously discharge his duties as agent and friend.

In a letter addressed to the Secretary of War, Jan. 17th, 1858, Jefferson Davis, then a United States Senator, testifies to the "zeal, intelligence, and, *to the hour of his death*, devotion of the late Captain Casey . . . . The circumstances of Captain Casey's death are no doubt

*Transfer of the Indian Bureau to the War Department, *American Catholic Quarterly Review*, April 1894.

† Captain Casey's body was temporarily buried at Fort Brooke By a strange coincidence, the same steamer that conveyed the last emigrating party of Seminoles away from their o d home, also bore the remains of their former agent and friend, for reinterment at Philadelphia, Pa.

known to you, and his efforts, as his mortal career was being closed, to guard the public service from injury by his death, presented to my mind an example which cannot be too highly appreciated or too much enforced on the attention of others." *

An army officer writing from Fort Brooke, gives the following high tribute paid to Captain Casey by Billy Bowlegs—a eulogy condensed into nine words:

"Billy Bowlegs repeatedly said to the army officers, 'Casey was a good man—never tell Indian lie;' a sentiment—coming from such a man, the recognized head of a people bitterly deceived and betrayed—that is worthy of being inscribed on the Captain's tombstone." †

Perhaps the highest testimony of all—that which speaks volumes—is recorded in the Captain's private diary for the year 1850.‡ From several entries we learn that General Twiggs had on the 18th of April informed Captain Casey of his intention to "grab" Billy Bowlegs, employing the same treacherous means that had enabled Jesup to secure Osceola and other chiefs and warriors. When General Twiggs first asked the Captain's assistance in the seizure, the latter officer at once declined to have any part in it. From an entry two days later it is evident that Bowlegs received a hint of possible treachery. On the 21st, the subject was again introduced, and the agent makes this entry: "I advised Twiggs not to 'grab,' on principle and policy, but he *says* he has reported to the Secretary of War that he shall do so." 30th—"Twiggs says he is more and more determined to 'grab' Billy; implore him not to do so." The General was evidently dissuaded from his purpose,

* War Department records.

† Boston *Herald*, May, 1858.

‡ Consulted by the author.

for three days later this significant reference to the matter appears: " He will *not* 'grab.' "

Resuming the thread of our story, we find that Captain Casey, stationed at Fort Brooke, had visited various points along the coast, at different times, and sailed up and down the Caloosahatchee River for a week or two, but not an Indian was seen. Finally he left a number of " peace signs " at different places, and returned to the fort.

Not long afterward, his guide Felipe, found at the south end of Sarasota Bay an Indian peace-token, which was supposed to have been left in reply to the peace-signs. The token was a snow-white flag, about six inches square, ingeniously made by attaching heron's feathers to a stick. At the top of the little staff was fastened a small string of white beads and a twist of tobacco.* The flag was placed on a tall pole and left in a conspicuous place. It was meant and understood that the sender desired to communicate with the agent and smoke the pipe of peace. Felipe left signs that it would be answered at the full of the moon. At the appointed time Captain Casey repaired to the place in a small sloop and was hailed by three Indians on the shore. The meeting is thus described by the Captain, in a letter written to his mother on the following day (Sept. 4th, 1849) :

" All who prate of Indian treachery, and all who desire another Seminole War, predicted a failure, and most people assured me that my scalp would be taken if I gave the Indians a chance. Well, now for the facts. Yesterday evening three Indians on the shore hailed my little vessel . . . . with my servant we rowed within twenty yards of the beach, when I stopped, and my boy

---

* Major Beebe has the identical flag in his possession.

carried me ashore on his back (to keep dry). I bore the Indian white flag (which I was certain had been sent me by the head chief) in my hand, and as I approached, the chief Indian waved one in his hand.

"Leaving my boy on the beach with orders to make for the boat if anything went wrong, I walked up to the three Indians who awaited me. They received me with more than mere cordiality, and when I extended my hand, the principal one said, 'more great friends do thus,' and he took hold of both my arms above the elbow, while I did the same with his, and we shook each other heartily. Each of the other two then shook me in the same way . . . ."

As it was late in the day, a meeting was appointed for the next morning. The Indians were promptly on hand, and a long talk ensued. They said their chief had placed the flag on the bay, and that he had sent them now to see if it had been removed. They had been instructed to inform Captain Casey that the murder on Indian River in July was committed by five young Indians who lived on the Kissimmee River; that one of these was an outlaw who desired to cause a war and thus save himself from the Indian law. The criminals had remained on the eastern side of the State for two or three days, and had then crossed over to Pea River in less than forty-eight hours and committed two murders there. Bowlegs had received information of the outrages through Sam Jones, and had immediately sent a party under the leadership of Assunwah, second chief of the remnant, to arrest the murderers. Assunwah reached Pea River on the day after the crimes had been committed, but the criminals had left. They were overtaken by another chief, Chittahajo.

The messengers had been instructed to say that the

tribe were unanimously opposed to hostilities, and that they utterly disavowed the murders and regretted their occurrence. Bowlegs desired a meeting to be appointed at which he would be present and would be able to settle the trouble to the entire satisfaction of the whites.

Captain Casey sent word to Bowlegs that he must settle the affair with General Twiggs in person, and appointed a time and place for the meeting. He also stated that "the General pledged his word for their safety under the white flag, and that in no event would he 'grab' them; and I pledged my own word to the same effect."

Billy Bowlegs (Holatamico), sometimes called "King" or "General" Bowlegs, was the last chief of prominence to leave Florida, as the reader will learn in another chapter. At the time of his emigration he was about fifty years of age. He had a fine countenance, expressive of intellect and great firmness. He could speak English quite fluently. He became the recognized chief of the remnant in 1842, at which time the Indians renounced the authority of the aged chief Sam Jones, and the influence of the Prophet.

Bowlegs was promptly on hand at the time appointed for the meeting with General Twiggs, when he offered to surrender the five murderers, who were, he said, watched by Chittahajo at their homes on the Kissimmee. Another meeting was appointed for the delivery of the criminals, October 19th.

After the interview just recorded, General Twiggs, who evidently had some sympathy for the Seminoles, wrote the Secretary of War:

"In 1842 General Worth made a convention with these people. For seven years its terms were kept by

BILLY BOWLEGS.
(From a Daguerrotype Taken in Washington in 1852.

every individual in the nation. The nation has not yet violated one stipulation. In seven years, unexampled in our history, not a murder was committed on an Indian frontier of some three hundred miles. In July, 1849, three murders were committed, the deed disclaimed by the nation, and the offenders offered to our justice. Will this justice now press hardly on a nation so acting?''

General Twiggs went to the place of meeting two days before the appointed time, where he found Bowlegs already on hand. The latter informed the General that he had three of the murderers with him at his camp near by, ready for delivery; that one of the others had been killed, and the fifth had escaped.

The next day the chief visited General Twiggs, accompanied by twenty young warriors, and delivered the three criminals, together with the severed hand of another, as proof that the fourth was dead. Bowlegs stated that he had made strict laws in his nation to prevent the recurrence of such deeds, and that he had brought his young warriors with him to witness the delivery of the murderers, as a warning lesson.*

General Twiggs assured Bowlegs that the tribe had made all the reparation in their power, and the President also afterward sent his approval of their action. The General wrote the Secretary of War that ''the prisoners had been surrendered unconditionally, and with the be·lief that they would be immediately executed.''

Before the detection of the murderers, and while it was believed that a general uprising of the Indians had again commenced, the Secretary of War had written General Twiggs: ''In every aspect of the condition of the Indian, so long as he remains in Florida, his speedy removal to the West appears desirable and necessary.

*Letter of General Twiggs to the Secretary of War.

The administration being thus impressed has concluded that their removal, voluntary or forcible, is to be effected."

In order to bring about this object peaceably, the Secretary proposed, in the above letter, to offer each person, without regard to age, sex or color, a hundred dollars as an inducement.   A few days later, he authorized General Twiggs to offer the tribe the sum of $215,000.*   The latter replied on the 6th of October. After referring to the love the Seminoles bore for their native soil, and to the long period of peace, he says :

"To approach them now with an offer of a million of money and all the prairies of the West, and war the alternative, there would not be a moment's hesitation in deciding on war.   Proclaim war, and within a week ten thousand men would not secure the planter and his family from Cape Sable to Georgia.† . . . If I am expected to submit to the Indians the alternative of instant emigration or war, let me be so informed . . . At the same time, so surely do I foresee the choice they will make, that for the safety of the inhabitants I must have an adequate force in position before the alternative is presented."

But war was not proclaimed, and the settlers returned to their plantations in perfect security.

At the meeting with Bowlegs in October, the subject of emigration had been broached.   The Indians showed great surprise, and their only answer "was an appeal to their last act as evidence of their claims on our consideration."   They were perfectly satisfied with the territory which had been assigned them in Southern Florida, and in which they had been living since the

*Annual Report, 1849.

†At this period there were less than 400 Indians in the country.

war. Another meeting was finally appointed with them to discuss the subject.

Soon after the talk on the 19th of October, a delegation of Western Seminoles arrived for the purpose of inducing their brethren in Florida to emigrate. Their efforts met with only partial success, for only two or three small parties could be prevailed upon to remove.

The Government continued its efforts, however, but with discouraging results, for in April 1850, Bowlegs came into Fort Brooke and told Captain Casey that "he could not go West, nor could he induce his people to go. He desired peace and could not make war, but he could not leave his country. If we did not molest them they would never make any trouble, or he would promptly bring in and surrender any offenders." On receiving this positive statement, Captain Casey reported four days later, "I regret to say that I now see no hope of inducing these people to go West in a body by any pecuniary temptation."*

In August 1850, a white boy was believed to have been killed by the Indians. The tribe disclaimed any knowledge of the affair, but signified their willingness to hunt up the criminal. Three Indians were finally proved to have committed the crime, and these the tribe willingly brought in and surrendered to Captain Casey at Fort Myers, who turned them over to the civil authorities. Three days later the prisoners were found dead in jail, having hung themselves.†

The famous Kit Carson, who probably knew the Indian better than any other person except George Catlin, claimed that in times of continued peace the red men never killed a white man without he deserved it. If the

---

*Unpublished letters of Captain Casey in the Indian Office.

†So stated by Captain Casey, in a private letter dated July 23d, 1854.

truth were known, it is probable that the crimes recorded in this chapter had been provoked by acts of
injustice or indignity. The crime is traced to the
Indians, and on this evidence the invariable verdict of the
neighborhood is, that it was wanton and unprovoked.
The lips of the only one who could disclose the whole
truth are sealed in death.

CHAPTER II.

In his annual report for 1850, the Secretary of War
states that peace had prevailed since the conference
with General Twiggs in the previous year, and that the
willing surrender of the three Indians, who had committed the murder in August, was good evidence of
their desire to live at peace with the white people. A
portion of the troops had been withdrawn, a few companies only being left to guard against a possible outbreak. No efforts will be spared, says the Secretary, to
induce the Indians to emigrate, which will be effected
"sooner by peaceable means than by employment of
force."

Captain Casey reported about this time that "no
outrages have been committed, *nor are any likely to be
so long as we leave them alone.*"

The movements of the United States Government,
however, were too slow for the Florida Legislature. In
1851, the Governor signed an act "to provide for the
removal of the Indians now remaining in Florida," a
removal which was aimed to be "speedy and final."
The act provided for raising a regiment of mounted volunteers to aid the forces of the United States. If the

latter Government refused to proclaim war, the Governor of the State was empowered to "undertake the removal for the sum of two million dollars," provided the United States would furnish transportation to the West.

A copy of this act was enclosed in a letter from the Governor to the Secretary of War. The latter official's reply was no doubt unsatisfactory. It stated that if the removal of the Seminoles by force would cost two million dollars, (and the writer "presumed that the Legislature was well informed on this subject,") it would be better to effect the desired end by peaceful measures ; that such proceedings (war) would rather retard than expedite the accomplishment of the object they have in view.

An entirely new scheme was inaugurated by the United States Government in the spring of 1851, at which time it was decided to " test the efficacy of individual enterprise stimulated by the hope of gain contingent on success." An arrangement, or more properly speaking a contract, was now made with Luther Blake, of Alabama, by which he was appointed a special agent to proceed to Florida and endeavor to effect, by judicious efforts, the removal of the Indians.* In his letter of instructions to this agent, the Commissioner of Indian Affairs says :

" Experience has shown the inutility and wasteful expenditure of attempts to remove them by force. . . . There is but one other humane course which, after the most mature consideration, the Department can devise or think of that seems to hold any promise of success. It is to engage some reliable and proper person willing

*Mr. Blake had been concerned years before in the removal of the Creeks.

to encounter the toil and peril incident to the service, who will go among them and by personal association secure their confidence, gain an influence over the leading and more prominent individuals, and thus gradually incline them to consider the subject of removal more favorably and to acquiesce in the wishes of the Government."

Mr. Blake was allowed expenses not to exceed $10,000, and a per diem compensation of five dollars; as an additional reward and incentive, he was to receive $800 for each warrior, and $450 for each woman and child removed, to be paid over to him on their delivery in the West among their brethren. All expenses of transportation were to be paid by the Government, which also agreed to subsist the Indians for one year after their arrival in their new home.*

The presumption was that the agent would pay the Indians whom he succeeded in inducing to emigrate a portion of the sums he was to receive, but the loose "arrangement" did not compel him to pay them a cent.

The first step of the agent in his new enterprise, was a visit to the Western Seminoles, a delegation of whom he finally induced to accompany him to Florida to assist him in the work. While at New Orleans, in January 1852, he wrote the Commissioner of Indian Affairs as follows: "If there are none opposed to the emigration but the Indians themselves, I will have them off, and hope to become of enviable reputation in doing so."

Arriving at Tampa, in March, Mr. Blake repaired to Fort Myers, on the Caloosahatchee River, where he established his headquarters. Soon after, he reported to the Indian Office that "things do not look half as

---

* Annual Report Commissioner of Indian Affairs, 1851.

bad as they have been represented," referring to the complaints of the whites against the Indians.

In the same month of the agent's landing in Florida, an event took place that caused the Indians to retire to their swamps and remain there in hiding for several months. In that month, Captain Jernigan, in command of a small party of Florida volunteers, reported to Mr. Blake that he had a few days before "charged upon some Indians near his (Jernigan's) residence and taken one old woman and a small child," since which " the old woman had hung herself, that the child was in good keeping, and that he would turn it over to me as soon as I could find its mother. . . . Whether Jernigan and his men charging on the Indians *without cause** will injure emigration or not, I cannot say. I have asked him not to do it again."†

The gallant Jernigan also reported this affair—no doubt with great elation over his prowess—to the Governor of Florida, and by the latter it was mentioned in a letter to the Commissioner at Washington as "strange and deplorable." The Governor added that he had taken steps to prevent a recurrence of such affairs, as he wished to co-operate with the Government and Mr Blake in their new project.

The poor old woman's violent act was indeed "deplorable," but there was nothing "strange" in the fact that she preferred death by hanging to imprisonment and banishment from the home of her youth.

By the aid of presents and flattering promises, Mr. Blake prevailed upon Billy Bowlegs and three other chiefs to accompany him and the Western delegation to

---

* How many such unprovoked assaults the Seminoles passively endured can only be imagined; the wonder is that they did not commit a hundred times the amount of bloodshed that was charged to them.

† Letter of Mr. Blake to the Indian Office.

Washington, in September 1852. The object of this visit, as stated by Blake, was to give the Florida Indians some idea of our strength, numbers and wealth, as a nation, and thus impress upon them the folly of further resistance.

While in Washington, Bowlegs and his companions signed a paper in which they acknowledged their obligation to remove to the West, and agreed, on their return to Florida, "to use all their influence for the purpose of getting their people to emigrate at the earliest possible day." The agent took the Indians to Baltimore, Philadelphia, and New York, before they returned home.

It may be stated that this visit to Washington was unauthorized by the Government. The first intimation the Indian Office had of it was contained in a telegram from Mr. Blake, dated at Savannah, which stated that he was on the way with Bowlegs and his party. After their arrival, the Government accorded full approval to the plan and visit. On the final settlement, however, the agent had considerable difficulty in securing payment for this item of his bill.

Mr. Blake had not been in Florida long before he wrote the Commissioner of Indian affairs that Captain Casey had been interfering with his plans; and that he had gone so far as to advise the Indians against emigration. He added that Casey had been overheard to characterize the Secretary of War as a "pettifogging lawyer from Mississippi." By such representations, Blake finally induced the Secretary to recall the trusted agent of the Seminoles.

In a letter to the Adjutant General of the Army, Captain Casey speaks of the trouble between himself and Blake "as similar to that between the sheriff and the criminal that he pursues, or between the rogue and the witness to his rascality, and the Government should have been thankful to me for calling its attention to a gross fraud being committed in open day, instead of rebuking me for doing my duty."

The removal of this conscientious and zealous officer was a colossal mistake, which the Department afterward discovered and rectified, as will be seen.

A gentleman who was in Florida at this period informed the author that most of the women and children, who formed two-thirds of the party taken to the West by Blake, were seized on the coast by him or his agents. The affidavit of an army officer bears out this assertion. He says that Blake was overheard in a public place to offer to pay for each Indian captured and delivered to him.

This dishonorable action, in time of peace, against a people who had said that "they would not be first to renew hostilities," was sufficient in itself to defeat the the best-laid plans. And it had this effect, for the result of the united labors of Blake and the Western delegation,* was that only thirty-six Indians were embarked for Indian Territory, and seven of these died on the passage.

Mr. Blake was finally compelled to report to the Commissioner of Indian Affairs that his efforts were unsuccessful, and his agency was terminated in the spring of 1853. Thus another ambitious project, started with quite a flourish of trumpets on his part, came to naught.

As an indication of the extent to which the people's money was squandered in carrying on the Seminole War and in transferring the Indians to the West, we may note the expenses incurred by the Government in connection

* See letter of the delegates to the President, Chapter 18.

with Blake's operations in Florida. In a statement filed by
that agent in the Indian Office, he claims the following
amounts: For expenses of visit to Washington. $1,490;
incident to preliminary arrangements in Florida, $10,000;
total expenses of Western delegation, $12,075.39; for
removal of thirty-six Indians, deliv·red in the West,
$20,230; and for his own compensation, at $5 per day,
$4,230.   Total, $48.025.39, not including the cost of
transporting the emigrants, which was at least $5,000
more.*

Seminole emigration, even by "peaceful" measures,
was a costly undertaking.

After the retirement of Blake and his scheme for
gaining "notoriety," the valuable services of Captain
Casey were again continued in Florida, as formerly, to
the great satisfaction of the Seminoles.   One of his first
acts was to send for another delegation to come from the
West, in the summer of 1853.   The late General. (then
Lieutenant) John Gibbon was detailed for this duty, and
succeeded in inducing a number of the chiefs to return
with him to Florida. Their efforts could scarcely be called
successful, however, as only a small party was induced
to emigrate in the following spring.

* See Senate Doc. 71, 1st Ses.. 33d Cong., for a full report of the Blake
affair Also records at Indian Office, from which this chapter is largely
prepared.

CHAPTER III.

About two years now elapsed without the occurrence of special events to vary the monotony of the situation. The Indians kept to themselves in their swampy fast-nesses, far removed from the whites. The State author-ities, however, continued to demand the entire removal of the tribe, and the United States Government kept troops actively engaged in exploring the southern part of the State, and opening up roads. A small steamboat was also provided for navigating Lake Okeechobee and adjacent waters, the pioneer in the business, to which were added nine small metallic boats for the same pur-pose.

The object of all these operations was to secure more complete knowledge of the country occupied by the Indians, in order that future projected plans might thus be facilitated. All intercourse with the red men was forbidden and their trade cut off. Nevertheless, they did not appear to be entirely isolated, for in De-cember 1857, Col. Gustavus Loomis, Commander of the

Department of Florida, reported that he "had strong reason to believe that an illicit trade was kept up between the inhabitants of the Bahama Islands and the Seminoles of Florida."

The Seminoles had faithfully adhered to the promises made to General Worth in 1842, and later to General Twiggs. They desired above all things to be left to themselves, believing that the country they occupied was theirs by right. They had learned what to expect if they should remove beyond the Mississippi River. Therefore, when even the contracted territory to which they had been driven was at last invaded by armed forces and exploring parties, consisting of United States Regulars and State Volunteers, they did just what any other brave and liberty-loving people would do under similar circumstances—they vigorously opposed all who would drive them from their last foothold on Florida soil. They exemplified the truth,

"Who would be free, *themselves* must strike the blow."

After thirteen years of peace, general hostilities were renewed in December, 1855, by the presence of, and aggravating acts of, a squad of men under the command of Lieutenant Hartsuff, a United States Civil Engineer, who was exploring and surveying east of Fort Keais, on the borders of the Everglades and the Big Cypress, in the very heart of the Seminole country. Regarding the immediate cause of this last warfare with the Seminoles, we submit the valued testimony of Andrew P. Canova, a native Floridian, who served in the campaign. He says:

"Hartsuff and his corps of assistants were encamped near a small body of water known as Bonnet Pond. Billy Bowlegs had a garden in the Cypress about two miles away.   Among other products of this garden were some magnificent banana plants, which were the delight of the chief's heart.   He had reared them with parental care until they were fully fifteen feet high . . . . But some of Hartsuff's men (like a good many of us) could not keep our hands off the beauties.   When Bowlegs visited his garden one morning, he was surprised and shocked to find the banana plants, once so tall and graceful, with leaves torn to shreds and some of the stalks broken short off at the ground by some ruthless hand.   Bowlegs knew at once where the blame lay. Going to Hartsuff's camp, he accused the men of the outrage.   They admitted it with the utmost coolness, but signified no intention of making good the loss, nor of giving any cause for their actions, other than that they wanted to see ' how Old Billy would cut up.'   When Billy saw that remonstrance and complaint were useless, he went back and summoned his braves together . . . . Early next morning Lieutenant Hartsuff and his men were fired upon, and some of them were wounded.'' *

Notwithstanding that the skirmish with Lieutenant Hartsuff had been clearly provoked by his men, and that the Indians had retired to their homes immediately after taking revenge, war was at once proclaimed, and Jefferson Davis, then Secretary of War, authorized Col. John Munroe, in charge of military affairs in Florida, to call on the Governor of the State for an auxiliary volunteer force of five companies, '' to serve six months unless sooner discharged.''

In January and March, 1856, two encounters took place between the soldiers and Indians, one on the Caloosahatchee River, east of Fort Denaud, and the other near Chokoliskee Key, at which two were killed

* Life and Adventures in South Florida, Canova, 1885.

and several wounded on both sides. The last battle of the year occurred on April 7th. While our troops were scouting near Bowleg's town, on the eastern border of the Big Cypress, they were attacked by a considerable force of Indians, who killed two of our men and wounded six others. The Indians then retired into a dense hammock.

Nothing had been accomplished thus far toward removal or extermination, and as the warm months were at hand, the red men were again enabled to enjoy a temporary peace.

A delegation of Western Seminoles visited Washington in the spring of 1856 to confer with the Indian Commissioner regarding a separate country for themselves. While in Washington they also addressed that official a letter in regard to their Florida brethren, from which we quote as follows:

" To remove our brethren in Florida by force will cost many hundreds of thousands, perhaps millions, of dollars, and many valuable lives." If the just claims of those in the West could be settled, and the nation given a separate country, " then we believe we can with little trouble persuade our brethren to emigrate peacefully and become peaceful and industrious citizens of the Seminole country West. But while those already West are discontented, and destitution stares them in the face, it is idle to think of inducing those now in arms to emigrate." *

Jefferson Davis saw the truth of this, and in the same year addressed a letter to the Secretary of the Interior on the subject. He said:

" I think that the condition of a separate organization (from the Creeks), securing distinct chiefs and

* On file in the Indian Office.

village laws, will be insisted on by the Seminoles of
Florida, and that, until they are secure of this, all other
inducements to emigrate voluntarily will prove in-
effectual." *

Later in the year, the Commissioner of Indian Affairs
thus referred to the same pressing subject, in his annual
report:

" The Seminoles of the West have been denatioual-
ized, and in a manner degraded, by being placed among
the Creeks and made subject to their laws. They felt
the humiliation of their position, which not only discouraged them from all efforts at improvement, but engendered a recklessness of disposition and conduct . . .
In this situation, which was well known to their brethren
in Florida, the latter were totally averse to removing
and joining them."

The Commissioner also says that one of the leading
objects of the treaty of Aug. 7th, 1856, was to enable
the Department to overcome this chief obstacle to the
removal of those in Florida. Under this treaty the
Seminoles in the West were now living on their own
lands, with their nationality preserved, as the reader
learned in a former chapter, and it was confidently
expected and believed that the others would at last agree
to join them.

If our Government had, in the first place, faithfully
fulfilled with those in the West its promises, and our
troops had never been allowed to enter the region occupied by the Indians in Southern Florida, the renewal of
hostilities would not have occurred. A delegation from
the West would then have experienced comparatively
little difficulty in inducing their brethren to return home
with them, after the treaty of 1856.

* Ibid.

During the summer of 1856, Captain John T. Sprague, then stationed in New Mexico, tendered his services to assist in the removal of the Seminoles. In a letter to the Secretary of the Interior, he says:

"I entertain an interest in the welfare of these Indians from the fact of my having been brought personally and intimately in contact with them—in the time of danger have been protected by their chiefs, and when in their camps treated with the utmost kindness. My impression is that with proper assistance I could aid in effecting the removal of the Seminoles by emigration . . . . "*

Unfortunately, perhaps, the offer of Captain Sprague was not accepted; the Seminoles continued to be hunted like wild beasts. On the 5th of March 1857, a detachment of troops were scouting in the Big Cypress, when a band of Indians were encountered and a brisk engagement took place, which resulted in a loss on our side of one killed and three wounded. Our troops withdrew and despatched an express to a point twenty miles distant for reinforcements. When these arrived, the attack was renewed, with a further loss of three killed and five wounded, before the Indians retired.

This was the last battle fought with this invincible foe, but they were kept on the defensive until the following January. Scouting parties continued to explore the southern part of the State,† destroying the camps and fields of the Indians, and capturing women and children. As these encounters were the last hostile efforts of the whites to conquer the Seminoles, brief notice of each will be given.

Capt. Jacob E. Mickler was ascending a small creek

* Ibid.

† Twenty companies of Florida Volunteers, ten of which were mounted, were in service until the spring of 1858. Three companies of the latter were not mustered out until the month of August.

that emptied into Lake Okeechobee, with a little steamer in July 1857, when he saw a broad Indian trail leading away from the water. Leaving his craft, he followed the trail with a party of armed men, and discovered an Indian camp on an island near the lake. The party approached this from two sides, and finally captured nine women and six children, without seeing a warrior. One of the women gave them a great deal of trouble, requiring four men to carry her through the saw-grass which surrounded the island, to the boat. The prisoners were conveyed to Fort Myers, where they were confined.*

In August, Capt. Wm. H. Kendrick, who commanded an independent company of Florida Volunteers, reported that while he was reconnoitering near Lake Istokpoga he came across a party of ''about six Indians.'' These were pursued and one killed, and a child between three and four years old captured!

While scouting south of Fort Doane on November 21st, Capt. W. H. Cone and command of one hundred and fifteen men, surprised a party of Indians, killing one warrior and capturing eighteen women and children and large quantities of provisions.

No loss had been sustained on the part of the soldiers, except from sickness and exhaustion, for eight months, but in the next encounter, which took place in the Big Cypress Swamp, north of Chokoliskee Key, on November 28th, Capt. J. Parkhill was killed and five others wounded. A large Indian settlement had been discovered by the troops, situated in a palm hammock. ''There were about thirty lodges, and about forty acres of land cleared and in cultivation. Large quantities of

* The Government had offered a reward or premium of from one hundred to five hundred dollars each for living Indians delivered at Fort Brooke or Fort Myers.

pumpkins, potatoes, peas, corn and rice, were found—the corn, peas, and rice hid away carefully in houses built off in the swamp, the trail leading to which was carefully concealed. The pumpkins were housed in fields, also the ground was literally covered with them, of all ages and sizes; even the trees were full, the vines having run over them. The ground was full of potatoes. Everything was destroyed that could be." The next day, about thirty houses and many fields were found. The Indians, as before, had taken alarm and fled before the arrival of the soldiers. They were overtaken, however, when the above punishment was inflicted on those who had destroyed their homes.

About one month later, Capt. W. Stephens, Florida Mounted Volunteers, who was scouting in the Big Cypress with about ninety men, discovered a large town "with fifty neatly built palmetto houses," and many cultivated fields. The Indians had fled, but they were finally overtaken, when one of our men was killed. Shortly afterward, the Indians were decoyed to an ambuscade and five of their number killed and two mortally wounded. This encounter terminated the hostilities with the Seminoles.

A number of lives had been sacrificed and enormous sums expended by the Government in its warfare during the years 1855 to 1858, but to no great purpose. As the Secretary of the Interior stated in summing up the situation at the beginning of the year 1858, the Seminoles had completely "baffled the energetic efforts of our army to effect their subjugation and removal."

It was this hopeless condition of things that finally induced the Government to desist from its vain efforts, and to adopt a plan that might have been tried with success months before. Col. Elias Rector, Superintendent of the Western Seminoles, had indeed been ordered some time previous to proceed to Florida with a delegation for the purpose of effecting, if possible, by peaceful means what could not be accomplished otherwise.

The party which finally set out with this end in view, consisted of Colonel Rector, two assistants, and forty-six Indians,—forty Seminoles, under John Jumper, chief of the nation, and six Creeks. They arrived at Tampa Bay on the 19th of January, 1858, and a few days later departed for Fort Myers, where they made their headquarters. All hostilities on the part of our forces had ceased, and scouting parties had been called in.

Soon after the arrival of the mediators at the fort, a niece of Billy Bowlegs, named Polly, who had accompanied the party from the West, was despatched to the Everglades with a message to her uncle, informing him of the presence of his Western brethren, and their desire for a "talk." The chief soon after appointed a meeting, which took place at a certain point on the edge of the Everglades.

The result of this and a later conference, held on March 27th, was that Bowlegs accepted the terms offered him on behalf of the Government, and entered into an agreement to be at Myers with his people on the 4th of May, for transportation to Indian Territory. The pecuniary inducements offered the chief and his followers, were as follows: Bowlegs was to receive the sum of $6,500; his four sub-chiefs, $1,000 each; warriors, $500 each; and each woman and child $100.

Before the appointed day the greater part of the emigrants had left their swampy homes and encamped near Fort Myers, in readiness to depart. It was understood that all were to be at the fort at nine o'clock on the morning of May 4th, for embarkation on the United States steamer Grey Cloud. An army officer who was present, writing from Fort Brooke, May 13th, thus describes the scene on the appointed day:

"At the hour set, the troops of the post, under Captain Brannan, were judiciously posted, without the knowledge of the Indians, at points selected, to meet and prevent any treachery that might be contemplated. As the appointed hour drew nigh the excitement on the part of the whites was intense. But soon all fears were at an end. The head of the procession was seen to emerge from the hammock and slowly wend its way to the wharf.

"Silently they took leave of their much loved Florida. Warriors who had defended their country to the last shed tears, and with aching hearts passed on to the deck of the steamer. The scene was one to be remembered, and calculated to excite the sympathies of the most inveterate Indian hater."*

The emigrating party numbered one hundred and sixty-four persons, all told. Of these, one hundred and twenty-three had come in voluntarily with Bowlegs, and forty-one had been captured. About one hundred persons, as near as could be ascertained, were left behind, having secreted themselves in remote parts of the Everglades. This remnant consisted of the followers of Sam Jones, and a few Indians distinguished as the "Tallahassees."† The expense incurred by Colonel Rector in effecting this emigration, was $70,352.

Two days after the departure of the Grey Cloud from Fort Myers, the party arrived at Egmont Key, at the entrance of Tampa Bay, where they were met by the

* Boston *Herald.*
† The Cow Creek branch of the present Seminoles.

United States steamer Ranger. On board of the latter was a party of invited guests, including army officers, citizens, and several ladies, to witness the Seminoles' final adieu to their old home.

At 11 a. m. on the following day, both steamers got under way, the Grey Cloud for New Orleans, and the Ranger to return to Tampa. The two kept company until the outer entrance of the bay was reached, when parting salutes were exchanged, and, as the steamers rapidly separated, a mighty and thrilling war-whoop burst from the combined throats of the Indians, and echoed and re-echoed over the waters.

> "My native Florida! adieu! adieu!
> I'm looking at the last pine on thy shore!
> Soon other climes must come upon my view,
> And thy sweet landscape meet my eyes no more!"*

On the 8th of May, Colonel Loomis issued a proclamation, in which he stated that the remaining Seminoles "being very widely scattered upon the islands, in the swamps of the country, and no trace of them having been discovered for some months back—no depredations having been committed, and no hostile gun fired by them for some months, except in defense of their fastnesses, and hiding places, I now consider it unnecessary and unwise, in view of the rapid settlement of the country, to prosecute scouting the swamps and Everglades to hunt up the few remaining families. . . ."

The Seminole War was therefore (once more and for the last time) declared ended, and the troops were soon afterward discharged. The army officer at Fort Brooke, previously quoted, thus comments upon the final termination of hostilities with the Seminoles, and the emigration of the main body from Florida :

"The agonizing struggle, extending through a

*Twasinta's Seminoles; or Rape of Florida, Albery Whitman, 1885.

period of twenty-three years, has at last terminated in the ruin and destruction of the gallant Seminole. . . . It is idle to seek to correct the errors and injustice of a past generation. To us is left the enjoyment of the Christian duties of mercy and sympathy : and in this, their last hour of tribulation and sorrow, we can, whilst remembering their sufferings and extenuating their cruelties, shed a tear over their departed hopes, and point our children to the example of what a united people can do in defense of their homes.

"Patience, heroism, and fidelity, such as the world may admire, have been exhibited to us, inculcating a lesson not to be lost upon us now that our national councils are torn by intestine strife. The Seminoles as a nation (in Florida) have been destroyed, but what an array of glory, faith, horrors, and anguish does this retrospect present! Conquered, they yet leave us proud and defiant."

"Though drearily, and wearily, and mournfully, and slow,
Towards a far off spot our exiled footsteps go ;
Across that track of dismal length our hearts shall never
    roam,
But still evade oppression's strength, and lingering dwell
    at home."

CHAPTER IV.

How shall we fitly characterize the little band of perhaps a hundred—the remnant of a remnant—whose intense love of home, and determination to remain in their native land, showed them worthy descendants of the immortal Osceola. We might call them the flower of the nation, with patriotism and fidelity the most deep-rooted of all!

This remnant lived in peace and plenty in remote recesses of the Everglades and Big Cypress, into which few white men ever penetrated. Game and fish were abundant there, the soil was productive, and the climate salubrious. Happy in their seclusion,

"The world forgetting, by the world forgot,"

their numbers slowly increased and their settlements extended. White neighborhoods were only visited when necessity compelled them to procure ammunition and other indispensable supplies, in exchange for hides and furs.

The new constitution adopted by the State in 1868, entitled the Seminoles to representation in each house of the Legislature, with all the rights, privileges, and remuneration accorded to other members. Such members were to be elected by the tribe, and in no case was a white man to represent them.* It is needless to say that the remnant have never availed themselves of this privilege; in view of their ignorance of the white man's language, it is doubtful if any legislator ever expected that they would do so. However, wonderful advancement may be made by this remarkable people in the not distant future.

An effort was made about the year 1870, by a Rev. Mr. Frost, to establish a school among the Seminoles. This was the first attempt to instruct these people, but the project met with discouragement and was abandoned. This result of earnest missionary endeavor was largely due to the opposition of traders† among the Indians, who, from selfish motives, were constantly adding to the natural distrust and resentment of the latter whenever strangers appeared among them. The object of this interference will appear later.

In 1872, an agent was appointed by the Commissioner of Indian Affairs to visit the Seminoles and report on their number, character, and manner of life. This was induced by representations that an outbreak might occur at any time. The malice and falsity of such reports were shown by the after statement of the Commissioner that these Indians ''were peaceable and lived together by themselves.''

It had never seemed to occur to the National or State Governments that lands ought to be provided for these refugees before the encroachments and injustice of the whites exasperated them to a renewal of hostili-

---

*Article XVI Section 7.

† The trader referred to here and in following pages are not those permanently located at different points along the coasts, but men who go out among the Indian camps, more properly called "peddlers."

ties. It is true that in 1875 the Commissioner strongly advised that public lands be secured at an early day for their occupation, "to save them from the fate of the Mission Indians of California." Even then nine years passed before any active steps were taken.

Up to the year 1880, very little was known of these secluded people. But in the fall of that year, the Bureau of Ethnology sent a trusted agent to Southern Florida to study the Seminoles in their homes.* This gentleman was the Rev. Clay MacCauley, a person well qualified for the undertaking.

Mr. MacCauley succeeded, after much trouble and delay, in reaching the camps of the Indians, where he spent portions of three months in earnest work. He estimated that their total population was about two hundred persons.† An accurate count was impossible, because all were never present in their camps at one time. They lived in twenty-two camps, grouped into five distinct towns, located as follows :

In Lee County, on the northwest edge of the Big Cypress; in Dade County, on the Little Miami River, about ten miles north of old Fort Dallas; in DeSoto County, on Fish Eating Creek, five miles from Lake Okeechobee; and in Polk County, between lakes Pierce and Rosalie.

The Indians were found to be industrious, in their way, and self-supporting, and their numbers were undoubtedly increasing. They had made clearings on which were raised corn, sweet potatoes, pumpkins, melons, bananas, oranges, and some sugar cane. They also kept cattle and hogs and a few ponies. The clothing of the Seminoles at this time was scanty, but adap-

----

*The agent's report was not published until three years later—Fifth Annual Report Bureau of Ethnology.

† This estimate was far too low for that period; see Chapter VI, Part II

ted to the climate.   The males generally wore a cotton
or calico shirt, belted at the waist and reaching within
several inches of the knees.   A kerchief about the neck,
and a turban made of one or more bright-colored shawls,
folded and wound several times about the head, with
ends neatly tucked away, completed the dress. The
women wore a skirt; with short waist of calico or gingham, but no covering for head or feet.

Mr. MacCauley bore high testimony to the honesty
and truthfulness of these Indians.   He also asserted
that "their sexual morality is a matter of common notoriety.   The white half-breed does not exist among the
Florida Seminoles, and nowhere could I learn that the
Seminole woman is other than virtuous and modest."

Especial attention was paid to the Seminoles' personal appearance and characteristics.   The observations
on these points are of great interest and value, and have
since been corroborated by various persons. "Physi-
cally both men and women are remarkable," says Mr.
MacCauley. "The men, as a rule, attract attention by
their height, fullness and symmetry of development,
and the regularity and agreeableness of their features.
In muscular power and constitutional ability to endure
they excel."

The valuable report of Mr. MacCauley was the
means of attracting attention to the almost forgotton
Seminoles.   When it was shown by his undoubted testimony that these people, who had been cheated, robbed,
and murdered, under former administrations, were industrious and self-supporting, morally our equals if not
superiors, and endowed with exceptional abilities for
their race, while still living in constant fear that they
might at any time be driven from their homes, the Gov-

ernment conscience felt a decided twinge, and it was forthwith resolved that atonement should be made.

In the same year in which the MacCauley report was issued (1884), Congress appropriated $6,000 to "enable the Seminoles in Florida to obtain homesteads upon the public lands of Florida, and to establish themselves thereon." An agent was afterward appointed by the Commissioner of Indian Affairs to visit the Indians and induce them to take advantage of the act. The agent found a number who were willing to take homesteads under its provisions. Many of them had valuable clearings upon which they had been living for years, and to which they desired to obtain a "white man's title."

But when inquiry was made by the agent at the land office in Florida, it was learned that no public lands could be found on which to locate the Indians, and that the lands they were occupying at that time were owned by the State or by Improvement Companies. Nothing, therefore, was accomplished, and the agent was recalled. Nine years before this time, as already mentioned, the Commissioner of Indian Affairs had recommended that lands be secured for these Indians at an early day, but this sound and humane advice had passed unheeded, and now it was too late.

Efforts in this direction, however, were not yet abandoned. In 1886, another special agent was dispatched to Florida to hunt up vacant public lands, but his mission terminated in December of the same year. His report was the same old story; no lands could be found suitable for the location of the Indians—the white man had appropriated all. The Commissioner of Indian Affairs had recommended in 1886, in accordance with a previous suggestion from the Governor of Florida, that the National Government should purchase lands of the

State. It was evident now, more than ever, that this course would be necessary.

But when Congress, in 1888, again appropriated $6,000 "for support and education of the Seminoles and Creek (?) Indians in Florida, for erection and furnishing of a school house, for employment of teachers, and for purchase of seeds and agricultural implements and other necessary articles," no provision was made for the one thing most sorely needed to enable the poor Seminole to become a man in *law* as well as in *fact*—namely, the purchase of lands.

Notwithstanding the repeated and unsuccessful efforts to find public lands, two more attempts were made before the project was finally abandoned. The first of these was the appointment of a lady agent, Miss Lily Pierpont, of Winter Haven, Fla., in November, 1888. This lady, however, like her predecessor, was unable to accomplish anything, and in the following July her resignation was accepted. Her successor, a gentleman, was equally unfortunate.

The Commissioner now reported that nothing could be accomplished without legislation authorizing the purchase of lands from the State. And here the matter rested. Congress renewed its appropriation of $6,000, year after year, with one exception, but as the money was unused, it reverted to the Treasury, until active hands and willing hearts appealed to apply it where it would do the most good for the deserving Seminole.

CHAPTER V.

The more favorable condition of the Seminole today
is largely due to the persevering efforts of the Womens'
National Indian Association, the pioneer on the field to
inaugurate effective work. Since the year 1888, this
Association, through its energetic President, Mrs.
Amelia S. Quinton, and the Missionary Committee, had
been investigating the Florida Indians. The result was
a firm resolve to gather this worthy remnant of a once
powerful nation from the swamps to which their fathers
had fled, and lift them up to the enjoyment of a better
life, that should include all the rights of the white man.

In March 1891, Mrs. Quinton went to the outskirts
of civilization, and beyond, on the western border of
—the Everglades, to visit the Indians in their native
wild, and to purchase lands for them if possible. She
was accompanied by two other ladies and a gentleman
—the well known Captain F. A. Hendry, a native Floridian. Captain Hendry conducted the party through
an uninhabited wilderness to several camps of the Seminoles, who were distinguished from those in other parts
of the country as the "Big Cypress" settlement.

With all their acquired distrust of the white man

and the white man's government* these intelligent red men quickly realized that the presence of ladies in their midst could only be for their good; the party were therefore cordially received wherever they went. Interesting talks were had with several of the leading men who understood and spoke sufficient English for the purpose. In this way, good impressions were made regarding the proposed work for these long neglected people.

During this visit, Mrs. Quinton, with the authority of the Association she represented, purchased four hundred acres of land on which to commence operations. The tract thus chosen is situated in Lee County, just east of Lake Trafford, and forty-five miles southeast of the town of Myers.† This location was chosen because it was practically central, at that time, to the camps of the Indians, also equally to the fact that it was not subject to overflow, like the greater part of the surrounding country, in the annual rainy season. Having thus made a good beginning, and greatly pleased with their reception and the prospects for the success of the work thus inaugurated, the party returned to civilization.

The active missionary work of the Association was commenced in June, 1891, when Dr. J. E. Brecht and his wife, of St. Louis, Mo., who had been appointed to the difficult task, arrived in the wilderness and took up their residence in a small log cabin, with the nearest neighbors and post-office forty-five miles away. Let the reader imagine the self-denial exhibited by this devoted couple in thus leaving a populous community and the society of friends, with all the resources of civilization, for a life among people with whom they could not even

* "Their resentment against the Government is perfectly justifiable" —Annual Report Commissioner of Indian Affairs, 1888.

† Sec. 4, Tp. 47 South, Range 29 East.

converse, and in a section of country which the white man had shunned partly on account of its unhealthfulness. Yet such, in many lands, has been the chosen lot of many a devoted and self-sacrificing missionary, "of whom the world was not worthy."

The purchase of land was made on the previous assurance of the United States Government that it would co-operate with the Association. After the four hundred acres were secured by Mrs. Quinton, eighty acres of the tract were sold to the United States, on which, after months of unavoidable delay, a saw-mill was erected by the Government, to furnish lumber for needed buildings.

Soon after the arrival of Dr. Brecht, he was appointed Industrial Teacher and Disbursing Agent, at the request of the Association, to superintend the operations of the Government, and to instruct the Indians in mechanical and other work. Thus the Association and the Government, each on its own land, worked side by side with one object.

For the first two and a half years, the Association provided the sole means for carrying on the work at the Mission. At the end of that period, the project having been successfully established, the plant was transferred, according to the original intention, and as a free gift, to the Missionary Board of the Protestant Episcopal Church of Southern Florida, under the oversight of Bishop Wm. Crane Gray, who have since had charge of the religious and school work. Doctor and Mrs. Brecht both continued in the field until January, 1898, when the latter withdrew, for reasons which will appear later. The financial support of Mrs. Brecht was provided by the Association and its auxiliaries.

The method of the Association was to first gain the confidence of these extremely shy and distrustful

Dr. J. E. Brecht.

Indians, and then induce them to occupy lands in severalty on the tract provided, which would be secured to them and their heirs forever, under titles that would protect. The first purchase of land was only a beginning; much more would be required. Therefore, before she left Florida, Mrs. Quinton organized branches of her Association at different points, to agitate the matter, and later on an appeal was made to the Governor and the Legislature for a donation of land.

The good example set by the Womens' National Indian Association in thus inaugurating the work among the Seminoles, and the petitions of their friends at Tallahassee, finally aroused the Legislature to its long-neglected duty. In May of that year (1891), "a joint resolution relating to the donation of certain swamp and overflowed lands to the Seminole Indians in South Florida," was passed, and on the 8th of June was signed by the Governor. The full text of this resolution is as follows:

" Whereas, The Seminole Indians in South Florida have no lands which can be called their own upon which they can settle permanently, for the purpose of homestead and cultivation, without fear of disturbance and molestation; and,

"Whereas, It is deemed a matter of public policy and justice to encourage them to become educated, and to interest them in securing permanent homes for themselves and their children; therefore, be it resolved by the Legislature of the State of Florida:

" Sec. 1. That the Board of Trustees of the Internal Improvement Fund be, and is hereby authorized, to set apart not to exceed five thousand acres of land donated by act of Congress (to the State) of September

28, 1850, for the sole and permanent use and benefit of the Seminole Indians in South Florida.

" Sec. 2.   Be it further resolved, That the said lands shall be conveyed to three trustees and their successors, to be appointed by the Governor, in trust for said Indians.

" Sec. 3.   Be it further resolved, That the trustees so appointed shall select said lands, and shall endeavor to induce said Indians to enter upon and cultivate the same, and the said trustees shall carry out the purposes of said trust without expense to the State of Florida or to the said Seminole Indians."

A few weeks later, the Governor issued commissions, in accordance with the second section of the above resolutions, to the following well known citizens of the State: James E. Ingraham, Frances A. Hendry, and Garabaldi Niles—the latter succeeded by a Mr. Ditmar. The tract donated would not be sufficient, but it was at least a good beginning, and, as it had cost the State nothing, it was hoped that more would be added.

Some account of the first few years' work for the Seminoles may prove of interest.   At the commencement of the enterprise, the National Government furnished farming implements, two mules and a wagon, ten oxen and a cart, two logging carts, and other articles necessary for carrying on the industrial work, in addition to the saw-mill before mentioned.   Work went on very slowly at first, owing to the small force of men allowed, and the magnitude of the necessary preliminary steps in an unbroken wilderness.   Nothwithstanding these obstacles, however, considerable progress was made. An unfortunate loss and set-back occurred by fire in October, 1892, by which a new and permanent mill-house, a planing machine, and a large quantity of shingles were totally destroyed, laying waste the hard labor of months. This loss was replaced the following year.

While the industrial work of this pioneer mission, remote from civilization, was being carried on, visits were made to the camps of the Indians, five to twenty-five miles to the southward, and every pains taken to gain their confidence. The first visits of Dr. Brecht to their settlements were somewhat unwelcome. Natural distrust and resentment, handed down from father to son, could not be overcome in a day. On this point, Mrs. Quinton, whose experience among Indian tribes has been long and extensive, says "the Seminoles were more timid and distrustful than any tribe I have ever known."

The distrust of the Indians was intensified by the malicious stories of white traders and whiskey peddlers, who for years had been buying their deer hides and other skins, and selling them an inferior grade of goods, including the vilest whiskey, at prices far above the actual value. This class of robbers—for they deserve no better name—realized that missionary work among the Indians would expose their own nefarious dealings, and cut off their highly remunerative trade. For this reason these unprincipled traders did their utmost to prejudice the red men against the mission and Government work. One old Indian, who had been told that the United States troops were again coming to remove them to Indian Territory, wept like a child at the prospect of another war.

The missionaries succeeded in assuring many of the Indians of the falsity of such reports, and prevailed upon them to visit the mission more frequently. Mrs. Brecht thus writes of the visit of an interesting family :

"The last family that visited us was a most interesting one; the father and two daughters (attractive maidens of fourteen and seventeen years) had been here several times before, but this time the mother, a boy and a younger girl, and a bright, five-months old baby too. They were a devoted family; the father proud of them all, the mother kind, faithful and loving—a real motherly face; the girls bright and respectful, relieving the mother of the care of the little one, yet full of fun and frolic."

In another letter, the same writer says:

"They often take meals with us, and it is gratifying to see how quickly they learn to use knife and fork; and to watch their improvement in manners. They seem to enjoy the white man's food. . . . Visiting among the camps we find them hospitable; soon after we arrive they offer us something to eat—whatever they have ready prepared. . . . They come to us, not because they are in need, but as guests. It is their custom to eat where they visit, and so we ask them to our table and find that their shyness and reserve disappear more rapidly, and they talk more freely at the table and after they have eaten with us."

On the Fourth of July of the years 1895–6, the Indians were invited to come in and help celebrate. Twenty-two, including several families, accepted the invitation on the former occasion, and camped at the mission from one to three days beforehand. Here, in the wilds of the Seminole country, separated from the rest of the world by miles of unbroken forest, Independence Day was celebrated in good old New England style, including fire-works in the evening. The most impressive and significant part of the day's proceedings was the raising of a large flag which had been provided expressly for the occasion by Dr. Brecht. After a short patriotic talk by the doctor, six little Indian boys and girls, with four children of white parents, who had moved into the neighborhood, grasped the halyards and hoisted the stars and stripes to the breeze, amid the cheers of the crowd. The fact that the Indian parents willingly allowed their children to raise a United States flag, and on Government soil, was in itself a great gain.

A year later the Indians again gathered to celebrate the day at a grand barbecue, which had been provided by Bishop Gray, through his missionary, Rev. Mr. Gibbs, who, with his wife, had commenced his labors among the Seminoles in the summer of 1895. Large tables had been arranged, around which the Indians and whites mingled freely, to the complete enjoyment of all. In the evening, during intervals of fire-works, the young Indians sang a number of their native songs, standing up before the crowd and conducting themselves in a manly fashion.

At the beginning of the mission work, a small stock of general merchandise was kept on hand, which proved to be one of the greatest attractions for the Indians. They brought in deer, alligator and otter skins, which the mission purchased, and in return sold them such articles as they desired, at actual cost. This prevented the Indians from being cheated by dishonest traders, and aided to guard them from the temptation to buy whiskey, which beverage many of the red men have learned to regard as one of their worst enemies.

The saw mill also proved an attraction, for many of the Seminoles seem to be fond of machinery and quite handy with tools, although they do not use the latter to a great extent. At first the noise of the mill, and especially the shrill whistle, frightened and repelled many of these simple children of nature. But their curiosity gradually overcame their fears, and they frequently visited the building and inspected the works, now and then sawing a board and blowing the whistle.

Dr. Brecht, being a physician, furnished many of the Indians with medicines and treatment, always gratis and almost wholly at his own expense. For a long time they refused to accept anything, even the smallest article, unless they were allowed to pay for it, thinking that the acceptance of a gift would compromise them with the Government. This feeling, however, disappeared as their confidence was gained.

A regularly organized school was impossible, owing to the fact that no Indians could be prevailed upon to accept the lands and settle around the mission. But on their visits there, and especially during the return visits of the missionaries to the permanent camps of the red men, instruction, both religious and secular, was given them with encouraging success.

During their eight years' residence among the Seminoles, Dr. and Mrs. Brecht have labored hard and unceasingly— while undergoing the severest personal trials and privations—for the elevation of these deserving Indians. They have sown seeds which will have a powerful influence, under certain conditions, toward helping these people to draw nearer to our civilization, forming a band of native Americans of whom the whole country may be proud. The main obstacle in the way of a more complete realization of the hopes of all who are interested in the welfare of these Indians, has been the ever-present opposition of a certain class of selfish whites—men who are as corrupt as the Seminoles are undefiled.

Leaving the pioneer work of the mission and the Government, we will now give, in the following chapter, some account of the Seminole of to-day.

CHAPTER VI.

At the present time the Seminoles are grouped in
three or four principal settlements, as follows: On Cow
Creek, west of Fort Pierce and north of Lake Okeechobee, in Brevard County; on certain islands in the
Everglades, west of Lauderdale, Dade County; in the
neighborhood of Fort Shackelford, on the western edge
of the Everglades, and of Chokoliskee Bay, south of
the Big Cypress, Lee County.   The general location of
these settlements is permanent, but the camps are not
infrequently changed.   Two of the old settlements occupied at the time of Mr. MacCauley's observations, in
1880, were abandoned a few years later, on the advance
of civilization.

For years there has been much speculation as to
the number of Indians in this remnant.   It has been
impossible to ascertain the exact population, owing
to their scattered location over a wide extent of country,
and also equally owing to the fact that all are never
present in either of the settlements at one time.   But,
judging from the careful observations of Doctor
Brecht, the Government agent, and others, and from
statements of intelligent Indians, the approximate

number is between three hundred and fifty and five hundred souls. These are distributed about as follows: Fifty to seventy-five west of Lauderdale; eighty to one hundred west of Fort Pierce; and the balance in the Big Cypress region.

According to the United States Census of 1870, the population of the Seminoles was five hundred and two. Twenty years later the census reported the total number of Indians in Florida as one hundred and seventy-one, located as follows: "Brevard County, 23; Dade County, 134; other counties with three or less in each, 14." No mention whatever was made of the largest settlement, in the Big Cypress!

Five individuals bear the name of the famous chief Osceola; they are known as Charlie, Robert or Billy, Jimmie, Tom, and Little Johnnie Osceola. Their ages range from fifty to twenty-five years. The father of these "Osceola boys," as they are called, died over twenty years ago. His name was John Osceola, and his sons claim that he was cousin to the great chief. The truth of this claim, however, may well be questioned. Their mother, Old Nancy Osceola, now about eighty years of age, lives with the Big Cypress Indians. It is a difficult matter to learn the relationship of many of the Seminoles, owing to the fact that the children do not all retain their father's name, but in numerous cases adopt one entirely different.

At various times since the immortal Lincoln's proclamation of emancipation, it has been claimed by newspaper writers and others that the Florida Seminoles still retained possession of negro slaves, as formerly. The latest assertion to this effect was published in the New York *World* a few months since, and the article was reprinted throughout the country. The substance of the writer's claim is contained in two paragraphs, as follows:

"Before the late war they (the Seminoles) had their negro slaves, and to-day they have slaves, though the white planter had to give his up over a third of a century ago. . . . That slavery does exist among the the Seminole Indians of Florida is susceptible of unequivocal proof. That the United States Government should interfere, and at this late day enforce to the full the freedom granted the colored man. . . . is just as undoubted."

The author has taken great pains to ascertain the fact in regard to this mooted "slave" question, and assures the reader that there is no real foundation for such reports as the above. In proof of this, we subjoin the statements of Dr. Brecht and Kirk Munroe, two of the highest authorities, contained in letters to the author. Says the former:

"According to the best information obtainable from the Indians themselves, and others, there are, all told, full and mixed-bloods, not over seven negroes among the Seminoles ; this includes the three distinct settlements. There is one full-blooded negro woman in the Big Cypress settlement; she has one son, now about twenty-five years old, by an Indian; the negro predominates in him. This woman has no other children to my knowledge. The boy is large, well built, and very industrious, and is a favorite among the Indians. He is not regarded or treated as a slave by any one; on the contrary, he sells his own produce and uses his money and time as he pleases. I think this is the case with all of their presumed or so-called 'slaves.' "

Kirk Munroe strongly corroborates the above, as follows:

"I would state most emphatically that there is no such thing as negro slavery among the Seminoles of Florida. During eighteen years of acquaintance with these Indians, I have always been on the lookout for the slaves reported to be held by them, and have not thus far found the least basis for the belief that they exist. I have gone freely and unexpectedly into scores of camps, and into fields where the Indians themselves were working, but have never so much as seen a negro working with them. . . . I know of but one full-blooded negress now living among the Indians, and she was stolen as a child during the Seminole War. Of half-bloods there are less than half a dozen. I know of but three. Full-blood negro men none."

This effectua'ly settles the "slave" question.

The tribe has no regularly constituted chiefs, as formerly, but in each settlement a certain prominent individual is respected as the leading authority. A noted Indian in the Big Cypress settlement, known as Old Doctor Tommy, seems to possess considerable influence over all of the different ban's.

Two prominent and influential members of the Cow Creek Seminoles are known, respectively, as Tallahaskee (pronounced Ta'lahass e by the whit s) and Tom Tiger. The former is a very old man—one of the few connecting links between the Seminoles of the past and those of the present day. Tom Tiger attracts great attention wherever he goes among the white people by his magnificent physique, being over six feet in height and weighing two hundred and thirty pounds. His face expresses great intelligence and strength of character. Both of these Indians and others have visited Mr. and Mrs. J. M.

Willson, Jr., at their home in Kissimmee, Florida, whom they regard as their friends.*

During the late war with Spain, Mr. Willson asked permission of the Governor of Florida to raise a company of Seminoles, some of them having expressed a desire or willingness to go and fight the Spaniards. Referring to this desire, on one of his visits to the Willson's, Tom Tiger said:

"Jimmie Willson (meaning his white friend) go; me go; Tallahaskee go; Little Tiger (his own son, about fourteen years of age) go." When told that Tallahassee was too old to go, Tom replied, "No; Tallahaskee shoot good."† The Governor's consent, however, was not obtained, and the Seminoles therefore lost an opportunity to prove their prowess in battle and their loyalty to their country.

The Seminoles are governed by unwritten laws of great strictness, and each individual regards it his first duty to himself and the tribe to assist in enforcing these regulations. Nothing is put under lock and key, as in white communities, for no Indian fears losses through the dishonesty of another. Their hogs, running wild in the woods, are sometimes stolen by unprincipled whites, but never by red men.

The perfect physical development of the Seminole men, as a rule, attracts the admiration of every observer. Their height, full bust, and well-shaped hands and feet; their strong and yet attractive features, and above all, their erect and self-confident bearing, all combined indicate a remarkable people. The wild and free yet highly moral life of these children of the Everglades, and their

*Among other residents of the State who have for years past taken an active interest in the welfare of the Seminoles, special mention may be made of the following persons, Colonel James E. Ingraham, Dr. DeWitt Webb, and Mrs. Marcotte, of St. Augustine; and Kirk Munroe, of Cocoanut Grove.

† So reported to the author by Mrs. Willson.

TOM TIGER.

SEMINOLE CHILDREN.

practical isolation from the whites, has developed and preserved in them the best characteristics of the true native American.

The women, while sharing to a considerable extent the above qualities of the men, are under the average height of their sex. Their features arc regular and uncommonly attractive for Indians, indeed, some of them are actually handsome.

The Western Seminoles, as a rule, both male and female, but especially the latter, are inferior to their Florida brethren in physical excellence.* The reader is already aware of the conditions in the West, as well as in Florida, which have caused this inequality.

The domestic life of the Florida Seminoles offers a great contrast to that of most other Indians. The women are treated with much consideration, and their wishes control all matters to a considerable degree. While they do most of the work about the camps, they are not treated as slaves in any manner; indeed, they are quite independent, the majority of whom own and dispose of pigs and chickens, and spend the proceeds as they choose. The children are almost perfect models of parental control, such a thing as willful disobedience being of rare occurrence; and this condition is secured without the harshness and severe punishments common in many white families. The different families are very sociable among themselves, and visit freely back and forth from camp to camp, where they entertain with a free and generous hospitality. The women and girls do not speak English as well as the men, and are far more reserved, both among themselves and in the presence of strangers.

The Seminole women are adepts at cooking such

* See **Five Civilized Tribes, U. S. Census Bulletin, 1894.**

food as they commonly use, although the usual manner of serving it is not inv ti g to white tastes. Their method of roasting a wild turkey, or a haunch of venison, preserves its rich juices and flavor with a skill which few white cooks can rival. The cooking is done over an open fire on the ground near the main habitation. The fires are built and kept burning after the common plan among oth r Indian tribes, namely, the logs are so arranged that the inner ends point toward each other, smaller wood being used to keep up a blaze. In this way the wood burns slowly and economically, moreover the heat and blaze are under better control. One of the most common dishes of these Indians is a meat and vege-table stew, made thick with hominy or crushed corn; sometimes, however, with one or the other of these ingredients left out. This is called "sofs-kee," an old Creek word signifying food or provisions.*

The common attire of the Seminole men is unlike that of any other inhabitants of America. Besides the gingham or calico shirt, belted at the waist and reach-ing nearly to the knees, as noted by Mr. MacCauley in 1880, many of the men wear an overvest of woolen or cotton cloth. When they are at home, or off hunting, their lower limbs are commonly without covering, but they are becoming shy about visiting the white settle-ments in this fashion, and on such occasions most of them now wear buckskin leggins or regular trousers.

The male Seminole has always been partial to a tur-ban, made of neatly folded shawls of bright colors and always open at the top. At the present day the turban is much larger than it was in Osceola's time. While the greater number still adhere to this curious head-dress, for several years past ordinary hats of felt or straw

*Gazetteer of the State of Georgia, Sherwood, 1826.

have been adopted by many, especially by the younger members of the tribe. The plumes of the white and the blue heron are often added to the turban, giving it a picturesque appearance. As a rule the males wear their hair cut short, with the forelock "banged," though some have a small plait or cue, commencing at the crown. Shoes are quite common among the men and boys, although many still wear moccasins, while others go without either.

While the dress of the men has undergone a considerable change within the past twenty years, that of the women remains the same. A long skirt, and an absurdly short sack waist which fails to meet the other garment, is the universal feminine fashion. To this is sometimes added a small shoulder cape, worn over the waist. The material used is calico or gingham of bright colors, made up in a showy manner. No females of any age wear covering on either head or feet. Boys and girls dress like their parents. The Seminoles are all fond of personal ornaments, as formerly; a remarkable habit of the women and girls, in this connection, is the wearing of several pounds of colored beads, in coils, about their necks. Other ornaments include ear rings and silver coin, the latter being commonly attached to one or more of the lower strings of beads.

In the early days of the tribe, when they inhabited the northern part of the peninsula, the Seminoles lived in log houses; but with the present remnant, situated as they are in a low latitude, the habitation is generally nothing more than a low palmetto shelter, or so-called "shack," usually open on all sides. This is the prevailing style of dwelling, but there are exceptions. In March 1892, Col. James E. Ingraham, with a party of twenty men, traversed the Seminole country from Myers to Fort

Shackelford, and thence across the Everglades to Miami.
One day they accepted the hospitality of an Indian
named Billy Harney, who was living in a good frame
house, all floored and wainscoted.   It was furnished
with excellent beds and mattresses, mosquito bars, cooking utensils, a sewing machine, and other conveniences
rarely seen in an Indian's habitation.

The "shack" is made by setting posts in the
ground and constructing on these a gabled frame-work
for the roof.   The covering consists of the broad leaves
of the cabbage palmetto, layer after layer of which
overlap each other like shingles.   These roofs turn
water "like a duck's back," and last until the fibre of
the leaves decays and breaks away, usually serving for
three or four years.   Inside of the shelters platforms
are erected for sleeping purposes.   As the mosquitoes
and sandflies are often very annoying, each bunk is
provided with nets or protections of cheese-cloth.   The
shacks, as above described, are built with open sides
for the purpose of allowing a free circulation of air, and
also to enable the occupants to look out on all sides
and thus readily detect the approach of strangers.

The cultivated fields of the Indians are usually
located in rich hammocks, while their places of abode
are in the open pine woods near by.   The crops raised
include nearly everything that the white settler produces.

As might be expected of a people driven to a wilderness and thrown upon their own resources, the Seminoles are successful hunters.   Their common method is
"still" hunting; they seldom if ever fire-hunt or use
dogs.   Large numbers of alligators and otter are killed
for their skins, and these animals are generally hunted
with the dug-out canoe, among the Everglades and
streams of that region.   As a rule the Indians hunt

Seminole Shacks.

singly, and use the Winchester rifle of 22 to 44 calibre. Their main source of revenue is from the sale of skins, furs, and the plumes of birds. The white traders induce them to kill the birds.

The white man has his Thanksgiving, Christmas and Fourth of July holidays, and the Seminole his annual festival known as the Green Corn Dance. There is a vast difference in the object of these observances, although all have some prominent features in common. While the former occasions are given over to joyous commemorations, the Seminoles' festival also includes ceremonies for cleansing the body of corruption, and for testing the endurance, both of which are confined to the men and boys.

Briefly stated, the Green Corn Festival continues four days and nights, and consists (in the order named) of ball playing; dancing; great feasting, followed by long fasting; partaking freely of a vegetable emetic, and going through a sweating process, to purify the body; and the test of endurance—scratching the body, legs and arms with needles inserted through a thin block. The ceremony for purging the body of evil, taken in connection with the fact that the Seminole recognizes a Great Spirit or God (E-shock-e-tom-e-see), and that he is highly moral, indicates a keen sense of wrong-doing and evil.

Dr. Brecht was present, by invitation, during one of these annual festivals, and was treated with great respect and consideration for his comfort and enjoyment. This was an honor which the Seminoles have not conferred upon many white men. The Doctor was also invited to the last festival (1898).

We will close the chapter with the following quotation from a letter received from Dr. Brecht:

"The old men talk but little of their past history, sorrows and great wrongs. If one refers to their past, it is plainly evident that sorrow fills their hearts; they show no anger, only they become quiet and look sad. I seldom speak of such things; only did a few times to see what effect it would produce. It is touching to hear the old men say, 'white man take away my squaw and pickaninnies, and no more bring-um back.'"

CHAPTER VII.

The baleful influence that has followed the red man
from the first settlement of the country, has for many
years past been darkening the prospects of the Florida
Seminoles. Before the steady advance of civilization
along the far southeastern coast, the dusky Floridians
who inhabited that section in considerable numbers were
happy in the peaceful possession of their homes. But
with the arrival of the white settler a radical change
takes place. Not far from the humble little dwelling
of the former, another, of more pretentious character, is
erected by pale-face hands. Others spring up as if by
magic, and then follows the serpentine track of the iron
steed—the last death-knell to the Indians' hopes in that
locality.

From the commencement of this change the Indians
were crowded farther and farther away from their old
haunts. In many cases they were actually robbed of
their hard-earned homes by unprincipled whites, who
homesteaded the coveted land and claimed the improve-

ments as their own; or who drove the rightful owners away by direful threats. One o d Indian who had been compelled to leave, asked a true friend whether he would be allowed to take from his own field the crops then nearing maturity, adding, "then if white man want field he take it; all right, Indian no want it."

Thus they have meekly submitted, in most cases, and removed to new and far less desirable lands within or near the borders of the Everglades. The author is unable to learn that one ever retaliated, as in former times, for these heartless acts. That we are stating facts can be proved by abundant testimony of the highest character.

Congress finally (1894) set apart one-half of the regular annual appropriation of $6,000, and required that it should be used for the purchase of permanent homes for the Seminoles. This division of the money necessitated a reduction in the force at the Government station, and besides left no funds for carrying on camp-work among the Indians, which Dr. Brecht rightly considered one of the best means of gaining their confidence. However, the acquisition of lands was of first importance, and to this effort a large part of the agent's time was devoted during three years.

Up to the close of the fiscal year 1897, nearly ten thousand acres of land had been located by Dr. Brecht and secured to the Government, for the Indians. Most of the tracts lie in Lee County, southeast of the station, and include several of the old homesteads of the latter, the owners of which seem to feel more secure. None of the others, however, have yet abandoned their old locations and settled on the lands provided for them.

In May, 1897, Hon. F. A. Hendry, a representative in the lower branch of the Florida Legislature, from Lee

County, introduced a bill which provided that a township of the unsurveyed lands of the State be set apart and held in trust in perpetuity for the Seminole Indians. The sum of $1,000 was also appropriated to pay the expenses connected with locating and surveying the said tract. The bill was unanimously passed by the House on the 31st of the month, but failed to pass the Senate.

During the frequent absence of Dr. Brecht in connection with land matters, and the discontinuance of camp work, the visits of the Indians to the Station grew less and less frequent, and finally ceased altogether. This discouraging feature was largely due to the malicious work of the traders and whiskey venders, who circulated false stories among the red men regarding the Government's intentions, and also to a proposition made by State officials for locating them on a reservation.

As **we** have stated, the Governor of Florida appointed trustees in the year 1891 to select 5,000 acres of land which had been donated to the Seminoles by an act of the Legislature. No funds were appropriated for the purpose of carrying out the trust, and nothing was attempted in this direction until six years afterward. In April, 1897, the trustees met to discuss the subject, at which time "it was resolved that they do now recommend the reservation of the whole of Long Key, an island situated partly in Lee, Monroe, and Dade Counties .... the same to be set aside and reserved from sale, and to be a reservation for the Seminole Indians, during their lives .... *They are a brave, independent and an intelligent body of men;* they have steadily refused to become the wards of the Nation. They support themselves by hunting, fishing and planting; their habits are clean and *they are honest and reliable.*"

The trustees claimed that Long Key contained "some five thousand acres of land," and a variety of soils, and that it was sufficiently high for health. Friends of the Seminoles now came forward and urged against their exile to an island so worthless that it had not attracted the cupidity of the white man. This evidently had some influence with the Governor, for the project was abandoned.

It is believed by some that the trustees had reference to a small island in the Sam Jones' group, situated on the eastern edge of the Everglades in Dade County, northeast of Miami. The error of this, however, is very apparent from the clear statements contained in the official report to the Governor, as accurately quoted above; also, from the fact that the entire group of islands referred to would only support a few families. The only large island bearing the name "Long Key," is situated in the southern part of the Glades, and wholly in Dade County. It has never been surveyed. hence its exact location has always been in considerable doubt. It has borne the name since 1838.*

Friends of the traders and whiskey men now violently attacked the conscientious efforts and personal integrity of Dr. Brecht, through the columns of a Myers newspaper. The object of this was to cause the removal of the agent and a discontinuance of the Government's work. Neither hope was realized, however; on the contrary the effort only served to further impress upon the Indian Commissioner the true state of affairs, and cause him to seek a remedy for the evil which had acted like a clog since the commencement of the endeavor to uplift those Indians.

---

* The Indians informed Dr. Brecht that Long Key was *holawahgus* (no good), and furthermore said that the island was inhabited by an enormous snake!

The primary steps toward a new project for helping the Seminoles were taken in the fall of 1896. In the month of October of that year, the Secretary of the Interior decided that the unsurveyed territory known as the Everglades was swamp land, and that it might be patented to the State under the Swamp Acts of 1848-50.* As soon as this decision was made public, Dr. Brecht and others appealed to the Indian Office to reserve all lands on which the Indians were living, before a patent for the tract was issued to the State.

The Commissioner of Indian Affairs, Hon. Wm. A. Jones, strongly favored such a plan, and in his annual report for 1897 to the Secretary of the Interior, recommended "that there be inserted in the patent to be issued to the State a clause expressly reserving the rights of the Indians to the occupancy of lands possessed and improved by them at the date of the patent. . . . The insertion of such provision in the patent would make the rights of the Indians clear, and would be a measure of protection to those people, who have excited the sympathy of all who have become cognizant of their situation."

The grant was therefore held up pending an investigation, by the Assistant Attorney-General for the Department, regarding two leading questions—first, as to whether the Seminoles had any valid claim to the lands; and, second, whether the department had a right to reconsider the approval of the grant. As to the first question, it was decided (in January 1898) that the only right the Seminoles had was that of occupancy. (How such a decision could be reached, in view of the overwhelming proof against it, we leave to the imagination of the reader.) Regarding the other point, it was

* See Sen. Rep. 242, 1st Ses., 50th Cong.

decided that the department had a right to revise the list of lands granted under the Swamp Act, since part of these lands could not be classed as "swamp."

Dr. Brecht was now called to Washington for conference with the department officials. He had resided in the Seminole country continuously since his appointment in 1891, and was therefore glad of an opportunity to verbally discuss the situation. His earnest and valuable testimony on various matters connected with his office, strengthened the plans of Commissioner Jones and Secretary Bliss for helping the Florida Indians.

It had been determined some time before to send an inspector from the office of the Interior Department to make a thorough investigation of the land question and of the situation, condition and needs of the Seminoles. The person chosen for this important mission was Mr. A. J. Duncan, brother-in-law of President McKinley, a gentleman of keen perceptions and ability. In company with Dr. Brecht, Mr. Duncan made a tour of the Seminole country. He visited the former homes of the Indians on the east coast, including several islands along the edge of the Everglades, from which they had been driven in some cases. Thence, crossing the State, he went among the Big Cypress settlements, near old Fort Shackelford and elsewhere in Lee County. Nearly two months were spent in careful study of the question of lands; of the Indian himself and his home life; of the obstacles that stand in the way, at present, of efforts to help him; and of the views of the better class of whites who have the welfare of the Indian at heart.

The author had several very interesting talks with Mr. Duncan after his return from Florida, and found him deeply interested in the people whom he was sent to investigate. His views of the Seminoles' moral and physical attainments were found to correspond with those of every competent witness who has been among them in the past twenty years. On these points, he says:

"The character of the Florida Seminoles makes them an easy prey to unscrupulous white men. They are peaceable, law-abiding and moral. Under the strongest provocation they have refrained from doing violence. Morally considered, they are far in advance of many white communities which boast of their civilization. Their physical perfection is remarkable, undoubtedly stamping them as superior to any other Indians in North America."

Mr. Duncan truly declares that the time is fast approaching—distant only a comparatively few years—when the Seminoles must of necessity rely almost altogether upon the soil for a livelihood. This is owing to the fact that the game is gradually disappearing, also the alligators upon which they now depend to a great extent for their revenue.

Along the western margin of the Everglades, from Fort Shackelford southward, are numerous small bodies of rich hammock lands, bordered by pine and cypress, which would support the entire number of these Indians. Between these lands and the nearest white settlements are vast barren and worthless tracts, which are more or less subject to annual overflow during the rainy season. Owing to the uninviting character of this region, it is probable that it will remain a wilderness for a long period, and that it will never attract and support more than a small and scattered number of whites.

After a careful consideration of every phase of the perplexing question, including their scattered condition, Mr. Duncan has recommended in his report to the Secretary of the Interior what is undoubtedly the only humane and practical plan for permanently protecting and assisting the Seminoles, viz: that a tract consisting of not less than 300,000 acres, embracing one of their main settlements, and extending south and west of old Fort Shackelford, be purchased by the United States Government and reserved for the permanent occupancy of these Indians. Here they could retire when the encroachment of the whites crowds them away from other sections, and under stringent laws to protect them from the evils which have always beset their race in Indian Territory, they may be taught the advantages of a higher civilization.

It is also recommended by Mr. Duncan that certain islands and hammocks on the eastern side of the Everglades, which have been inhabited by the Indians for generations, be reserved from the Swamp Act grant, and included in the above mentioned tract.*

It is not to be doubted that the Honorable Secretary of the Interior (who is perhaps more deeply interested in the Seminoles than were any of his predecessors) will see the justice and force of Inspector Duncan's suggestions, and that he will strongly recommend the matter to the favorable consideration of Congress. But Congress is ever composed of "many men of many minds;" among its members are not a few who, having no real sympathy for the red men, may favor the removal of the Florida Seminoles to the lands occupied by their brethren in Indian Territory.

The leading object of this Story of the Seminoles is to emphasize the injustice and cruelty of such an attempt, should it ever be made, especially in view of our past relations with this tribe—not to mention our deal-

* Mr. Duncan made a second trip to Florida, accompanied by a surveyor, in the middle of the summer (1898), at which time several of the islands were located and surveyed.

ings with others. It would be heartless in the extreme to remove these worthy native Americans—the last link that connects Florida with her ancient inhabitants—from the genial land they are so strongly attached to, and for which their ancestors fought with such patriotism and dogged determination, to the comparatively bleak and barren Western highlands. A large majority of the residents of Florida, and most of her newspapers, are undoubtedly opposed to the removal of the Indians. On the other hand, it is alleged that capitalists interested in the drainage of the Everglades, and in railroads, will strongly favor such a plan.

It has been claimed by some that the only hope for the Florida Seminoles lies in emigration to Indian Territory, for the reason (say those who entertain this view) that as long as they remain in the State they will be demoralized by whiskey peddlers. A little reflection, however, will convince any sincere friend of these Indians of the absurdity of this claim. Emigration would be worse than the proverbial "jumping out of the frying-pan into the fire," owing to the fact that demoralizing influences are far more numerous and active, for obvious reasons, in the Territory, than they are in the Everglades. The best proof of this is the high moral character and splendid physical development of the Florida Seminoles, in comparison with the Western Indians.

The author earnestly appeals to every reader of these pages to use his or her influence with members of Congress, and of the Florida Legislature, to the end that the Seminoles may be allowed to permanently remain in the State, and that an extensive tract of land may be secured to them and their descendants for all time.

We can well afford to turn over a new leaf in our
dealings with the Indian, by permitting this worthy
remnant of Osceola's warriors to live and die in the land
of their choice and of the graves of their fathers.   In
so doing the last chapter of the Seminole War can be
contemplated with honor to the Nation and the State,
and credit to our civilization in these closing years of
the century.

THE END.

YOUNG SEMINOLE WOMAN.

APPENDIX.

OSCEOLA NIKKANOOCHEE.

In the fore part of the Seminole War, our troops
captured a little Indian boy on one of their trips in the
interior. An Englishman by the name of Dr. Welch,
residing at Jacksonville, took a fancy to the boy, and
was allowed to care for him in his own family. A short
time after the child was placed in the doctor's charge
the latter learned that he was a nephew of the great
chief Osceola, and that his name was Osceola Nikkanoochee, and his mother a sister of the chief. These facts
were established by the boy himself, and by a prominent
doctor then residing at St. Augustine. Dr. Welch says
that "the conduct of little Osceola so far gained upon
my regard that I fully determined to adopt and cherish
him as my own child," which he finally did, in October
1837, by authority of the War Department.

Dr. Welch remained at Jacksonville about a year,
and then purchased an estate at the mouth of the St.
Johns River, where he retired with his protege. In
this secluded part of the State, the doctor took great

pains and pleasure in bringing up his charge to civilized
ways, teaching him to read and write among other ac-
complishments. For a long time, we are told, the boy
was extremely shy and scarcely ever spoke except to say
yes or no, but gradually he became less reserved, and a
mutual attachment resulted.

In 1840 Dr. Welch returned to England, accompanied by young Osceola. The following year the
former published a book* relating to his adopted son and
to the chief Osceola, from which we have drawn for this
sketch. In the preface to his book the writer says
that his object was "to record all events relating to the
life and capture of my protege with which I was
acquainted, . . . in order that in the event of my death
the manuscript might inform him of his origin and history, and at the same time remind him of one who loved
him with the fondness of a father."

Catlin painted young Osceola's portrait in 1840.
While the great artist was in England in 1842, he met
Dr. Welch and his charge on numerous occasions, and
afterward referred to the great pains the doctor was
taking with the boy's education.†

It would be interesting to learn what became of this
remarkably fine boy; if he is still living his age is about
sixty-five years. The author has endeavored to trace his
history in London after 1842, but without successful
results. Any information on this point, or regarding
Dr. Welch, will be gladly received.

THE TREATY OF TALLAHASSEE.

The reader will remember that certain reservations
of land were granted by the Treaty of Camp Moultrie

* Osceola Nikkanoochee, Prince of Econchattimico, London, 1841.
† Catlin's Eight Years, Vol. II.

(1823) to six of the old chiefs, who desired the privilege of remaining in West Florida, where they had lived for generations. (See page 39). These chiefs lived on their reservations in peace and contentment, with their families and more or less followers, for about twelve years. They were not parties to the Treaty of Payne's Landing (1832); having been granted lands separate from the bulk of the tribe, the Government seemed to regard them as a distinct people, referring to them in the treaties of Tallahassee and Pope's as "Appalachicola" Indians, although they were really Seminoles.

Accordingly, on the 11th of October, 1832, the Treaty of Tallahassee was negotiated at that place with John Blunt, (one of the six chiefs favored,) O-sa-hajo, and Cochrane, by which these chiefs surrendered to the United States all right and title to the reservation of land granted them under the Treaty of Camp Moultrie, and agreed to remove with their families and warriors, amounting to two hundred and fifty-six souls, to the west of the Mississippi River, not later than October 1st, 1834.

In consideration of this surrender and removal, the United States agreed, among other stipulations to their benefit, to pay them $13,000; three thousand cash and the balance when they had commenced the removal of their whole party. This Treaty was ratified February 13th, 1833. The author is unable to state positively whether its conditions were ever fulfilled by either party, but he believes that this band represented the first emigrating party prior to the commencement of the war. (See foot-note, page 55).

TREATY OF POPE'S.

Eight months after the foregoing Treaty was signed, another was negotiated with two other bands of the so-called "Appalachicola Indians." This is a curious document in several respects. It was signed by Mulatto King and Tustenuggee Hajo, head chiefs of Emath-locnee's town (the latter having died), with seven of their warriors, and Econchattimico and seven of his warriors. The chiefs agreed to surrender to the United States all their right and title to the reservations of land granted them under the Treaty of Camp Moultrie. The tracts surrendered consisted of four sections (2,560 acres) from each of the two bands.

In consideration of this, the United States agreed to grant and convey in three years by patent, three sections of land to each band, to be laid off so as to embrace their old improvements. At the same time the chiefs had the privilege of selling the said tracts prior to the expiration of the three years, if they desired to emigrate to another country. If, however, they continued to remain on their lands, the United States was to withdraw its immediate protection* as soon as Blunt's band and the main tribe had emigrated, and they would thereafter become subject to the Government and laws of Florida. This Treaty was ratified in April 1834.

Strange to say, by this agreement those who signed it had the privilege of remaining in Florida, while all other members of the tribe were to be banished from the country! Why these bands were thus favored, the author is unable to say. They did not remain, however, but finally emigrated with the rest.

---

* The "protection of the United States" has been a prominent clause of every treaty negotiated with our Indian tribes, but it amounted to little more than a farce—the red men were *not* "protected;" had they been no one would have had cause to complain of their acts of retaliation.

LIST OF BATTLES AND OTHER ENGAGEMENTS OCCURRING DURING THE SEMINOLE WAR.*

1835—Near Alachua Savanna, Alachua County, Dec. 19. Near Micanopy, Alachua Co., Dec. 20. At Fort King, Marion Co., Dec. 28. Dade's Massacre. Sumter Co., Dec. 28. At the ford of the Withlacoochee River, Sumter Co., Dec. 31.

1836—At Dunlawton plantation, back of Port Orange, Volusia Co., Jan. 18. Near the ford of the Withlacoochee River, Sumter Co., Feb. 27, 28, 29, and Mar. 5. Withlacoochee River, at Oloklikaha, Sumter Co., Mar. 31. At Cooper's Post, Citrus Co., April 5 to 17. At Thlonotosassa Creek, Hillsborough Co., April 27. At Micanopy, Alachua Co., June 9. At Welika Pond, Putnam Co., July 9. Near Ridgeley's Mill, July 27. At Fort Drane, Marion Co., Aug. 21. Near San Velasco Hammock, Alachua Co., Sept. 18. Near Wahoo Swamp, Citrus and Sumter Co's., Nov. 17, 18, and 21.

1837—Near Hatcheelustee Creek, Osceola Co., Jan. 27. At Camp Monroe, Orange Co., Feb. 8. Near Clear River, Feb. 9. Near Port Orange, Volusia Co., Sept. 10 Near Lake Okeechobee, Dade Co., Dec. 25. Near Waccasassa River, Levy Co., Dec. 26.

1838—At Jupiter Creek, Dade Co., Jan. 15. Near Jupiter Inlet, Dade Co., Jan. 24. At Newnansville, Alachua Co., June 17.

1839—On the Caloosahatchee River, Lee Co., July 23.

1840—Near Fort King, Marion Co., April 28. On Levy's Prairie, Levy Co., May 19. At Waccahoota, Levy Co., Sept. 6. Everglades, Lee Co., several engagements between Dec. 3 and 24. Near Micanopy, Alachua Co., Dec. 28.

1841—Near Fort Brooks, Putnam Co., Mar. 2.

1842—At Haw Creek, Volusia Co., Jan. 25. At Pilaklikaha hammock, Lake Co., April 19.

1855—In the Big Cypress, Lee Co., December.

1856—Caloosahatchee River, near Lake Flirt, Lee Co., Jan. 18. At the mouth of Chokoliskee River, Lee Co., Mar. 29. At Bowleg's town, Big Cypress, Lee Co., April 6.

* From the records of the War Department.

1857—In the Big Cypress, Lee Co., Mar. 5 to 7. Last hostilities.

FORTS ESTABLISHED IN FLORIDA DURING THE WAR.*

Adams, T. B.—Temporary; Lee County, right bank of Caloosahatchee.

Alabama—Temp; Hillsborough Co., same river, 23 miles from Tampa.

Andrews—Taylor Co., left bank Fenahallawa, 6 miles above mouth; established Mar. 2, 1839.

Ann—Brevard Co., at " Haulover " canal; est. Nov. 30, 1837.

Annutteeliga—Hernando Co.; est. Nov. 30, 1840.

Appalachicola—Gadsden Co., junction of Flint and Appalachicolo rivers; est. in 1833.

Arbuckle—Polk Co., on Lake Arbuckle, east side; est. Jan. 23, 1850.

Armistead—Est. Nov. 30, 1840.

Armstrong—Sumter Co., on Dade's old battleground; est. in 1836.

Atkinson—Taylor Co., on Suwanee River, 3m west of Charles Ferry; est. Jan 18, 1839.

Barbour—Gadsden Co., on Appalachicola River, 9m south of Flint River; est. May 16, 1841.

Barker—Lafayette Co., head waters Esteinhatchee River; est. Feb. 1, 1840.

Basinger—Temp; DeSoto Co., west bank Kissimmee River, 17m above Lake Okeechobee; est. Dec. 1837.

Braden—Leon Co., on Ocklockonee River, 16m west of Tallahassee; est. Dec. 31, 1839.

Brooke—Hillsborough Co.,head of Hillsborough Bay, adjoining present town of Tampa on southeast; est. in 1821.

Brooke, Frank—Temp.; Lafayette Co., mouth of Esteinhatchee River.

Brooks—Temp.; Putnam Co., junction of Ocklawaha River and Orange Creek.

* Authorities: Various Military Maps published during the war; Land Office Maps of early surveys; Dictionary of the Army, Gardner, 1853; Army Register of the United States, Hamersley, 1880.

Brown—St. Johns Co., 10 m east of Palatka; est. Feb. 24, 1840.

Buckeye—Temp.; Lafayette Co., headwaters Estcinhatchee River.

Butler—Lake Co., west side St. Johns River, op. Volusia; est. Nov. 5, 1838.

Call—Volusia Co., St Johns River, at Volusia; est. Dec. 10, 1836.

Capron—Brevard Co., op. Indian River Inlet; est. Mar. 1850.

Carroll—Temp.; Polk Co., 4m southeast of Lake Hancock.

Casey—Manatee Co., Charlotte Harbor; est. June 3, 1850.

Center--DeSoto Co., 2m west of Lake Okeechobee; est. June 25, 1856.

Chipola—Calhoun Co., east bank Chipola River; est. Nov. 9, 1841.

Chokonikla—DeSoto Co., near Bowling Green; est. Oct. 26, 1849.

Christmas—Temp.; Orange Co., south of Lake Harney.

Clarke—Temp.; Jefferson Co., on Ocilla River, 10m above its mouth.

Crabbe—Bradford Co., on New River.

Call—Bradford Co., 10m north of Newnansville.

Clarke—Alachua Co., 6m west of Gainesville.

Clinch—Nassua Co., on Amelia Island, north of Fernandina; est. Feb. 9, 1842.

Clinch—Polk Co., south of Crooked Lake; est. Jan. 13, 1850.

Clinch—Levy Co., north bank Withlacoochee, 9m from mouth; est. Oct. 22, 1836.

Cooper—Temp.; Citrus Co., on the Withlacoochee.

Crane—Temp.; Alachua Co., on Lake Pithlochoco.

Crawford--Temp.; Manatee River, 19m east of Manatee.

Cross—Hernando Co., near Brooksville; est. Dec. 25, 1838.

Cummings--Polk Co., 16m southwest of Davenport; est. Jan. 22, 1839.

Dade—Pasco Co , 2m southwest of Dade City; est. Jan 1837.

Dallas—Dade Co., on Biscayne Bay, est. Jan. 1838.

Davenport—Polk Co., 10m east of Lake Tohopekaliga; est. June 9, 1839.

Denaud—Lee Co., south bank Caloosahatchee River, 27m above Myers.

Doane—Temp., Lee Co., western part of Big Cypress.

Downing—Lafayette Co., 9m above Santa Fe River; est.
    Jan. 30, 1840.
Drane—Marion Co., 10m south of Micanopy; est. Dec. 1835.
Drum, Simon—Lee Co., 7m east of Lake Trafford; est. Mar.
    11, 1855.
Drum—Brevard Co., west side, due west of Fort Capron.
Dulany—Lee Co.. near mouth of the Caloosahatchee River;
    est. Nov. 23, 1837.
Econfinee—Taylor Co., 5m above mouth of Econfinee River;
    est. Mar. 10, 1840.
Fanning—Levy Co., 23m from mouth of Suwanee River; est.
    Nov 30, 1838.
Foster—Hillsborough Co., on Hillsborough River, north of
    Lake Thlonotosassa; est. Sept. 23, 1849.
Fowle—Temp.; Marion Co., 6m east of Ocala.
Frazer—Polk Co., near Lake Hancock; est. Dec. 1837.
Fulton—St. Johns Co , right bank Pelicier Creek; est. Feb.
    21, 1840.
Gadsden—Site of " Negro Fort," Calhoun Co., left bank of
    Appalachicola River; est. in 1817.
Gamble—Jefferson Co., 30m southeast of Tallahassee; est.
    Aug. 24, 1839.
Gardner—Temp.; Osceola Co., between Lakes Kissimmee
    and Hatchineha; est. in Dec. 1837.
Garey's Ferry—Duval Co , on Black Creek; est. in 1837.
Gates—Temp.; Putnam Co., west bank of St. Johns, north
    of Lake George.
Gatlin—Orange Co., 10m southeast of Lake Ahapopka; est.
    Nov. 9 1838.
Green—Temp.; DeSoto Co., northwest corner.
Griffin- -Lafayette Co., west of Suwanee River, 6m north
    of mouth; est. Jan. 30, 1840.
Hamer—Manatee Co., near mouth of Manatee River; est.
    Nov. 1849.
Hanson—Temp.; St. Johns Co., headwaters of Deep Creek.
Harlee--Bradford Co., 6m northwest of Santa Fe Lake;
    est. Mar. 1837.
Harrell—Temp.; Lee Co., southern extremity Big Cypress.
Harriet—Leon Co., 17m northwest of St. Marks; est. Mar.
    13, 1840.

Harrison—Hillsborough Co., Clear Water Harbor; est. April 2, 1841.

Harvie—Lee Co., 19m above mouth of Caloosahatchee; est. in 1841; afterward called Fort Myers.

Heilman—Duval Co., Black Creek, 8m from mouth; est. May 5, 1836.

Henry—Temp.; Dade Co , in Everglades, west of Biscayne Bay.

Holmes—Putnam Co., on Deep Creek, 11m southwest of Palatka; est. Feb. 9, 1840.

Hook—Temp.; Marion Co., 12m west of Ocala.

Hulbert—Taylor Co., 3m from coast, 15m northwest of Deadman's Bay; est. Feb. 2, 1840.

Hunter—Temp.; Putnam Co., 1 1-2m south of Palatka.

Jackson—Madison Co., 13m southwest of Columbus; est. Nov. 11, 1838.

Jennings—Temp.; Levy Co., east bank of Wacasassa River, 12m from coast.

Jones—Temp.; Taylor Co., Ocilla River, 23m from coast.

Jupiter—Dade Co., near Jupiter Inlet; est. Feb. 21, 1855; old Fort Jupiter was one-half mile to the west.

King—Marion Co., 2 1-2m east of Ocala; est. in March 1827.

Kissimmee—DeSoto Co., on Kissimmee River, 15m south of the lake; est. Mar. 23, 1852.

Kingsbury—Temp.; Volusia Co., north side of Lake Monroe.

Lane—Temp.; Orange Co., west shore of Lake Harney.

Lauderdale—Dade Co., on peninsula, 6m north of New River Inlet; est. Feb. 14, 1839.

Lawson—Putnam Co., 4m west-southwest of Palatka.

Loyd—Temp.; Brevard Co., 7m north-northeast of Lake Okeechobee.

Mackay—Marion Co., near Ocklawaha River, 10m south of Orange Lake Creek.

Macomb – Lafayette Co., west bank of Suwanee River; est. April 16, 1839.

Macomb—Temp.; Leon Co., 10m north of St. Marks.

Maitland—Temp.; Orange Co., south of Lake Monroe.

Many—Wakulla Co., 16m southwest of Tallahassee; est. Aug. 3, 1841.

Mason—Temp.; Orange Co., 14m southwest of Volusia.

McClure—Temp.; Sumter Co., near Sumterville.

McCrabb—Lafayette Co., on Suwanee River, south of Fayetteville; est. Jan. 31, 1840.

McNeill – Temp., Orange Co., near Lake Poinsett.

McRae—Dade Co., south side of Lake Okeechobee; est. in 1838.

Meade – Polk Co., near town of Ft. Meade; est. Dec. 19, 1849.

Mellon—Orange Co., on Lake Monroe, adjoining Sanford; est. Jan. 1837.

Micanopy—Alachua Co., near town of same name; est. April 30, 1837.

Mitchell—Taylor Co., south branch of Finalawa River; est. Feb. 2, 1840.

Moniac—Baker Co., on St. Marys River, south of Ellicott's Mound; est. July 24, 1838.

Myakka—Manatee Co., southeast of Fort Green; est. Nov. 16, 1849.

Myers—Lee Co., 19m above mouth of Caloosahatchee River; est. Feb. 20, 1850; formerly Fort Harvie.

New Smyrna—Volusia Co., near Mosquito Inlet; est. in Nov. 1838, and again Feb. 18, 1852.

Noel—Temp.; Madison Co., 6m northwest of Fort Pleasant.

Ocilla Jefferson Co., 2m southwest of Fort Gamble; est. in July 1843.

Ogden DeSoto Co., town of Ogden.

Peyton—St. Johns Co., right bank of Moultrie Creek, 5m southwest of St. Augustine; est. July 17, 1837.

Pierce—Brevard Co., 5m below Indian River Inlet; est. in Jan. 1838.

Pleasant—Madison Co., on Econfinee River, 22m from mouth; est. Nov. 12, 1838.

Poinsett—Monroe Co., at Cape Sable; est. Oct. 16, 1839.

Preston—Temp.; Gadsden Co., left bank of Appalachicola River, 13m from Aspalaga.

Russell—Temp., Marion Co., 3m east of Orange Lake, on Orange Lake Creek.

Sanderson—Duval Co., near Gary's Ferry; est. July 12, 1840.

Searle - St. Johns Co., 6m east of Picolata; est. Dec. 28, 1839.

Shackelford—Temp.; Lee Co., on edge of the Everglades, middle of the Co.; Waxy Hajo's old landing.

Shannon – Putnam Co., at Palatka; est. in May 1838.

Simmons—Lee Co., on Caloosahatchee River, 5m east of Alva; est. Nov. 5, 1841.

Stansbury—Leon Co., on Wakulla River, 9m above St. Marks; est. Mar. 15, 1839.

Starke—Manatee Co., mouth of Manatee River; est. Nov. 25, 1840.

St. Marks—Wakulla Co., near junction of Wakulla and St. Marks Rivers.

Sullivan—Hillsborough Co., 11m east of Lake Thonotosassa; est. Jan. 20, 1839.

Thompson—Lee Co., on Caloosahatchee River, near Thompson; est. Nov. 23, 1854.

VanCourtland—Temp.; Clay Co., head of Kingsley's Pond.

VanSwearingen—Temp.; Brevard Co., 6m northeast of Lake Okeechobee.

Vinton—Brevard Co., 18m northwest of Indian River Inlet; est. April 7, 1839.

Vose—Taylor Co., near Ocilla River, 24m from mouth; est. Nov. 5, 1841.

Waccahoota—Levy Co., 10m west-southwest of Micanopy; est. May 1840.

Wacasassa—Levy Co., mouth of Wacasassa River; est. Mar. 17, 1839.

Walker—Temp.; Alachua Co., 9m west of Micanopy.

Ward—Temp.; Bradford Co., east bank of Olustee Creek.

Wekiwa—Temp.; Levy Co., above mouth of Spring Creek.

Westcott—Temp.; Monroe Co., 18m east of Ten Thousand Islands.

Wheelock—Marion Co., on Orange Lake; est. July 7, 1840.

White—Alachua Co., on Santa Fe River, 7m from mouth; est. in Jan. 1838.

Wool—Temp.; Lafayette Co., near Suwanee River, 9m from mouth.

BIBLIOGRAPHY.

The following authorities have been of more or less assistance in the preparation of the present volume:

Aboriginal History of America, McCulloh, 1829.
Aboriginal Races of North America, Drake, 1880.
Across the Everglades, Willoughby, 1898.
American Antiquities, Bradford, 1843.
American State Papers.
Antiquities of the Southern Indians, Jones, 1873.
Army Register of the United States, Hamersley, 1880.
Bartram's Travels, 1773.
Bench and Bar of Georgia, Miller, 1858.
Biographical Register, Cullum, 1868.
Biography and History of American Indians, Drake, 1834.
Book of the Indians, Frost, 1844.
Camp-Fires of the Everglades, Whitehead, 1891.
Camp-Life in Florida, Hallock, 1876.
Catlin's Works.
Catlin's Indian Gallery, Donaldson, 1884.
Century of Dishonor, Jackson, 1881.
Civil War on the Border, Britton, 1890.
Congressional Documents and Reports.
Conquest of Florida, Irving, 1851.
Court of Inquiry Regarding Generals Scott and Gaines, 1835-6.
Creek War, Halbert and Ball, 1895.
Debate in Congress on the Seminole War, 1819.
DeBow's Review, 1858.
Dictionary of the Army, Gardner, 1853.
Exiles of Florida, Giddings, 1858.
Fairbanks History of Florida, 1871.
Five Civilized Tribes, U. S. Census Bulletin, 1894.
Florida Gazetteer, Hawks, 1871.
Florida War, Drake, 1832.
Foreign Relations of the United States.
From Everglades to Canon, Rodenbough, 1875.
Gazetteer of the State of Georgia, Sherwood, 1826.
History of American Indians, Adair, 1775.
History of Alabama, Pickett, 1851.

Historical Collections of Louisiana and Florida, French, 1875.
History of Carolina, Florida, &c., Catesby, 1763.
History of Catholic Missions, Shea, 1854.
History of the Indian Tribes of the United States, McKenney & Hall, 1844.
History of the Indian Wars, Trumbull, 1846.
Historical Sketch of Tomo-chi-chi, Jones, 1868.
History of South Carolina, Ramsey, 1858.
Histories of the United States, Bancroft, Lossing, Trumbull, Winsor, &c.
Indian Miscellany, Beach, 1877.
Indian Races of North and South America, Brownell, 1857.
Land Office Reports and Surveyor's Field Notes.
Literature of Aboriginal Languages, Ludewig, 1858.
Life and Adventures in South Florida, Canova, 1885.
Life of Kit Carson, Ellis.
Lives of Generals Jackson, Scott, Taylor and Worth.
Migration Legend of the Creek Indians, Gatschet, 1884.
Magazines of various years.
Malte Brun's Universal Geography, 1832.
Memoirs and Travels Among the Indians, McKenny, 1846.
North American Indians of Antiquity, Short, 1880.
Notes of the Floridian Peninsula, Brinton, 1859.
Notices of East Florida, By a Recent Traveler in the Province, 1822.
Notices of Florida and the Campaigns, Cohen, 1836.
Observations on the Floridas, Vignoles, 1823.
Origin, Progress and Conclusion of the Florida War, Sprague, 1847.
Origin of American Indians, McIntosh, 1843.
Osceola, or Fact and Fiction, By a Southerner, 1838.
Osceola Nikkanoochee, Prince of Econchattimico, Welch, 1841.
Our Indian Wards, Manypenny, 1880.
Proceedings of the Legislative Council of Florida.
Red Man and the White Man, Ellis, 1882.
Report on the Indian Tribes, Morse, 1822.
Record of the Killed and Wounded in the Florida War, 1881.
Report of the Mexican Commission, 1873.
Reports and Records of the Indian Office, War and Navy Departments, and Bureau of Ethnology.

Roman's History of Florida, 1775.

Seminoles of Florida, Willson, 1896.

Schoolcraft's Works.

Sketches of the Creek Country, Hawkins, (1798-9), 1848.

Sketches of the Seminole War, by a Lieutenant of the Left
    Wing, 1836.

Territory of Florida, Williams, 1837.

Treaties with Indian Tribes, 1830.

Traditions of the North American Indians, Jones, 1830.

Twasinta's Seminoles, or Rape of Florida, Whitman, 1885.

U. S. and Mexican Boundary Survey, 1857.

View of West Florida, Williams, 1827.

Vindication of General Jackson's Attack on the Seminoles,
    by a Citizen of the State of Tennessee, 1819.

Wild Life in Florida, Townsend, 1875.

War in Florida, by a Staff Officer, 1836.

FILES OF EARLY NEWSPAPERS.

Advertiser, Bahama, N. P.

Army and Navy Chronicle, Washington, D. C.

Bulletin, New Orleans, La.

Congressional Globe, Washington, D. C.

Courier, Charleston, S. C.

Courier, Jacksonville, Fla.

Commercial Advertiser, New York City.

Daily Intelligencer, Washington, D. C.

Intelligencer, Van Buren, Ark.

Floridian, Tallahassee, Fla.

Gazette, Charleston, S. C.

Gazette, Pensacola, Fla.

Georgian, Savannah, Ga.

Herald, New York City.

Herald, St. Augustine, Fla.

Herald, Boston, Mass.

News, New York City.

News, St. Augustine, Fla.

National Intelligencer, Washington, D. C.

Niles' Register, Baltimore, Md.

Republican, Washington, Miss.

Republican, Charleston, S. C.

Republican, Savannah, Ga.

Star, New York City.

Star, Washington, D. C.

INDEX.

Florida, 160; succeeds General Armistead, 157; terminates the war, 158–159; testifies to the peaceable character of the Seminoles, 191.

ERRATA.

Page 18—The second footnote should be credited to General Clinch's official report.

Page 19—The fort contained about 300 persons, (200 of whom were women and children), nearly all of whom were killed.

Page 25—Footnote to Governor Duval's letter: Previous to June 30, 1834, the Governors of the Territory had also acted as Superintendent of Indian Affairs.

Page 66—10th line from bottom, read murdered instead of "unharmed."

Page 183—First line of chapter head, read 1866 instead of "1886."

www.ingramcontent.com/pod-product-compliance
Lightning Source LLC
Chambersburg PA
CBHW031021120726
47905CB00007B/1999